John Murray Forbes, Sarah (Forbes) Hughes

Letters and Recollections of John Murray Forbes

Vol. I.

John Murray Forbes, Sarah (Forbes) Hughes

Letters and Recollections of John Murray Forbes
Vol. I.

ISBN/EAN: 9783744764971

Printed in Europe, USA, Canada, Australia, Japan

Cover: Foto ©Andreas Hilbeck / pixelio.de

More available books at **www.hansebooks.com**

LETTERS
AND RECOLLECTIONS
OF
JOHN MURRAY FORBES

EDITED BY HIS DAUGHTER

SARAH FORBES HUGHES

IN TWO VOLUMES

VOL. I.

BOSTON AND NEW YORK

HOUGHTON, MIFFLIN AND COMPANY

The Riverside Press, Cambridge

1899

PREFACE

ABOUT twelve years ago my father put together in manuscript a couple of volumes of reminiscences of his life; and these, together with a vast collection of letters to him, press copies of letters from him, and other papers, he left in my charge, mainly that I might make selections from the whole and put them into more definite form for his grandchildren.

I am led to believe, however, that his life and character were exceptional enough to make some account of him of general interest. With the view of giving this to the public I have made extracts from such parts of his notes as seem to be to the purpose, and have selected from the letters and papers those which explain and give color to the scenes and events recalled. In a preliminary chapter I have given some general description of my father's habits and characteristics, such as may help a reader who did not know him the better to understand what follows. I publish these things as the record of an American citizen who, keeping himself

in the background, never stinted work, or money,
or service of any sort, for the country he loved so
well.

I wish to return most grateful thanks to all the
relatives, now surviving, of my father's correspondents, who have kindly permitted the use of letters
written to him. Above all, I wish to record my
deep obligation to Professor J. B. Thayer, to whom
I am indebted for all legal notes; and for endless
kindness and help, in more ways than I can here
enumerate, in the preparation of this work.

S. F. H.

Milton, *July,* 1899.

CONTENTS OF VOLUME I

CHAPTER I

INTRODUCTION

CHAPTER II

SCHOOL DAYS

CHAPTER III

FIRST VENTURES

CHAPTER IV

LIFE IN CHINA

CHAPTER V

TEN YEARS OF BUSINESS

CHAPTER VI

RAILROADS AND OTHER ENTERPRISES. — SLAVERY

CHAPTER VII

THE BUSINESS PANIC OF 1857. — THE IMPENDING POLITICAL CRISIS

CHAPTER VIII

THE BEGINNING OF WAR

CHAPTER XIII

THE PROSECUTION OF THE WAR

ILLUSTRATIONS

"I said never was such force, good meaning, good sense, good action, combined with such domestic lovely behavior, such modesty and persistent preference for others. Wherever he moved he was the benefactor. It is of course that he should ride well, shoot well, sail well, keep house well, administer affairs well; but he was the best talker, also, in the company : what with a perpetual practical wisdom, with an eye always to the working of the thing, what with the multitude and distinction of his facts (and one detected continually that he had a hand in everything that has been done), and in the temperance with which he parried all offense and opened the eyes of the person he talked with without contradicting him. Yet I said to myself, How little this man suspects, with his sympathy for men and his respect for lettered and scientific people, that he is not likely, in any company, to meet a man superior to himself. And I think this is a good country that can bear such a creature as he is."— R. W. EMERSON (of J. M. Forbes). — *Letters and Social Aims*, Riverside edition, p. 100. See, also, *Emerson in Concord*, p. 121.

LETTERS AND RECOLLECTIONS

OF

JOHN MURRAY FORBES

CHAPTER I

INTRODUCTION

IT is usual to give some account of a man's ancestors when beginning the story of his life; but in the present instance a memory of my father's feeling about the matter prevents my following such a precedent at any length.

No one ever spent less time in hunting up remote forbears than John Murray Forbes. His life was too full for such researches, which he declared were always likely to disclose facts quite as well forgotten; summing up his verdict with the proverb, "Let sleeping dogs lie." For instance, among the family traditions is one of a Robert Forbes who was said to have won his bride, Kate Cameron, by obeying her behest and killing her father's slayer, and then to have married her, red-handed from the fray. Of this and similar ancestors my father only remarked, when they were mentioned, that they were

probably a set of old cattle thieves; and he took
no trouble to find out how successful their forays
might have been. Friends in Scotland have sent
us an account of one Robert Bennet who, according
to authentic records, bore fine and imprisonment
from 1662 to 1681 and paid first £1200 and afterwards various other fines, amounting altogether to
5000 "marks," rather than give up going to hear
the "Revd. John Blackadder" and other beloved
covenanting preachers, and receiving them at his
house when, during brief periods of governmental
leniency, he was not in the Tolbooth gaol. This an-
cestor would have had my father's hearty approval;
but although he may have inherited from him much
of his determination of purpose and habit of carrying out his resolutions at all cost, I fear that he
would not have followed the old covenanter in any
martyrdom which necessitated the hearing of long
sermons on bleak hillsides.

However, I believe, although he would scarcely
have admitted it, that the well known Scotch feeling of "pride in being a Scotchman" lay hidden
in a corner of his heart. Be this as it may, at least
one trait came to him from the old Highland clan,
namely, an intense interest in all his relatives far
and near, and a feeling of his responsibility towards
them to the sixth generation. The thought of a
relation's becoming bankrupt was horrible to him,
and many a plunge he took into distasteful business
in order to prevent such a catastrophe, or to remedy
it, as far as possible, if it had already occurred.

The Forbeses and Bennets were united in America by the marriage, in 1769, of Dorothy Murray (whose mother was Barbara Bennet) and John Forbes, then of Florida but originally of Deskrie, Scotland, and this couple were the parents of Ralph Bennet Forbes, and grandparents of my father, John Murray Forbes. His mother was Margaret Perkins, and her people, to some of whom he owed his start in life, he valued and loved; but for all this he could never refrain from repeating a joke of his cousin, James Sturgis, apropos of a common ancestress on that side who had, according to Mr. Sturgis, made her grocery shop successful by inserting a large thumb into all her measures as she served her customers.[1] As a matter of fact this lady (*née* Elizabeth Peck), who had been left a widow early in life, with eight small children to bring up, had by most honorable means transformed the wholesale part of the grocery business left by her husband into one of large and general commerce, and had bequeathed this to her sons; and her character and ability had my father's warm

---

[1] The following epitaph on the father of the ancestress referred to has been sent me by another cousin, Mr. J. Elliot Cabot : —

> Here lies a Peck, who, some men say,
> Was first of all a Peck of clay.
> This, formed by Hand Divine, while fresh,
> Became a common Peck of flesh.
>
> Full forty years Peck felt life's bubbles,
> Till death relieved a Peck of troubles.
> And here he lies, as all men must,
> Though nothing but a Peck of dust.

esteem. Nevertheless, any hint of pride in ancestry, and through that in merits not one's own, would be sure to produce the profane story of the thumb.

For all this he was a man of the strongest family affection. In his own immediate circle he was, throughout life, all that one could be to his relatives.

For his grandmother Dorothy's sister, Mrs. Elizabeth Murray Robbins, and her kind husband, he had a grateful regard, saying that she stood in his grandmother's place to him.[1] And as she had delighted him by gifts of pill-boxes filled with small silver pieces, so he in his old age kept an assortment of like boxes for all sorts of little people, in memory of the pleasure she had given him so long ago ; after his death we found a bag of change and numberless little plush boxes ready for use. In all this good aunt's family, down to her great-grandchildren, he kept a deep interest, and would dwell constantly on Judge Robbins's kindness, or enumerate the virtues of his cousins, Mary Revere and Sally Howe, or smile over recollections of the pithy stories of their sister, Mrs. Lyman. And then he would mention with pleasure some good trait he had observed in their descendants.

Impatient, to a degree, of sloth, incompetency, and above all hypocrisy, I have seen him among kith and kin, and those who had any claim on him,

---

[1] Dorothy Murray Forbes died in 1811, two years before J. M. F.'s birth, after having been a cripple, from rheumatic gout, for nearly thirty years.

exhibit an endless patience and long-suffering with the foibles most distasteful to him; so that a cousin who had had many opportunities of watching him under **very trying** circumstances once **exclaimed,** " **The most patient** *im*patient man **I have ever seen !** "

It cannot be denied, however, that my father could be a good hater, and when once this feeling was excited he seemed never to be able to tolerate the persons who inspired it, often expending on them more thought than they were worth. As a rule this sentiment was confined to public characters of whose conduct and record he disapproved. Especially he detested sanctimonious rogues, or in fact pretense of any kind, whether of patriotism or religion. Toleration of newspapers which spread "bad doctrine," financial or political, or increased their circulation by personal scandals, was not among his virtues. His estimate of one of this order, which had attacked his business honor, was shown by his characteristic reply to some friends who had urged him at once to vindicate himself: " When the New York —— *praises* me, I shall sue it for libel, not before."

My father's really active business life in this country began on his return from China in the middle of the financial panic of 1837, but it was not till 1860, when the war cloud, so long in gathering, was about to burst, that the inordinate work began which I remember as going on continuously from that date. But whether busy or comparatively idle, he still found time for irksome duties to his children, and would walk the floor all night with an ailing, wide-awake baby, crooning old songs to it, and watching for the cold winter's dawn to refresh himself with bath and breakfast, — and then to his work in Boston. Before 1860 he had at least periods of leisure. He would go to his office in Boston early, return to Milton for dinner (also early), and drive with my mother afterwards, or ride with my sisters, mounted on his favorite horse Prince. And later on, when I was still quite a small child, he would often call me to a delightful game of hide and seek among the pine-trees behind the house; and when winter came he would appear with a wonderful pair of skates which he had had made with double runners, " to make him secure " as he said, and with these on his feet would teach me to skate on one of the meadows which he had had flooded by damming the brook that flowed through it; and so on this eminently safe pond we struggled about until the desired end was attained. Besides making the pond itself, he had built a large settle, with a high back, where we could put on and take off our skates and rest, sheltered from the north wind, a comfort for which we all were grateful, and the conception of which was very characteristic of himself. He always held it to be bad economy for any one to submit to a discomfort which could be reasonably avoided.

Afterward there was little of this leisure in Milton. The storm and stress had begun, and, although we all knew then, more or less, that he was hard-worked, it brings now a feeling of exhaustion to look through the letters and papers of those years and realize for the first time the amount and variety of work which must have been got through. I do not undertake to catalogue the immense mass of this material; the following pages will speak for themselves.

During the most exciting periods of the war letters were begun at six o'clock in the morning. After breakfast, rain or shine, he rode into Boston, and back to dinner. Then a short nap, and work until supper, followed by a game of cards; after which, work again until far into the night, sometimes until three o'clock the next morning. On other occasions all day would be spent in Boston. I can recollect my mother's anxiety over it all; and yet the work was to be done! He was often so weary that he would say he wished he could do something to get shut up in jail, as "the only place where he could be sure of rest."

He never liked it to be known that he wrote editorials, or inspired editors with his views, or that he drew up bills for congressmen; and he always declined any nomination for office. "Let them feel that I want nothing but the good of the country, and then I shall be trusted: if it is fancied that I work for any personal end I shall lose influence." And again, "Never mind who does it or gets the credit for it so long as the thing is done."

Any number of men, statesmen, men of the army

and navy, scientific men, business men having to do with steamboats, railroads, newspapers, and politics, were constantly invited by my father to his house. I can recollect an endless succession of them, from Emerson, Agassiz, Wyman, Sumner, Andrew, Fessenden, Chase, Cobden, Goldwin Smith, and James Bryce, to men whose names were never heard of out of their own business. All were made welcome; all who were in earnest were warmly received. His way of imparting his ideas to these various guests was very characteristic. Often he would grasp with his left hand the right arm of the person to be convinced and walk him off, earnestly talking, and emphasizing any telling point with a stroke executed in the air with the forefinger of his right hand. This forefinger so marked his sentences that one watched it, involuntarily, and grew quite sure that the views he tried to impress were being successfully driven home to the mind of his hearer by means of it.

I think that one of my father's strong points in his dealings with all sorts and conditions of men was his power of drawing out all they had in them of interest. This gift he sometimes humorously brought to bear on the modern newspaper reporter. On one of our Western trips, when we had Mr. Emerson with us and stopped at Salt Lake City, one of these gentlemen boarded our car and wanted my father's "impressions of the West," etc. He was received very pleasantly; but to our great amusement we soon found the reporter giving *his* views of the West, and my father listening with interest and attention, and continuing to ply him with questions till the end of the interview. The gentleman of the press went away much pleased, but without having discovered that we had the " Seer of Concord" with us, and quite in the dark as to Mr. Forbes's views on any subject.

But perhaps his strongest point was his power of " putting through " work. No obstacle seemed to daunt him, failure only to stimulate to fresh exertion. He used to declare that he was the laziest of men. We did not see it ! When, to his peculiar disappointment, General Butler was chosen governor of Massachusetts, he only said, " We must work harder next time ; " and while strength lasted he never thought the removal of a poor official, representative, or senator, too great an undertaking. No political machine ever made him fear to set about such a business.[1] " We must appeal to the people," he would say ; and with " Broadsides " and the " Spirit of the Campaign " (printed sheets containing articles from the best newspapers in the country) he would bombard local editors and postmasters, and through them the people, in his own and other States. " People," he insisted, " must be taught to think." Ready to own himself wrong, if so proved, yet, meantime, he had an intense belief

[1] See letter of October 29, 1884 (at page 207 of vol. ii.), to the Independents. In another letter to them, written during the same month, he says : " Better make a thousand mistakes in your method of action than to stand supinely and let the ship of state drift on, or be entirely in the hands of hack politicians."

in his own convictions, which brought victory in
many a hard-fought field.

That he impressed others with his power of carrying his point is clear from many of the letters to
him which I have read. The Rev. W. G. Eliot, of
St. Louis, wanting help in getting colored troops
enlisted, and in strengthening General Schofield's
hands in this matter, writes, "Your coming here
would do great good. You are a perfect firebrand.
Come prepared to speak for the powers if you can,
and get the bounty for the negro recruits, if possible;" and Mr. John Earl Williams, of the New
York Metropolitan Bank, writes on the same subject, "What do I think about your going to St.
Louis? Go by all means; don't fail to do it. Perhaps you know Schofield; but lest you may not I
inclose a line to him, which, of course, I know
to be unnecessary, as you will have St. Louis,
Schofield, and all, under your command twenty-four
hours after you get there!" And finally, Mr.
Robinson, the newspaper correspondent known as
" Warrington," in one of his " Pen Portraits " gives
the following account of my father's methods of
work at this time : " It is curious to see a meeting
of the Committee on the Enlistment of Colored
Troops. John M. Forbes is its chairman, a man of
headlong energy, long time an abolitionist, and
more than any other man the confidential adviser
and helper of Governor Andrew. He attends to
everything ; writes letters, raises money (liberally
contributing himself), sends messages to Washing-

ton to direct and organize congressional opinion, makes or persuades editors to write leading articles to enforce his views, hunts up members of Congress in vacation time, dines them at the club, and sends them back full of practical suggestions, which reappear in bills and resolves the month after."

Amidst the intense labor before, during, and after the civil war, I never knew how my father found time to give so much thought to his children as he did. A wise counselor, tender, patient friend, and cheery comrade, he was to us, one and all. Every reasonable wish of our hearts was granted, with a pleasure, in pleasing us, which made the sweetest part of the benefaction. His pride in his sons was good to see. When my younger brother proved himself a good sailor and won races, sailing his own boat, my father took the liveliest delight in his victories, throwing himself into the sport with the ardor of a boy. Later, the success of my elder brother, as president of the American Bell Telephone Company, was a source of great gratification; largely because, as he said to me, it showed that he had real ability, and " was not spoiled by his too easy surroundings." In after years his grandchildren became a great delight to him. He dwelt much on the pleasure they gave him, and showed as large a generosity to them, and sympathy with their joys and sorrows, as he had shown in the case of his own children. These, both sons and daughters, he had made independent of him, in money matters, — giving so simply and so much as a matter of

course that they scarcely realized how unusual such
liberality was.

This habit of making light of what he did for
others was a very strong one. "Mr. Forbes retires
behind his benefactions," one friend said of him;
and another, a young relative whom he greatly
valued and to whom he had given a house, told me,
"He handed me the deed as if it had been a ticket
to the opera." This recalls to me a transaction
which illustrates my father's ingenuity in devising means of making gifts so that no feeling of
delicacy on the part of the recipient should be
wounded. A near relative (Miss E.) and he had
a mutual friend, one of the rare souls that come to
bless the earth from time to time and show how
like heaven some people can make it. This lady
(Mrs. M.) was a widow with children, whose husband had left her but poorly off, so far as money
went. With that quiet dignity which graced our
old-time ladies of New England she had put gently
aside all offers of help. The house she rented
chanced to belong to my father, and he well knew
that he could give her nothing. Miss E. was ill,
dying, in fact, as both of them knew; he went to
her and talked over with her the matter of the
house, and they agreed that he should deed it and
its land to her, and that she should leave it to Mrs.
M.; and this was done, so that no feeling but that
of the dear memory of her friend was ever mingled
in the mind of the recipient with the gift of her
home. She may have suspected the transaction,
but in this world she never knew.

In smaller matters, his inability to enjoy the pleasant things of life without sharing them with others was a marked trait. No sail in the yacht was perfect unless a party could be gathered to enjoy it too; and after the Wild Duck, with her auxiliary screw, had taken the place of his old sailing yacht, the Azalea, and had made it possible to time his excursions more exactly, he took great pleasure in giving the clerks and other employees of the Chicago, Burlington and Quincy Railroad an outing on Boston Harbor or Buzzard's Bay, — in the latter case sending the yacht to meet them in New Bedford, landing them at Naushon, and taking them over the island. Then again, once a year the Wild Duck, well provisioned you may be sure, was lent to the Old Colony Railroad officials who served on the Wood's Hole branch, for a day's sail. And the island friends, farmers, sailors, servants, and all, had one afternoon in the course of the summer, with supper served them on the yacht.

This trait appeared occasionally in a "pious fraud" in which he took great satisfaction. He much enjoyed fruit, especially oranges; and at one time he owned an orange grove in Florida. It proved to be rather a poor one and was soon sold; but it served long as a pretext for the distribution of numberless boxes of Indian River oranges (sometimes shipped for him direct from Florida, sometimes secured in Boston) among dozens of friends and relatives, from his "Florida grove."

Never was a man more truly " born in *givey* weather," as the little girl in the story of " Poor Papa " called it. His last act of this sort, within a few weeks of his death, concerned a relative, for whom he had a great regard; but in talking over the prospective gift he was troubled by the thought of her virtues, and exclaimed, " M——— is so unselfish, she will give it all away." I comforted him with the assurance that M——— would do as he wished, for his sake; and then he took great pleasure in the thought that in future she would have a few more small comforts on her own account, and wound up with, " Her mother and grandmother were so good to me."

Our kind friend of many years, Professor Thayer, has spoken, in an article on my father in the " Boston Transcript," of his " sleepless benevolence." The Institute of Technology, schools for the freedmen, the Tuskegee School, the Hampton School, Milton Academy, funds for the families of various public men after their service was ended, and political campaign funds, were conspicuous objects of his generosity; but there were endless others, both public and private, of which we had at the time no knowledge. He always said that he wished to see money used while he lived; that he had seen too much mischief done by dull trustees to wish to tie up money in that way.[1]

[1] One of the codicils of his will reads : " I wish my heirs to understand that my policy has been, and I hope may continue to be, to do what I reasonably can for public objects, and for my near relatives and friends, while I am here and can myself observe the effect of what I do. I hope and believe that my heirs will continue the

With all this, he disliked to see his name in public donations, and seldom headed a subscription list unless he hoped to induce others to give by giving himself; as a rule he concealed the amount of his benefaction and let other people lead. Sometimes he would put his name and subscription on one line; and on the next "From a friend," with a second donation; and in some instances, when he took especial interest in the matter in hand, he would make this ruse cover several of these "friends," with a good amount attached to each.

But in spite of this concealment, it was natural that his habit of free giving, when there was any good reason for it, should have got abroad and led to scores of applications for aid, with no reason to show for them whatever. I will give two of these, as specimens, the one of innocence, the other of assurance. An old woman, well to do in appearance, whose name he had never heard before, called on him one day at his office and told him she had a grown-up son living with her, and it would be so nice for them to have a little home of their own. She did not want to have any mortgage on it, but to own it outright. She had heard that Mr. Forbes had more money than he knew what to do with; and now would he manage this for her? He hated to snub her, and said, very gravely, "Madam, I'll

same policy, within prudent limits, in the way of using their property for public and private beneficences under their own eyes ; my own experience having been that money can be much better used under the eye of the giver, than by bequeathing it, under attempted limitations, to public managers or to trustees' management."

think of it;" but when she replied, looking at him doubtfully, "I'm afraid you won't do it," he had to add, "I'm afraid I shan't." The other application was made by letter. It came from the fond mother of twins who had heard that his name was John Malcolm, and modestly offered, if he would send her $500, to name one of them John Malcolm and the other Malcolm John!

The Institute of Technology, on the board of which he served, always commanded his greatest respect and interest. He declared that the classics were of no use to half the community; while, in a new country, there must always be a call for technical training; and he held that a young man should be fitted to earn his own living at once on leaving his place of instruction. Then, again, Harvard, in his opinion, was a club for the favored few, not meant for those with whom he most sympathized, whose call was instant work on graduation; and although some of us used to urge that he underestimated the scope of Harvard and the good to be got there, no argument moved him, and he clung to his view of the respective merits of the two places of education with his usual tenacity.

From the year 1857 my father's long vacations were spent at Naushon, an island dividing Buzzard's Bay from Vineyard Sound, which he had some time before joined my mother's uncle, "Governor"[1] Swain, in buying. It is about seven miles long, with a surface varied by woods, hills, open downs,

[1] The governorship was that of Naushon. — ED.

and a number of ponds, — some hidden in the depths of tangled swamps, some along the shore or in little nooks in the hills, while Deerwood Lake, at the west or farthest end, is really a large sheet of water, and has always been the principal objective point for island picnics.

The same earnestness which filled my father's business life went with him when he left the office behind. Into play as into work, he threw himself with his whole soul; and it was this, and his absolute faith in the good-will of those about him, which inspired children, friends, and dependents with the strongest desire to do his bidding, and secured for him such service as is very rare. At the word of command men would rush to saddle horses, maids to prepare all sorts of unexpected meals, boatmen to get yachts ready and hoist sail; and the same inspiration reached to clerks, railway conductors, telegraph operators, and others with whom he came in contact; all sprang to do his bidding.

At Naushon my father usually wrote in the morning; and when, as he said, he had "cleared the decks" of his business letters, he drove with some of us to the South Shore of the island, where there were bathing-houses and a safe sandy beach, and where he taught us to swim. After early dinner, and then a short nap, came his afternoon ride, sometimes with the elders, who could go fast, sometimes taking me on Johnny Crapaud, the French pony, of whom more will be told later on. When I outgrew Johnny, there were two island ponies, Countess and

Rosabelle, to mount; and often, after a chapter of his favorite Sir Walter Scott, he took me with him through the woods and over the hills.

In our talks during these rides there came, naturally and without premeditation, opinions and precepts which I recall vividly to this day. He spoke of the civil war, then raging, and talked with much freedom of public men. President Lincoln, he always declared, was a follower, not a leader, of public opinion; but of Governor Andrew, whom during those anxious years he managed to bring once and again to the island for rest, he could not say enough in praise. There were talks on business matters, of which he held that girls were kept much too ignorant, adding that not one in a dozen knew, when grown up, the difference between stocks and bonds. He spoke of railroads, their policy and management, the difficulties of the " long and short haul " question, and the like. Business axioms were impressed, by the force of his opinion, on my mind. Never, he would say, for any business or other purpose, borrow more money than, by giving up all your property, you can repay, in case your venture should be a failure. He said that at one time he had to mortgage both his Milton and Naushon places in order to advance money to the railroads in which he was interested; but neither then, nor at any other time, would any one but himself have been a loser had his ventures failed.

He talked of the importance of always distinctly putting responsibility where it belonged. Apropos of this, I find a letter of his to a partner in Russell & Co. in which he says: "I have a great horror of a divided responsibility, preferring one common man, who has got to take all the credit or blame, to half a dozen geniuses, who can put it off on somebody else." I am inclined to think that his adherence to this maxim was an important element in his successful leadership.

There were discourses on the extreme care required in the treatment of trust funds placed in your hands, and the scrupulous avoidance by a business man of recommending as an investment for others any business in which he might be himself engaged, as one could not fail to be more or less biased in favor of his own projects. "Let investors judge by reports, by character, by the opinion of other good business men not in the venture; but withhold your own opinion." He was equally emphatic in his warning against the assumption that high interest on an investment could be either secure or permanent, and recommended as a precautionary measure the saving of anything over four per cent. interest on one's capital, for reinvestment, in order to be secure against risk and depreciation. A conservative business man, he said, should never invest in any property which has not real, intrinsic value. Nothing is more foolish than fancying yourself clever enough to speculate successfully in stocks that are for the moment "favorites," but not good for permanent investment. You are pitting your wits against those of men " on change," the keenest in the country, and are sure to fail in the end, as any other amateur gambler must do when playing with professionals. On the other hand, if a thing has real bottom buy it. Then, if it should fall ever so low, you can wait patiently for its rise, which will surely come, independently of stock market fluctuations; and when it does come, if you wish to sell, do not wait for what people consider the highest point, but be content with a moderate profit. These things point to that conservatism in business of which my father claimed to have no small share.

He had a vivid recollection of his own early work and struggles, and the strongest wish to help on young men who were having a hard time at their start in life. He would plan education, and provide places for boys; and cared more for those who were poor (if only they had energy and determination to work) than for those whose circumstances were easier. He enjoyed having such fellows at Naushon and giving them all the fun he could between their working times.

As to Naushon, my parents always felt that this "Paradise for children young and old" must be shared with all their cousins and friends, and their respective small people, and I may say, in passing, that in war time it became a convalescent hospital. A constant stream of guests poured through the house and took part in the joyous summer and autumn holiday time, and its boating, riding, fishing, and hunting. There was always room for one more, and the food was abundant and very simple. My father, with keen pleasure in the young folks about him, would sit at the long table, chaffing and teasing this one and that, or making game of any small mischance, such as the getting brushed off one's horse by some one not on the lookout for projecting boughs; and he would tell how this thing had happened, years before, to Miss Elizabeth Peabody of kindergarten fame, and how, on being asked whether she did not see the bough, she had replied, "Oh, yes, I saw it, but did not *realize* it!" All this in the kindliest spirit; and though some of the juniors were too shy to appreciate jokes at their own expense, the greater part gave as good as they got; and so the meals were very merry, pervaded with a sense of vivid life, of which all felt my father to be the centre. At times, interspersed with the chaff, came really good talk, when some of my parents' friends, for whose opinion they cared, were there. It was their wish that we should be listeners on such occasions, and the discussions which then took place have left many and delightful memories.

But the house was generally in the hands of the young people; and with such an army of them as I have indicated, the hurly-burly which occurred when an expedition to the West End was on foot was prodigious. My father would be writing for dear life at his table, while the punctual member of the family, book in hand, would wait, seated at one of the windows, and a concourse of boys and girls would tear through the rooms shouting for bait, hooks and lines, luncheon, and billhooks, or for choice of which should ride and which go in the wagons, — he continuing to write as rapidly as if perfect calm prevailed. But when once he was ready, double-quick was the order, and we were soon off and away. He used to go through the woods with the most murderous, curved, cutting knife, bare in his hand, lopping off such branches as grew too much over the road, — stopping from time to time and dropping his reins on his horse's neck, when a tougher bough than could be managed with one hand was encountered. As a rule, his horses learned to stand this manœuvre very well; · I ought to say, however, that on one occasion his horse did take offense at a large bough falling on his haunches, and dashed off among the trees with his rider; he, seeing a dangerous branch ahead, promptly kicked his feet out of the stirrups, dropped reins and billhook, caught the branch, and reached the ground unhurt. He impressed all the active young men into the service, and thus kept the paths well open, and insured their having an appetite for the lunch which was afterwards served under a great oak near the West End Pond. After lunch there was generally a fishing expedition for perch, and in later years for black bass, in a flat-bottomed boat on the lake. Then home, sometimes in the dark, when the horses were the best guides, and always brought us back safe and sound.

Next, in my Naushon holiday memories, comes the

autumn deer hunt. The precedents for this were handed down, somewhat modified in form, from the time when my mother's uncle was governor of the island. Matters went somewhat thus : breakfast, amid considerable confusion over orders for horses, arrangements for luncheon, guns, cartridges, etc. Next my father with a small hunting horn, very eager-eyed, hurrying on the juniors, and, it must be confessed, hustling those of the seniors who required it, giving prompt orders, in a rather low-pitched voice : "Tie up at the black gate! W., put H. on this stand, A. on that!" and the like. Then the piling into the wagons of the elder hunters, the younger going with my father ; and perhaps a couple of girls following on horseback. Then our leader sounds one sharp note on his horn : " I give you just fifteen minutes to be on your stands," and the cavalcade starts off pell-mell for the black gate. Here the horses are tied ; and then the hunters are hurried by my brothers to certain trees, rocks, or shrubs, all out of shot of one another and identified by name as separate stands, and are bidden, if raw hands, not to stir from their places lest they get within some one else's range, never to shoot a doe or fawn, nor move until the leader of the beaters winds his horn and Mr. Forbes answers with his ; this being the signal that the " drive is up," and that all have to repair again to the black gate. Promptly every man is on his stand, and we can hear the drivers shout and the dogs bark, as they come through the woods and swamps towards the hunters. The deer are supposed to run in front of the drivers, but the older and wiser ones, trained by long experience, crouch in the thick undergrowth and run back when the men have passed. However, there are always some unwary enough to run forward, and the drivers shout out, " Big buck to the right!" or, "Buck to the left!" as the case may be, and every one grows much excited. Sometimes there is a shot; but quite as often as not the deer makes off out of range, and no tangible result comes out of the great expectations stirred up in the hunters. When the drivers come in sight of the stands, the horn is sounded and responded to by my father, who comes up, eagerly asking what has been seen; and if a deer has been wounded, he sets men and dogs on its track. If nothing has been done, he decides at once on the next drive, hurries every one into his wagon or on to his horse with an energy that defies dawdling, — and so off through the gay autumn woods again as fast as horse and man can go. At noon comes a halt and lunch under some big oak, my father in the midst, stirring up every one to undo packages of sandwiches and open ginger-ale bottles, with an aside to A.: " There is more than we can manage; see that the extra sandwiches are handed over to the men; they have their own lunch, but these won't hurt them; they have the work to do." After luncheon the hunt is resumed until dusk, my father never allowing it to continue after that, lest a deer should be wounded and the men not able to track it and put an end to its pain. Back to the mansion house, the cold of the October evening nipping one's fingers and making the blazing wood fires in all the rooms most welcome. Then dinner at the long hunt table, with plenty of fun and the food seasoned with the appetite of an open-air day. After dinner my father, who never smoked, would call for a song and sit listening and marking time with his hand in the air, and vehemently applauding "Come brave the seas with me, love!" or some favorite war song. And so, with a game of cards thrown in, would pass the evening. The hunts usually lasted two days and a half, and at first my father used to ask to it all Governor Swain's old friends. As these began to fail him, my brothers' friends, and business or political allies of his own, took their places; but whoever the guests, there was always an atmosphere of outdoor freshness and cheer, even in the house, which both parents knew well how to give.

During the autumn months, we usually had one or more severe gales, followed the next day by a nor'wester, with a clear sky and a strong cold breeze, which covered the bay with white caps. Such a morning was sure to provoke this speech: "There must be black duck blown into the North Shore ponds by this time. Who wants a try after them with me?" Candidates were seldom wanting; but oh, how cold it could be! We would drive in an open wagon in the teeth of the wind to the north shore, and there my father would draw up his horse and lay his finger impressively on his lips to insure, silence, for the black duck were keen of sight and hearing, and very shy. Then he would get out of the vehicle, seize his gun, and creep over the hills, a single opera-glass in hand, and coming in sight of a pond would peer anxiously into it. If there were no duck, his charioteer was signaled to come on by a wave of the arm; but if there were duck, a gesture followed which was meant to keep you back, but was sometimes so like the other as to be mistaken for it. You soon discovered your error if you advanced, by the vehement gestures of his hand, this time toward the ground, and signifying absolute quiet. As a rule the ducks managed to see us and take themselves off just as he was ready to fire. But occasionally we had the glory of fetching one or two of them home. Once, on a cold, gray, autumn day, having left me in the woods near the West End Pond, he managed to wound a duck badly; and, not being able to stand seeing the poor creature flapping about on the pond, he stripped and swam to it, reclothed himself in the bitter wind, and came back to the wagon with his game, triumphant, but rather blue from the bleak bath!

It was always a source of gratitude to my father that none of his children or guests ever had any serious accident at Naushon. In spite of numerous hair-breadth escapes on his own part, he always declared that he was at bottom a very prudent man. I think that he was. Good riders were chosen for lively horses; we were commanded never to canter downhill; never to carry guns at full cock; never to lash the main sheet when sailing; and it was a frequent injunction, when any expedition was starting, to " be on the safe side."

These holiday times at Naushon, strenuous and over-active as they sometimes appeared to more placid natures, were always his chief points of rest. From them he set forth again to mercantile, railroad, and public work of all sorts, thoroughly refreshed.

I have scarcely touched on the romantic side of my father's nature. This appeared most strongly in his intense love of the sea. Whether it was due to his early voyages, or to his brother's profession, certain it is that " blue water " much attracted him; all ships were deeply interesting to him, and dashing through the waves on ship or yacht in a " wholesail breeze " made his spirits rise like a boy's.[1] This showed itself also in his regard for Sir Walter Scott's novels and poems, which had been the delight of his youth. There seemed to be, so to speak, an atmosphere of Scott about the place. Horses were named Ivanhoe, Redgauntlet, Douglas,

---

[1] In a letter to his mother, written while at sea, October 10, 1830, he says : " What can be more magnificent, for instance, than a strong gale (right astern, mind) of a clear winter's day — the ship springing forward under reefed topsails, and nothing to be seen around but the white foamy tops of the waves. There is nothing that elevates the spirits so much as this ; it is like riding a fiery horse ; he goes at his own speed, but he carries you where you guide."

Bruce, Rob Roy, and Mosstrooper; we children had
Scott read to us from seven years old onward; and
I can remember his coming frequently to my bed-
side, and half reciting, half chanting, the ballads,
until I grew too sleepy to listen.

In 1884, at our parents' golden wedding, we
took advantage of this passion for Scott to celebrate
it with the performance by his grandchildren, and
great nephews and nieces, of scenes from "The
Lady of the Lake," arranged by our friend, Dr.
Edward Emerson. And again, in 1894, on the
celebration of the sixtieth anniversary of the wedding day, "The Legend of Montrose," dramatized
by his grandchildren Edith and Cameron Forbes,
was performed, chiefly by some of the same company, grown from boys and girls into young men
and women. Dugald Dalgetty had always been a
great source of amusement to him. He was glad
to see this old friend on the stage, and when his
favorite songs, "Bonnie Dundee," "All the blue
bonnets are over the border," and "The MacGre-
gor's Gathering" were given, nothing was left to
be desired. To these and other Scotch songs, some
vivid and romantic chord in him always responded;
and while they were being sung he often found it
hard to keep back his tears. He much objected to
have this noticed, and would cover his forehead with
his hand, under pretense of listening intently, while
with his thumb he would surreptitiously wipe away
the unwelcome tear.

For Burns, also, he had a sincere affection, and a

weakness for divers minor poets. His "Old Scrap-Book,"[1] which he printed and distributed among his friends who came to the golden wedding, in

[1] I give the introduction as eminently characteristic of its writer : —

This volume is built up from the nucleus of an old scrap-book begun about 1830, and from a few old verses which had been either copied or impressed upon the memory much earlier. The original leaves still hold a few flowers, pressed fifty years ago, and a good many newspaper cuttings of various periods. To these last have been added contributions from friends, both in print and manuscript, many songs and gleanings from the then current literature of England and America, while some living authors, and the representatives of others, have generously permitted the free use of their treasures.

If I were to catalogue in a rough way the patchwork now printed, it would read something thus : —

Nursery hymns, having the tones of voices long silent, still ringing in one's ears with the distinctness of yesterday.

Stealings, from school and other books, accumulated in the desultory reading of a lifetime ; and, especially, large extracts from those poets who were universally recognized fifty years ago, and whom it seems to be the fashion of young America to forget or ignore.

Songs of the hunt, the yacht, the Indiaman's cabin or deck through trade-winds and Cape of Good Hope storms, or the coming typhoon, — some having for an accompaniment the rushing tide of Wood's Holl, or the squall hurrying down the sides of St. Michael's or Teneriffe's mountains ; the ripple of the Miami River pushing out of the Everglades, the foam along the Florida reefs, or the "burr" of the hurricane among the pines of the St. John's River.

Songs of the concert-room, theatre, and opera, — from the days of Mario and Grisi, Jenny Lind and Rachel (if the snake-like hissing of Rachel's "Marseillaise" can be called singing), down to the sturdy Badialli with his three encores of "Suoni la Tromba."

National, political, and war songs, — from the days of the Free-Soil campaign of 1856, up to those which rang through the camps of Grant, Sherman, and Sheridan, carrying the undertone which so many of the verses got from the outgoing regiments under Gordon, Lee, Williams, Shaw, Lowell, and Hallowell, and from the sadder march when they returned with thinned ranks and tattered flags.

1884, shows that alongside of the best poems he could find room for all sorts of jingle. His liking for either seemed to be quite independent of literary merit. Old association was decidedly the strongest factor in determining his preferences, and during his last years songs and poems from this " Old Scrap-Book " were among his keenest pleasures. This weakness for old associations extended even to his clothes. I have often wondered why one person's garments, irrespective of fashion, seemed to partake of their owner's individuality, while those of another

In short, to paraphrase Halleck, —

> Songs of the peasant and the peer,
> Songs of the bridal and the bier,
> The welcome and farewell.

Poems of the parlor, beginning under the low ceiling of the old Milton House, then through Pearl Street and Pine Bank, reaching over to Russell Sturgis's pleasant quarters on the Praya Grande of Macao, and onward still to my little ranch of Mt. St. George in California, — by no means forgetting Naushon and Swan Island.

Poems heard from the lips of Emerson, Lowell, Poe, Holmes, Fanny Kemble, and the beautiful Catherine Sedgwick, afterwards Mrs. Heine.

All these and a thousand more such threads run through the memory like echoes from the past, when one tries to string together the rhymes which have been floating in the mind through over half a century.

This crude medley of Poem and Song, Epigram and Charade, is offered with some hesitation as a token of remembrance to the few old friends who still surround me, and to the many younger ones who are so rapidly taking our places.

If it saves some eyes from straining over faded manuscript and fine print, or recalls scenes and tones of voice or of music connected with its verses, it will have answered the rather vague purpose with which it has been so loosely thrown together.

J. M. F.

did not appear to be so affected at all. My father's soft felt hats, after a few days' wear, grew into such characteristic shapes that one could swear to their identity anywhere. Capes took unmistakable folds, and boots almost turned in their toes of their own accord, as he did. He was scrupulously dainty about underwear, but habitually careless of the outer man, and loved his old raiment so dearly that one had almost to use force to get possession of it with a view to its transmission. On one occasion, when he seemed to be gaining flesh, a relative, who was aware of his peculiarity, declared that it was "an effort of nature to get rid of his old clothes."

He did not care for reading of a ponderous kind, saying that his "brain wanted rest." Travels, novels of adventure, the Indian mutiny, and all such contemporaneous history appealed to him; but he used to say that his mediæval history he got from Shakspere and Scott. Modern fiction of the introspective type he simply ignored, or, if he tried it, would put it down, declaring it to be "tedious." Of plays he must have been very fond, for he never tired of rehearsing Charles Kemble's excellences, but his hearing was just enough impaired, even in my childhood, to spoil for him this sort of enjoyment. Fanny Kemble's readings, too, he had very much admired. He cared for these more than her acting, and went to hear them whenever he could. I recollect his telling me how her rendering of the witches in "Macbeth" made his eyebrows stand on end, a fact of which he was unconscious until he felt them pushing against his theatre glasses! He had a warm personal feeling for Mrs. Kemble, and their friendship lasted until her death.

Music, save and except his favorite songs, ballads, and hymns, was a blank to him, and, though he liked many operas of the old school, he never went to instrumental concerts in my time. He suffered pretty poor singing sometimes at home, so long as no one sang a shrill, high note, and all confined themselves to his " particular vanities " as he called them. These he always greeted with immense enthusiasm, and our friend Miss Emma Ware, who survived him only a few days, used, as long as she was able, to come and play old song after old song to him, giving him a pleasure beyond words. Military bands excited and inspired him, and his musical preferences were, like those of Queen Elizabeth, " for stormy or lively " airs.

My father used to like pictures; and could never look enough at those of his friend, Mr. William Hunt; but in other cases the liking was largely for the artist's sake; and he often valued what seemed to others to be a fearful daub, if only it represented a scene he knew, or was painted by some one whom he liked and wished to help. Grand natural scenery, however, at all times delighted him, and gave him one of the greatest pleasures of his many journeys.

I suspect that his architectural ideas were very similar to his musical ones so far as the æsthetic sense went. In any building which he personally used he wanted room, warmth, and convenience; he did not like showy coloring, inside or out; but there ended his interest. I recollect, however, that he greatly enjoyed some old halls and castles in England. Time had never served for any early artistic training, neither do I think that his natural tastes lay at all in these directions.

I ought not, however, to forget among the arts one which my father did most heartily enjoy, namely, that of oratory. Daniel Webster's Seventh of March speech was well-nigh condoned for the sake of many another, which for both manner and matter had led my father captive. Wendell Phillips, too, was almost forgiven for his abuse of Andrew and his love of General Butler and the greenback party, for the sake of his wonderful power as an orator. George William Curtis was one whom my father enjoyed hearing speak, especially when, at the Convention of 1876 in Cincinnati, he appeared contrasted with General Logan. He faithfully attended Mr. Emerson's lectures, much admiring his grave, clear enunciation. Mr. Everett he cared less for; though, as he used to say, "he could speak smoothly." Perhaps he felt his own deficiency in these directions; and hence the more admired in others what he himself lacked. Be that as it may, I have seldom seen him stirred to more enthusiasm than when speaking of the occasions on which he had listened to some of these great men.

I should not forget to mention another source of

pleasure, namely, the society of the men composing the Saturday Club. This was a club whose members met in Boston, on the last Saturday of the month, during the greater part of the year, to dine together at the Parker House. So much has been told of those delightful gatherings in the biographies of some of the members as to relieve me from saying anything about them, except that my father regarded them as among the greatest pleasures of his life, — bringing, as they did, meetings with Emerson, Lowell, Longfellow, Holmes, Agassiz, Wyman, Judge Hoar, and others whose names are household words, not merely in Boston, but throughout the country. Besides all else, as each member could bring one guest, he had the opportunity of introducing any distinguished visitor to the best wits that were to be found in our good old town. At home we used to enjoy these occasions vicariously; and he would bring home to us the latest bit of literary, political, or scientific gossip, or the last *bon mot* of Judge Hoar or Dr. Holmes. It was this most genial of poets who wrote the verses given below, for the Saturday that fell next after my father's eightieth birthday, when they dined together at the club. I can only hope their kind author took as much pleasure in writing as his friend did in hearing them : —

TO J. M. F. ON HIS EIGHTIETH BIRTHDAY.

February 23, 1813—February 23, 1893.

I know thee well. From olden time
Thou hadst a weakness for a rhyme,
And wilt with gracious smile excuse
The languor of a laggard muse,
Whose gait betrays in every line
The weight of years outnumbering thine.
And who will care for blame or praise,
When love each syllable betrays?

The seven-barred gate has long been past,
The eighth tall decade cleared at last;
But when its topmost bar is crossed
Think not that life its charm hath lost:
Ginger will still be hot in mouth,
And winter winds blow sometimes south,
And youth might almost long to take
A slice of fourscore's frosted cake.

Thrice welcome to the chosen band,
Culled from the crowd by Nature's hand:
No warmer heart for us shall beat,
No freer hand in friendship meet.
Long may he breathe our mortal air,
For heaven has souls enough to spare.
Lay at his feet the fairest flowers —
Thank God he still is earth's and ours.

One subject remains for me to touch upon, and
this but lightly, as is due to one of his reserve with
regard to all matters on which he felt deeply. He
used to say that the Unitarian Church was the one
most liberal, and therefore likely to go forward,

that he knew, and he always contributed liberally
to the support of that church in Milton.   When I
was a child he always went to hear " Brother Putnam," as he called his friend, Dr. George Putnam,
the distinguished minister in Roxbury.   He also
much admired Theodore Parker, while for Mr.
Emerson his reverence was very deep.   Later on he
seemed not to care much about churches, saying,
" We all know very little."   Once he said to me
that " universal law presupposes a law-giver," and
that " somehow we must believe in thought behind
matter."   But in general he spoke seldom on such
subjects.   His creed might be said to be *Laborare
est orare.*

CHAPTER II

THE notes of which the present and succeeding chapters largely consist were written by my father in 1884; and had slight additions made to them by him in 1889. To explain their opening it should be said that my grandfather, Ralph Bennet Forbes, detained in France on business, was joined by his wife in 1811, and that after some troublesome adventures, all of which may be found in my uncle's book,[1] they found themselves at the beginning of 1813 in Bordeaux. It is to her voyage out that the following extract from a letter dated "Boston, March 23, 1812," refers.

WILLIAM STURGIS TO JOHN P. CUSHING.

. . . Most truly do I join in your wishes for the success of our friend Forbes; he is a most indefatigable fellow, and she a most extraordinary woman. She went from hence in January, 1811, in a little schooner laden with fish; and after encountering every species of distress and danger was finally landed, from a British frigate that captured

---

[1] Personal Reminiscences, by R. B. Forbes. Second edition, Boston, Little, Brown & Co., 1882.

her, on a small island near the coast of France, and reached her husband.

Here follow my father's own notes, necessarily much abridged : —

" They tell me I was born at Bordeaux, in France, on the 23d of February, 1813, and this is confirmed by a certificate ' *de naissance* ' from some officer of Napoleon the Great; while color is also given to the tale by my early recollections of being called Johnny Crapaud. As, however, my parents were merely travelers in France, I am assured that my title to citizenship is as good as anybody's.

" On our way home, when I was three months old, on the schooner Orders in Council, we were attacked by one or more Guernsey privateers, whom we repulsed after a spirited fight : an early experience in naval warfare which gave me the advantage in after life, when discussing such matters, of one speaking with authority, and on one occasion I used it very effectively. In 1861 a certain Mr. Smith, M. P., brought me letters of introduction, and at dinner he positively denied that England had been guilty of the barbarism of fitting out privateers. This was a very practical question then, as the rebels were preparing to send out this class of pirates from England. I answered Mr. Smith by telling him that I had been myself in action with a British privateer, and as I gave no particulars, he could only accept my evidence. There is a family tradition that on board the Orders in Council the baby was put down in the forecastle, with a dose of laudanum in his stomach and his ears stuffed with cotton wool to avoid harm from the noise of the cannon.

"My father had married, early in life, Margaret Perkins, the youngest child of one of the most prosperous Boston families. My two uncles, James and T. H. Perkins, were among the largest, if not the largest, East India merchants in the United States, having a branch house in China (then four to six months distant in time), which was managed by my cousin, J. P. Cushing, and later by my brother, Thomas Tunno Forbes. My other uncle, Samuel G. Perkins, was engaged in the Calcutta trade, when not occupied by his more congenial pursuit of gardening.

"I have heard my father spoken of as a man of great energy, and originally of the warmest feelings and the most genial and generous temperament, somewhat resembling in character my brother Bennet; but he had been prostrated by overwork at about forty-five years of age, after being unsuccessful in his very energetic business life, and as I remember him during my early days he was very much broken up by gout and a partial paralysis. He died in October, 1824, being then about fifty-one years old.

"The visible means of support of my parents, with five children at home, was, I remember, $1200 per annum, contributed by my three Perkins uncles. I well recall my mother's patient patching and darning, my sister Emma's vigilant eye to our wants, corporeal and spiritual, and especially the latter on Sunday afternoons, when she always read to us our Bible and hymns.

"My earliest recollection now (1884) is of the little low-roofed house in Milton between the cemetery and the Randolph turnpike, — still standing and still called the Peggy Howe house,[1] — which my father had hired. Later comes in the more comfortable home, on Milton Hill, given or lent to my father by his brother, 'The Consul,' John Murray Forbes, where my childhood and early school days were passed. My first school experience was under the not severe rod of Miss Polly Crane, who ruled with steady hand and literally a very long stick, with which she used to reach the whole class without leaving her post; and my next school was under Master Pierce in the town schoolhouse.

"It stands recorded by the elder members of the family that I was good at my letters and had a marked taste for the Bible, which led them fondly to predict the church as my vocation and to give me the agreeable name of 'The Bishop,' which I much preferred to the older one, hinting at my foreign birthplace. I ought to add, however, that the possibility of such a fate was averted in my case by the forcing of the Bible upon me in early life, in season and out of season, so that it became to me even as salts and senna in the mouth. I hope that my descendants may be treated with more discre-

---

[1] Pulled down and rebuilt in 1889.

tion and that it may become food to them instead of physic.

"Among our pleasures I remember the drives, when I first learned to hold the reins, squeezed in between my father and mother, the vehicle being old Jerry Crane's yellow two-wheeled chaise with no top, shabby and henspecked, drawn by his old white horse which looked the very image of the pale horse in Scripture lore. For a very small payment this team was hired occasionally from its daily routine of peddling fowls and vegetables, and with great enjoyment we drove about the town.

"This early life of strict economy, with each member of the family obliged to make little sacrifices for the others, and especially for our sick father, was the best training that could have been given. My mother so regarded it, and not merely from pride, but from forethought and principle, she refused the larger aid which her brothers would have furnished, and would only accept what seemed absolutely necessary.

"As my brothers Tom and Bennet got up in the world, they were able to help, and more comfortable housekeeping followed, but never more cheerfulness nor more unbounded hospitality than the little old house with its narrow limits and narrow means always supplied. Where the numbers who came there slept, and how they were fed, even on our plain fare, the Lord only knows."

The following letter from my father to his eldest brother, Tom, in Canton, is the earliest which has been preserved. It is dated Milton, June, 1821 : —

"Ben has been with us a week, and is in very good health. The Canton Packet ran on shore on the southern part of George's Island, but received no injury, as she was aground only nine hours. It happened on a dark rainy night with a pilot. We are all writing to you except sister Peg, who left her letter to ride on horseback. I went to Boston to spend election. In the morning I went on the Common, and called for a glass of lemonade in high style, and the consequence was a dizziness in my head. I could get to cousin Nancy's without falling. As I have told you this secret, I should like to know whether you ever got tipsy. I received your painting by the Volunteer, which delighted us all very much, also the walking toys. My adventure[1] sells very well in the village. I shall send the money out by Ben if he goes direct. Mary and Fanny send their love to you : as for the rest, they must speak for themselves. Excuse this bad writing. Ben says you have a box of paints, which would be very acceptable to your humble servant and affectionate brother, J. M. F."

My father's notes continue : —

" The first break in this wholesome, hardy life at

---

[1] My uncle Tom had a "privilege," as it was called, of space in the Perkins vessels, and under it had given J. M. F. a little "adventure" in tea or silk or perhaps Chinese toys. These adventures gradually accumulated, until at seventeen, when he went out to China in the Lintin, he began his commercial life with above $1000 of his own. — Ed.

Milton was my transfer, when about eight and a half years old, to the Franklin Academy in the north parish of Andover, kept by Master, or as he was called, Preceptor, Putnam. He was, I suppose, a good teacher: certainly a sharp disciplinarian. It was altogether a rough place. Under a leaning roof of not a large room were three large beds, and in each not less than two, and sometimes I think three, boys of nine to twelve years old; and as washing was included in the board bill there was some premium or bonus of cake or extra bread and butter applied to reward those who wore their shirts longest!

"In those days wrestling at arm's length was the chief game with young and old, and on election days and other holidays the young men used to collect and try their strength. Andover gave me such good training at it that I afterwards held my own among bigger boys at Round Hill, and I never lost my skill at it. After my own boys had got to be twice as strong and much heavier than I, I have often laid Will and Malcolm on their backs at arm's length, or elbow and collar grip as it was called at Andover."

The following account, condensed from my father's notes, covers the remaining five years of his school life : —

"In October, 1823, I was sent to the famous school at Round Hill, Northampton, then lately opened by Messrs. Cogswell and Bancroft. The grounds covered perhaps a hundred acres, with fine woodland and beautiful views of the Connecticut valley and of Mt. Holyoke and Mt. Tom. Mr. Cogswell was a learned man and a man of the world, and to him was largely due the breadth and liberality of the school, and its great success. The teaching was of no meagre kind, for Germany, Italy, France, and Spain each gave us of its best. But it was the pleasant and friendly relations of Mr. Cogswell and his masters with the boys, and the gymnastic and out-of-door education, which made Round Hill peculiar. The boys were taught to ride, had skating and swimming in their seasons, and wrestling, baseball, and football; and, during the summer, excursions on the 'ride and tie' plan, of sometimes over a hundred miles and back, were undertaken, accompanied by Mr. Cogswell, who was himself a great walker. He and some of the boys carried hammers, and he would give us a geological lecture when we sat down to rest. Under the excellent rules I am sure no schoolboys ever did less mischief to the farmers' orchards and fences; indeed, we were warmly welcomed everywhere, and the only uncomfortable reminiscence which remains is that of some blistered feet and sunburned faces from those long summer walks.

"I must not forget the little town — 'Cronytown' — which we built. In parties of twos and threes we burrowed into the side hill, made a low chimney, and front door, looking south, with height enough to stand erect and a real lock and key. Here many rabbits and an occasional partridge, the product of our traps or our bows, were cooked, and many an ear of sweet corn roasted, especially on Saturday afternoons; and while there was much fun I never knew of any harm growing out of the indulgence. If it did no other good, it helped to confine us to the killing of game which we could eat. Let me not forget, however, our once catching a tartar. Visiting one of our steel traps, the foremost boy, hearing a scratching of the ground as we approached, jumped boldly forward to secure the prize, when instead of bunny he was met by the pungent salute of the black and white American sable, and beat an ignominious retreat amid the jeers of his companions.

"Strange as it may seem to the youngsters who have made fun of my misses in later life with the gun, I was one of the best archers among the hundred and fifty, and only remember T. G. Appleton as a successful competitor.

"The history of my life at Round Hill School would not be complete if I forgot fisticuffs. I think there was no teaching of boxing as an art there, and fighting was discountenanced without being too rigidly punished, but one encounter I remember in which I took a hand, and this was a regular duel with two seconds on each side. My antagonist was a boy rather bigger than I, but by no means so quick as I then was, and after two or three bouts I was decided the victor, having closed my opponent's eyes, but at the expense of dislocating both my thumbs, which in my unskillful fashion I had extended too far. Another threatened attack from one of the bullies of the school I once stopped with my bat, as he was entirely too strong for a fair fight with fists. My notion then as now was, after Polonius' advice, — Avoid getting into a fight by all honorable means, but, once in, so conduct the war that your adversary would not soon hanker after another. From this principle of action, as much as anything, I had very few quarrels in school or since ; and both theory and practice I strongly recommend to my descendants.

"To sum up the physical results of Round Hill. When I left it in 1828 to enter my uncles' Boston office, I was strong, healthy, and self-reliant, though not remarkable in any degree; a fair swimmer, a good shot, and best of all a good rider; and I never can be grateful enough for the advantages which Mr. Cogswell conferred."

I now give a selection from my father's schoolboy letters to different members of his family, together with extracts from two letters written by Mr. Cogswell to my grandmother, when his pupil was leaving Round Hill : —

TO HIS MOTHER.

NORTHAMPTON, *November* 2, 1823.

DEAR MOTHER, — I hope to receive my pictures and bed-quilt. I mean to write you a long letter, therefore you will not have another for a fortnight. . . . Last Sunday I fell down and hurt my knee, and last Saturday I climbed a large tree and strained the cords so that I can hardly walk. I hope that

you will write me a good long letter with the pictures. I find that none of the boys are very good
climbers, so that I gained the prize for climbing,
which was a fine crossbow. I now study with Mr.
Cogswell, which I like very much. We are getting
to be very fine runners; we have run half a mile in
three minutes and a half; we run twice a day. . . .
My leg has prevented my going to meeting to-day,
therefore I can find time to write another letter to
you. . . . If there should be an opportunity for
China do tell me, that I may write a handsome long
letter to Tom. If you send me up any cake or
sweetmeats, depend upon it I will let you have them
again or I will give them to the boys, as I now want
only manly things. . . . You must send your letters, which I suppose you have received before this
time, from Tom and Ben. I continue to feel very
happy here. I do not think that Mary will write
me a separate letter now, I don't want her to ; however, I hope that she will sometimes put into your
letters a specimen, to see whether she can beat the
writing in the letter which I sent you by Emma, if
she dares to try. I hope that little F. goes on better than she did when I left home. I hope there is
some good schoolmistress in Milton, for I am certain
if they go to Daddy Fairbanks much longer they
will be spoilt forever. Tell Emma that I think she
could manage them better than any lady, as she has
a pretty good head. . . . I suppose you will come
to Northampton in the spring vacation. I hope
that you will follow the plan I am going to propose,

which is that you set out with me about a week
before the end of the vacation, then I can drive you
all around.   J. M. F.

TO T. T. FORBES, CANTON, CHINA.

NORTHAMPTON, January 16, 1825.

MY DEAR BROTHER, — . . . Mr. Cogswell is as
fine a man as there is to be found; he is very amia-
ble and pleasant and has much knowledge, not only
of the languages, but of natural history; he was a
lawyer, but disliked it; he has traveled over almost
all Europe and part of Asia and Africa; he has
been as kind to me as possible. . . . I am reading
Cicero's orations, which is pretty hard to me. . . . I
sleep in Mr. Cogswell's house, in which point I think
I am very lucky, as he is so kind to me.   Once one
or two of us dressed ourselves as quickly as we
could when we were called, and went down into the
place where we wash.   I having some paper, we got
some wood in the fireplace, I made a fire, then
Mr. C. came down to tell us it was school time.
He asked who made the fire; we told him we did.
He then told us we might make one every A. M.
if wanted, and might keep it there all day.   We
thanked him and told him we would like it.   We
then got all the boys together and got our own
wood, for there is plenty round in the woods, and
we take turns every A. M.   This may show what kind
of a man he is.   I suppose you know all the news
better than I do.   I am as ignorant as if I were a
hermit in the Indian forest. . . . I should like to

ask a favor, though you may think it foolish. It is that you would send me some Chinese insects, of which I should like to make a present to Mr. Hentz. He has a very fine collection of insects and seems to prize those he had from China very much. He has always been very kind to me. I hope you will not put yourself to any trouble about it.

Your grateful and affectionate brother,

J. M. F.

TO THE SAME.

ROUND HILL, NORTHAMPTON, *June 6,* 1828.

. . . . You may be sure that I shall receive [your] advice and wishes as to my conduct as anything rather than those of a taskmaster, and I trust that I shall observe them more strictly than if they were so. I can hardly say that I was surprised at your determination as to my going to Canton. I have thought much of it since you left and had almost come to the same conclusion myself, and I have thought for some time that whether I went into the Perkins's store in Boston or not, I must end by going to Canton. It is true that it must be painful to me to leave all our friends here, but I feel that it is better to make any sacrifice than to be a useless member of our family. It is true that in a little while I might make myself useful in the Perkins's store ; but I know from some examples, and perhaps from my own little experience, how difficult it is to give my attention to anything in a place like Boston, though I think I could do it. These are my

sentiments at present, and were they otherwise, I
should not hesitate to give up my judgment to
yours : and I think they will not change. . . . As to
manners, etc., I have a couple of monitors, mother
and Emma, who are always ready to add theory to
practice when I am under their jurisdiction, and are
always ready to direct and restrain my boyish propensity to slovenliness, and also to bring me into
all the society possible while I am with them.   The
former is here now, staying with Mrs. Howe.   She
thinks I had better follow my former plan of going
into the store in Boston in October, if they will take
me for one year, that I may see something of the
world before going to Canton, and perhaps to see
something of society and to correct any carelessness
about appearance which I may have contracted during my residence under the aristocratical and free-
thinking government of Round Hill.   I have read
your letter to Emma, and must own that I almost
envy you the pleasure of being able to render one
so dear to us all independent, and hope most sincerely that, if fortune is favorable to me, it may be
my first pleasure, as it is yours, to share it with those
I love.   My obligations to *you* can never be repaid,
but I hope to show you at least by my conduct that
I am not insensible to them.[1]   I shall, as you wish,

---

[1] This refers to the help that his brother Thomas gave towards
his education.   In a letter dated September 11, 1823, addressed to
this brother in Canton, he says: "Mother intends paying half my
expenses at Northampton, — and to your goodness I must be indebted for the rest; I hope to repay you in part by my diligence and
good conduct, and to show you on your return that I have been nei-

pay a good deal of attention to my French and Spanish. In the former I feel quite secure and even prepared to put it into immediate use; as to the latter, I have not nearly so general knowledge either in reading, writing, or speaking, either from not having so good a teacher or from an idea when I began of its not being of so much consequence. For this deficiency I shall endeavor to make up in the time I have left. . . .

Your ever affectionate brother,

J. M. F.

JOSEPH G. COGSWELL TO MRS. R. B. FORBES, MILTON.

NORTHAMPTON, *July* 17, 1828.

MY DEAR MADAM, — I should not doubt for a moment of the plan to be pursued with John if Colonel Perkins could give him a place in his compting room. . . . I consider him as possessor of a far better education than nine tenths of the young men who have received degrees at our colleges, and feel no scruples about sending him out on the great theatre of life, either as to principles or knowledge. In both respects his condition is entirely satisfactory to me, and I hope you will have reason to accord with me in opinion. . . . It is not mere length of time in which he has been my pupil, that attaches me strongly to him; a stronger tie is the uncommon worth and irreproachable character he has maintained in this relation. . . .

ther idle nor ungrateful for the high privilege you have afforded me on this occasion."

THE SAME TO THE SAME.

[*September* 29, 1828.]

. . . . " Were I to leave off my calling to-morrow I should feel that I had not engaged in it in vain to have aided in producing even one so excellent a character as your son." . . .

CHAPTER III

My father's Boston counting-house recollections refer largely to traits of the sea-captains employed by the firm and of others connected with it. These, however interesting to those whose recollections stretch as far back as the beginning of the century, can hardly appeal to more modern readers, and I have therefore confined my selections to memories of his own life : —

"From Round Hill school I went almost directly (October, 1828) to the counting-room of my uncles, Messrs. J. and T. H. Perkins, in Boston. My brother Tom was either head clerk, or possibly junior partner, of the Canton house, under J. P. Cushing (our cousin), who had been some twenty-five years in China, and was about returning home with a fortune.

"The Boston house was at this time — 1828, 1829 — occupying two large stores, Nos. 52 and 54, near the end of Central Wharf in Boston, in front of which their ships engaged in the China trade discharged and received cargoes.

"As I was the youngest clerk, my duty at first consisted largely in sweeping the store, making the fire, closing up at night, and taking home to the active partner the large journal or book which formed the basis of the house's accounts. This, incased in a green baize bag, I used to deposit, with the keys of the store, at his house the last thing at night, going for them the first thing in the morning. Later, but I cannot say exactly when, my duties were lightened by having an old retainer of the firm installed as porter.

"Mr. Samuel Cabot was the active managing partner of the firm and bore the brunt of the work at Central Wharf.

"My immediate superiors were my cousin, J. H. Perkins, a year or two my senior, and J. T. Hayward, the head bookkeeper. They were on the whole kind and considerate to the awkward boy they were doomed to lead in the ways of mammon, admitting me to more of companionship than I had any right to expect.

"It may be heterodox and a bad example, but I cannot refrain from recording one sketch which still lingers of the three parties last referred to. It was customary when discharging our ships to stow away in the lofts any wines or liquors which were left from their stores, and on very rare occasions my seniors used to test the goodness of these remnants from an East India voyage. On one stormy afternoon, when the blustering snow seemed to insure Mr. Cabot's absence, I had been sent up for a bottle of whiskey, — the sugar was also always saved, — and the tin pot used for testing tea was well

filled with water and on the office fire, just beginning to warm, when a hurried step on the stairs and
a stamping of snowy feet outside the office door
announced Mr. Cabot! With presence of mind
worthy of a better cause, James P. seized the blower
and adroitly hid the teapot, just as his superior
entered and seated himself at his desk to write one
of those interminable letters to China which we all
dreaded. Hayward, on his high stool, worked away
at his books, while the two junior sinners watched
with trembling the issue. For minutes, which
seemed hours, Mr. Cabot worked away at his desk,
the fire roaring in the chimney and the air getting
more and more heated, until at last he pushed back
his chair, exclaiming, ' What on earth have you got
such a fire for; take off that blower !' Jim ran to
the blower, now red hot, and with the tongs managed to extract it from its place, and to our great
relief the tin pot, water and all, had disappeared,
no doubt shriveled up by that fiery blast, and the
dreaded explanation, or explosion, was no longer to
be feared.

"My boarding place was with Mrs. Mellus, first
in Otis Place, and afterwards in Hamilton Place,
next the alley which still leads down to Winter
Street. At Otis Place I now only remember one
fellow-boarder, the once celebrated beauty of Boston, Miss Mattie Hatch. She was then a very well
preserved but somewhat portly lady of about sixty,
well-mannered, kindly and gracious to all about
her, but to my young eyes retaining little trace of

the beauty or charms which had made her celebrated.

"A boy of sixteen does not see much of society,
but besides my relatives, the Perkinses and Cabots,
I remember the welcome I always received at Mr.
William Sturgis's in Summer Street, and at a few
other houses.

"My Sundays, with part of Saturday afternoon,
always found me at Milton, and as my mother had
received from my cousin, Mr. Cabot, a present of
a horse, I think named Charlie Hardscrabble, and
had set up a carry-all, it was my practice to start at
a certain hour on foot out over the South Boston
turnpike, and about half way out to meet my sister
Emma with the carry-all. In those days Dunmore's
stage left Milton Mills every morning at about
eight, returning in the afternoon, and was the only
public conveyance between Boston and Milton.
Our letters were often carried back and forth by
Mr. Beal, the milkman."

The first of the letters which follow was written
directly after my father entered the Perkins counting-house. The second could scarcely have been
read by his brother, as he was drowned off Macao
only seven weeks after its date : —

J. M. FORBES TO THOMAS T. FORBES.

Milton, *October* 12, 1828.

Dear Brother, — I have at last taken leave of
Northampton for good. I was sorry of course to
part with Mr. Cogswell, for his treatment of me has

been uniformly kind and friendly. He says he thinks me prepared for the duties of an active life, and that I should derive more benefit from being in the store than from being any longer with him. I only want about four months of the age you mentioned and hope that you will be satisfied with my being in the store till shipped for Canton, to which event I look forward as the time at which I should commence my duties to you, and perhaps to mother, in a more efficient manner than heretofore. Mother is trying to procure a boarding place for me in some French family ; if she cannot I shall take lessons in French and Spanish in the evenings, by Mr. Cogswell's recommendation. By his advice I shall also read history and travels in my leisure time. *En passant*, a book has been lately translated from the French of Malte-Brun styled "Universal Geography," in five large volumes. . . . Should you not like to have me get it and send it out to you? I have studied the part relating to Hindostan and the Oceanica, as he calls all those islands, and think it as entertaining as any travels. I have of course seen Mr. Cushing and liked him better than I expected, for you know that we have always looked upon him as many degrees higher than the pope in all his glory, and I expected to feel a proportionate degree of awe in his presence. I think he has the faculty of making one feel easy, his manners are so calm and unostentatious. . . . Mother looks upon him as the only unexceptional object (except perhaps aunt Abbott) in this wide world of sin. . . .

I feel the sooner I go to Canton the sooner I can come back, and that perhaps **my** going **may have** some influence on your return.

>Your ever affectionate brother,
>
>J. M. F.

MILTON, *May* 30, **1829**, Sunday.

MY DEAR BROTHER, — I wrote you a short **letter** yesterday in case the Canton Packet should go **off** "*à la Française*," though it is not probable she **will** go before Tuesday. To-morrow is the "Election" day, and I shall **stay out of town.** It is the first holiday I have had since I have been in the store, and it seems as if I were going to stay here a week. . . . We have **not had** much pressing business at the **store this winter,** though you **know there is** always **employment** in making copies of invoices, etc. **If I** should **stay** another six months, however, I shall **have** much more work. As yet I have had but little to do with China cargoes except the Parthian, which gave me **a** pretty good dip into the art **of** stowing teas, **as I** had the whole management of hers. . . . Your part came out in excellent order, a **few** chests of Souchong **only being** damaged. I **should think** they would **sell pretty well** from what I **hear,** though **if you believe Mr. Cabot, the** times are so **bad that it is** better to make a bad than a **good bargain, from the** greater security of getting paid. Mr. Cabot talks **a** great deal about giving up trade and winding up the concern. James Perkins **says** he means to wind **up** the concern as he would a clock, "to make it go the longer." . . . I make out to keep on the fair-weather side of the colonel by always knowing how many brigs and ships are coming up, and which way the wind is. . . . I have been expecting by every vessel to hear something of your plans in regard to me, but I do not now hope to have anything before the Bashaw appears. . . . If she does not come here I shall expect orders to go by first ship direct, which will probably be Bryant & Sturgis's new ship, to sail by the last of June. If the Bashaw comes, it is said she will go off without landing any of her cargo, which consummation I hope you will have prevented by partly loading her with goods salable here, perhaps half a cargo of cheap teas for September, and some manila grass which I should calculate will go off then. . . The Smith place[1] has, I suppose you know, been sold. Mother is much disappointed at Mr. Cushing not getting it, and hopes to see it in your hands at some future day. Wishing with all my heart and soul and body that the aforesaid hope may be accomplished, . . . the great Bashaw prosper, and teas rise in these United States,

I remain your affectionate brother,

J. M. FORBES.

I now return to my father's recollections of the last part of his work in the Boston counting-house, and of his start for China : —

---

[1] Now known as the Russell Place, — the old estate of Governor Hutchinson on Milton Hill.

"Some time in February, 1830, the quiet and peace of my routine life was sadly interrupted by the news of the tragic death of my brother Tom in a typhoon near Macao, on the 10th of August, 1829, over five months previous. I remember carrying up the letters to Mr. Cabot's house without suspecting their contents. What marked the event more conspicuously was, that the night before I had been at a very gay party. It was one of the brightest evenings of my life, its tints perhaps colored by the cloud which so soon followed it.

"I was too young to know my brother Tom well, but everybody who did know him agreed in believing that in this last great crisis he had sacrificed his own safety in the hope of saving his friend, who was on his way with him, in a little schooner from Macao to Canton, to meet one of Perkins & Co.'s ships.

"Another incident will further indicate his character. Our father had been unlucky in business and failed, owing various parties money. As soon as my brother Tom had become prosperous his first duty had been to make his mother comfortable. His next was the pleasure of looking up his father's creditors and repaying, perhaps to all, but certainly to those who most needed the money, his father's debts, although of course there was not even the most remote legal obligation upon him to do so.

"From the time when we heard of my brother Tom's death I was in constant preparation for my voyage to China in the Lintin, commanded by my brother Bennet, during the coming summer.

"My brother **Tom's** death proved the turning-point in the affairs of Perkins & Co., for it left them not only without a partner in China, but also without any person who had been in training for such a position.[1]

"I remember the parting from home, saddened by the blow which Tom's death had inflicted on all our circle. I fancy that no boy ever left his native land with less enthusiasm or love of adventure than I did.

"The Lintin sailed on the 7th of July, 1830, my brother taking me as a passenger, and also Augustine Heard, who was engaged to take charge of the house of Russell & Co., in Canton. We also had with us a young physician, Dr. John Jennison, of Northampton, who went out to seek his fortune in China, and I think worked his passage as ship's surgeon.

"Our voyage to China was entirely without event. We anchored at Lintin about the middle of November, 1830, and went on the same night with our letter bag for Canton, seventy miles distant. My first impression of China was our passing in the dusk the splendid fleet of the English East India Company anchored at Whampoa, ten miles below Canton, some fifteen or twenty ships of the size and appearance of our large frigates, well armed and

---

[1] I find that Mr. Cushing, who was in Europe at the time, went by overland route at once to Canton, to look after the affairs of Perkins & Co. there, and merged their business in that of Russell & Co. before the arrival in China of my father and my uncle Bennet. —ED.

manned; in fact, perfectly able (as they had proved themselves) to beat off a powerful French squadron.

" My boyhood period ended sharply when I arrived in China, and was, by an arrangement made by Mr. J. P. Cushing, at once put into the office of Russell & Co. as their youngest clerk, but with a private understanding, not communicated to me until I reached China on my return in August, 1834, that if I proved competent I should be admitted to the firm on the 1st of January of that year. My salary was not large, but my quarters and position were good, as my fellow passenger, Mr. Heard, became the active manager of Russell & Co., and was very kind and indulgent to me. Before Mr. Cushing left (about the new year) he introduced me to his old friend Houqua, the chief of the Hong,[1] or company, which then managed all the foreign trade of China, and recommended me to his confidence.

" Houqua, who never did anything by halves, at once took me as Mr. Cushing's successor, and that of my brother Tom, who had been his intimate friend, and gave me his entire confidence. All his foreign letters, some of which were of almost national importance, were handed me to read, and to prepare such answers as he indicated, which, after being read to him, were usually signed and sent

[1] A Hong was technically a collection of business offices. The Russell & Co. Hong, or the "Swede" Hong, as it was called, consisted of five houses, one fronting the square, the rest behind, communicating by a sort of street, with verandas looking down. — Ed.

without alteration. It was his habit when he could not sell his tea or silks at satisfactory prices to ship them to Europe or America, and before I was eighteen years old it was not uncommon for him to order me to charter one or more entire ships at a time, and load them. The invoices were made out in my name, and the instructions as to sales and returns given just as if the shipments were my own property, and at one time I had as much as half a million dollars thus afloat, bringing me into very close correspondence with Baring Bros. & Co., and other great houses.

"Besides doing my work for Houqua, I had plenty to occupy me at the office, and as I had from various causes the appearance of being much older than I really was, I soon found myself playing a man's part. Russell & Co.'s business, swelled by that of Perkins & Co., was very large, and Mr. Heard, though untiring in his industry, was by no means rapid in his methods, so that a great deal came upon my shoulders. Old captains and supercargoes were often turned over to me for consultation without any suspicion of my inexperience, and as some of them were foreigners my French and Spanish lessons proved useful.

"In these days of steam and telegraph it is difficult to conceive of the state of isolation in which we lived. When a ship arrived she often brought news five or six months old from home, but as the success of her voyage depended upon keeping private all intimations about the market which she had

left behind, not a letter or newspaper was ever delivered until she had bought her cargo, very often
not until she lifted her anchor to go off."

Though my father seems to have recognized the
necessity for this rule with regard to letters, I find
from one of his, dated Canton, July 28, 1831, to
Mr. J. T. Hayward (bookkeeper in the Perkins
house at Boston, who appears to have taken care
there of his " adventures "), that he could not help
feeling indignant at the retention for some weeks,
by one of the captains, of private letters to himself
and his brother Bennet, which must have contained
news of three and a half months later date than
that of their last advices.

My father's work in Russell & Co.'s office was
very hard, for Mr. Heard was single-handed; but
he had time for occasional sailing and rowing on
the Canton River and trips to his cousin, Mr. James
P. Sturgis, at Macao, and to his brother Bennet,
who was making a great success of his receiving
ship, the Lintin, at the port of the same name.

Partners and clerks in Canton lived all together
on terms of social equality, but there was not much
outside sociability, nor was there any marked incident affecting my father's life. I must give short
space to the rest of his first stay in China. As to
his Chinese experience up to this date, he writes in
1884 : —

" What with hard work, tempered by boating
and an occasional run down to Lintin or Macao, I
managed to pass three years in China, and then, at

the age of twenty, the work or the climate proved
too much for me, and I was ordered home to re-
cruit.

"I took passage in the ship Alert, Captain J. W.
Sever, the same ship which R. H. Dana immortal-
ized by his admirable book, 'Two Years Before the
Mast.' We reached home about the 6th day of
June, 1833, and I think I carried the first news of
my coming, it being considered best not to awaken
the anxiety of my mother by announcing my intention."

He found all well at home, and then followed what
was most natural. He writes of the coming engagement of his brother Bennet, who had preceded him
from China, and adds, referring to himself : —

"It was hardly to be expected that a successful
young man who had been debarred all ladies' society for three years should escape the contagion.
I found my sister Mary had grown into a woman,
and was expecting a visit from two charming young
ladies of New Bedford who had been schoolmates
with her at Miss Elizabeth Peabody's school. They
were twins, and so much alike that nobody could
tell them apart. I had been to New York on some
business and expected to find them in the little old
house on my return. Accordingly one of them,
Miss Mary Hathaway, appeared, and I was introduced and much charmed ; but she soon went off
and in came her sister, differently dressed, but so
wonderfully like her that only the dress saved me
from making mistakes. This lasted a few hours,

when it turned out that Sarah had been prevented from coming and that Mary had been masquerading in her place by a change of dress. She completely took me in, but I don't think had the laugh on me for any bad blunders. It was some time in the summer of 1833 that Mary Hathaway was married to Robert Watson, at New Bedford, where I was one of the wedding guests and first saw Sarah Hathaway in her own person. . . . Later that season I made a memorable journey to New York with my sisters Emma and Mary, they stopping with Aunt Fanny Forbes. We went and called on Sarah Hathaway, then taking care of her sister, Mrs. Lydia Anthony, at Brooklyn, who was quite ill. We persuaded her to join us in a theatrical party, I think to see Fanny Kemble. During the play we encountered a party of New Bedford friends, whom I overheard telling her they were going to New Bedford by the Providence steamer next morning at eight; and as she had been waiting for an escort for some time she said she would avail herself of theirs. I listened, but said nothing until later in the evening, when I let out that business called me back to Boston. Had it been a voyage to Europe for next day, I think the business would have been there. So early next day I left my sisters (much, I fear, to their disgust) on their aunt's hands, and appeared at the Providence steamer! It was a very pleasant voyage to me, however, and somehow resulted in an invitation to Governor Swain's, at Naushon. . . . My next reminiscence is of starting on "The Judge," in the saddle, the night before Thanksgiving of 1833, sleeping at the Middleborough Pond Hotel, and riding into New Bedford, before breakfast, on Thanksgiving Day, but I was then engaged, and in high feather."

And so within eight months of landing he was very quietly married to Miss Sarah Hathaway at the house of her uncle, William Swain, of New Bedford. Of this marriage I can only say that for sixty-four years the good deeds of the husband were more than seconded by the wife; and that all who partook of their hospitalities, either at Milton or, later on, at Naushon, felt, and were grateful for, the cheeriness, buoyancy, and simple mode of life which had been brought from the Quaker city, and which gave a touch of something informal and original to all that was done for others in the home. My father refers to the wedding as follows:—

"When it came to the point we found that one formality had been omitted, in regard to publishing our 'intentions,' or as it was then called 'the banns;' which, as I was a minor, required some further certificate. Our regular pastor was absent, and we had to get a Baptist or Methodist clergyman, the Reverend Mr. Chowles, who found out the slip at the last moment, but who liberally gave out the Dogberry-like sentiment that the law was intended for law-breakers, and need not bind such worthy citizens as ourselves; and so he took the responsibility,—which indeed had penalties for him if for anybody."

My father continues : —

"Having these new responsibilities, I now had to look about me to earn a living, for though my China business had been reasonably successful, my salary had been small and I had not accumulated much money."

CHAPTER IV

BEFORE my father had been a month married there came the business offer of which the following account is given in his reminiscences : —

"My training in China was so entirely different from anything wanted for business in this country that when Bryant & Sturgis offered me the chance to go supercargo of the ship Logan which they were fitting out, and the prospect of another ship (the Tartar) following me, I could hardly avoid accepting it, cruel as it seemed to leave my wife so soon after marriage. Canton had just been opened to foreign ladies, but it was very unusual for any to accompany their husbands, and besides my wife was a martyr to seasickness, and the death of one of her sisters had been attributed to a sea voyage ; so it seemed impossible to take her with me, and leaving her in my mother's family at Milton I reluctantly embarked on the 7th of March, 1834, in the ship Logan, Captain Henry Bancroft, for Gibraltar and China. I took with me as clerk Handasyd Cabot, my cousin Mr. Samuel Cabot's eldest son, and there were some plans half formed of my joining Perkins & Co. on my return, after perhaps making some arrangements in China for their business; but, what has always seemed very strange, Mr. Cushing allowed me to embark without even having given me the slightest intimation of the provisional arrangement which he had made for my being admitted to the house of Russell & Co. in China, of which I have already spoken."

The Logan party arrived without incident at Gibraltar on March 28, 1834, and were most hospitably entertained by the U. S. Consul, Mr. Horatio Sprague. Here, as the ship took about three weeks to load the lead which she was to take to China, my father went through the usual round at "The Rock," burnt blue lights in St. Michael's cave, saw the pretty women strolling on the Alameda to hear the band play, followed the garrison fox hounds, was taken into custody for attempting to go in and out of that strictest of fortresses without a pass, and finally took the regulation trip to the cork wood convent, where he was kindly received by the prior and his company, and allowed to contribute some dollars towards "ransoming Christian slaves from the Moors."

The voyage of the Logan to the mouth of the Canton River was without excitement, with the exception of the occasional catching of a shark and an abortive attempt at mutiny, which was the more exciting because "a great lot of boxes of silver dollars" had been taken on board at Gibraltar and stowed under the captain's cabin. The mutiny was soon quelled and three of the mutineers put in irons, but released within a few days on the handing over by each of them of some cherished possession as security for good behavior, and " never was there a more quiet crew for the rest of the voyage," he writes. As to books on board ship, it so chances that Miss Edgeworth is the only author to whom reference is made in his journal, written at the time, and of her he says : —

" May 23d. I have been reading some of Miss Edgeworth's books lately; I did n't like them quite so well as I used to — there is too much windiness, her characters are too perfect, her plots hinge upon too slight and improbable contingencies; then there is always some grateful Irishman, or old woman, or six months old baby, or Jew boy, or beggar who comes in to the relief of the hero when he is in a strait. Good reputations are too easily gained and lost; and then she always furnishes her good people at the end with such a glorious set-out. Estates fall from the wicked to go to them, they have lots of creature comforts, and are perfectly happy. The moral is good, the plot bad; for truly the wicked are not always punished here, externally; nor the good always rewarded, as far as we can see."

On arriving at Canton early in August, 1834, my father found Mr. Heard longing to get away on account of the critical state of his health, and at odds with Mr. Green, the partner whom he had taken into the firm of Russell & Co. on account of its overwhelming increase of business. He also learned for the first time that he himself had been a partner in the firm since the first of the preceding January, so that his share in the profits of the house, should he assent to the arrangement, must be already much larger than all he could make as supercargo of the Logan and Tartar. Even this would not have decided him, " but," as he wrote, " Mr. Heard insisted that he would stay till he died unless I would take his place," and so " I took some time to consider the case, but finally decided to sign the articles and go to work." Mr. Heard left in search of health in the course of the autumn, and, as Mr. Coolidge, the only other partner in the house, was away in India, the whole work of the firm devolved on Mr. Green and my father. Houqua, after some demur, consented to transfer his business to Russell & Co., stipulating only that my father should give it his personal attention. On the 3d of February, 1835, Handasyd Cabot was attacked by small-pox, and nursed by my father and Mr. Francis Hathaway, my mother's cousin, till he died, early in the following April. As to one of the dreary distractions during his cousin's illness, my father writes in his journal : —

" April 5, 1835. Whenever I have found time lately I have been with Hathaway to a walk which we have discovered on the other side of the river. We land there at five in a sort of suburb, saluted by men, women, and children with ' Hillo, you foreign devils ! ' and besides by beggars for cumshas (presents), which we offer with our canes.

We come at last to the country, which is composed of barren hillocks covered with tombs, and between them paddy fields, which are overflowed at high tides — the same round day after day; even this dreary walk is better than pacing up and down in front of the factories."

On the day following the funeral of Handasyd Cabot, Francis Hathaway, having detained his ship Horatio for that purpose, took my father with him on a trip to Manila. As to this he writes : —

"After the confinement and the strain under which I had been, the voyage in a fine ship, with good company, good weather, and above all pure air, was simply delightful, and I was soon able to enjoy life again."

In a letter to one of his family in Milton, written on board ship and dated May 8, 1835, Lat. 17° N., Long. 11° E., he says of his Chinese servant : —

"Apee is my valet still. I take him to Manila, in the hope that he may run away when he gets there, or if not, fall overboard. I am really disgusted with him, he is such a clumsy cooly of a fellow, and it is only on account of the regard which mother has for him [1] that I have not turned him adrift fifty times. He cannot get a plate or a glass of water without running over a whole room and capsizing two or three boys and chairs."

In about a week they landed at Manila and were most hospitably received by Mr. Sturgis. They

[1] He had accompanied my father to Milton on his first return from China. — ED.

remained there two or three weeks and made an excursion as to which my father wrote: —

"June 1, 1835. Hathaway, Wood, and I got away at about six or seven A. M. in a carriage for Santa Anna, where we embarked in a canoe long and narrow, two feet by twenty-five; after two hours of quick pulling we reached the mouth of the lake, where we found another barca, or canoe, a little larger than the first; by three o'clock we reached Wood's house or hut, which is, like the Indian houses, built of plain wood, stuck upon posts six feet in the air, and very ordinary. We proceeded to the house of Don Pablo, the owner of all that district and also the head of the police. He received us well, and gave H. and myself quarters, and after supper we turned in. I had hardly lain down, when I heard the most awful noise, women screeching, with cries of 'Ladrones! Ladrones!' (robbers) mingled with prayers to the Holy Virgin. I seized my dirk, without which no one ever sleeps in this country, and ran into the hall, where all the household soon appeared, Don Pablo armed to the teeth. I was frightened to death, because I knew they had $2000 to $3000 in the house, and that there was in the neighborhood a band of thirty robbers. It turned out that the servant had seen a man climbing into her window, who had retreated when the alarm was sounded. Don Pablo caught him the next morning, and found that he had formerly been a servant in the house, and had climbed up to make love to one of the maids, but was seen by the wrong one. He was dismissed with thirty lashes. Don Pablo's dress, when he sallied out next morning, was a primitive one for a man in his station, checked shirt and pants, kept up by a leather belt, which also supported a most murderous knife, made to cut your way through the woods or through your enemies, as may be, and called a 'machete.' . . . We spent the next day in visiting Wood, and after dining at twelve started at three to visit the mountains. Hathaway was mounted on a one-eyed creature that strongly reminded one of the Naushon horses, while I had an animal that could only be got into a dog-trot by severe pummeling. We went on paths that seemed almost impracticable on foot, the beasts showing a most wonderful sure-footedness. Our guide, an Indian, bare to the waist and mounted on a horse without a bridle, led the way, with my gun and apparatus — for which arrangement I have been sorely laughed at, though I think it a very rational one under such a sun. We dragged on by by-paths, zigzag enough, to the top of the mountain, and then had a fine view of the lake and the sea. We undertook to return by a new path ten times worse than the first, had to dismount and lead our horses down hills and over gullies that would have puzzled a goat, and after getting a mile and seeing two deer we had to return, and at sunset found ourselves on the top of the mountain, completely at fault. I proposed leaving the horses and getting home while there was light, but after some trouble the

Indian found the path, and we got home at seven, after four hours of severe exertion on a very hot day. Hathaway was desperately done up, but I, though tired, was not fatigued, and could have walked half a dozen miles farther. We were both heartily tired of the lakes (a nasty muddy piece of water full of green stagnant weed and water snakes, which we saw, and alligators which we did not see). We had been eaten up by mosquitoes, there being no curtains, and had not had a moment's comfort since we left, so we got into a canoe at ten P. M., and arrived here at ten of the following A. M. I never saw Hathaway so completely miserable; there was no place to shave nor to bathe, no good tea, a thousand risks to health from midnight air and midday sun, and badly cooked dinners; and all on my poor head for leading him into such a scrape. I think I never passed three days of such constant and disagreeable exposure, and my escaping without even a headache proves that my constitution is of the strongest and that my days of illness are passed."

In Manila my father bought a pony, which he called Augustine in honor of Mr. Heard, and took back to Canton. For some time afterwards nothing worthy of notice seems to have occurred, but on 23d November, 1835, I find him writing to my mother : —

"Last evening, just as I was beginning to think of writing home letters, a tremendous row commenced; a fire had broken out about half a mile in the rear of the factories; the wind was blowing half a gale towards us. There has been no rain for many weeks, and all Canton is dry as tinder and as ready to take fire. We had about $300,000 in our treasury, and perhaps $50,000 worth of goods in the house. I instantly started for Houqua's, and such a scene as the narrow streets presented you cannot imagine. Bands of armed coolies forcing their way along with continued yells, each man having his master's name on his cap and on his lantern, and I suppose on his tongue; and the parties keeping close together and running, their numbers varying from ten to fifty in a party; the rest of the street filled with coolies carrying goods from the fire on their shoulders, and having in one hand a lantern, and in the other a glittering short sword which they flourished constantly, vociferating loudly all the while to clear the way. Through this dense mass, I shouldered my way, with the help of my cooly, to the Hongs, and there found old Houqua as cool as if nothing was the matter, surrounded by his men, with water and engines ready for the worst. He said there was no danger, but I insisted on his lending me a large cargo boat, which he sent opposite the factory. I then got home as quickly as possible, sent for Dumaresq and our other captains, made them write orders for the ships' boats to come up armed to protect us in case of need, and dispatched an express with their letters to Whampoa (ten miles distant) to alarm the fleet. By this time the fire had spread perhaps one

eighth of a mile in width and was rapidly increasing; we could hear the cracking of every house as
it fell, and the cinders and sparks flew over us in
showers; the whole sky was lighted, and the square
in front nearly as light as in the daytime. From
the top of Sturgis's house it was the most magnificent sight I ever witnessed, such a mass of red
flame, with a falling of houses and yells of the
Chinese, which made such a din as Babel never
knew; but it was no time to indulge in admiration
of the picturesque. We hired as many men as
could be found, and went to work packing up our
books and papers; this we completed before eleven,
and I then ordered supper for all hands, in the
full persuasion that it would be the last meal we
should eat in our house. Our specie all ready
for removal, I went once more to Houqua, found
him still up, but his spirits gone; he now advised
shipping everything but our money, which he said
would be safer in the vault than in a boat. We
returned to the factory, got all our coolies laden;
Dumaresq in the boat, armed to the teeth as guard;
clerks at our door and at the boat, to take account;
and were about starting, when the fire appeared to
abate. We waited an hour, and thinking the matter nearly settled in our favor, I gave my boy
orders to call me if anything new happened, and
lay down in hopes of getting a nap; this must have
been at two. I had not closed my eyes before the
clamor was renewed, and Green and Dumaresq hurried into my room to say all was lost and the fire

quite close to the factories in a new place. We scampered down, harnessed the coolies, and had got about half of our luggage into the boats, when the new flame was put out and the main fire seemed going down. I again stopped sending down to the boats, placed a watch, and laid down. In half an hour all was uproar again; we had to set to work again, and fairly cleared everything out, and at daylight I would not have given sixpence for the factories; the wind was high, the engines (?) had reached the city wall, and that was now our only protection against it; on this side were paltry wooden houses which, packed close together, extended to the factories, and seemed to form a train for the fire to take; but the daylight saved us, the streets were pulled down now that they could see the whole course of the fire, and the necessary measures to stop it were taken, and in half an hour from the point of greatest danger, we were safe, just as the boats from the ships arrived. By one P. M. we had our house to rights again, gave the sailors a jollification, and all parties were well pleased with the result except the poor devils of Chinese. The number of houses is estimated at from 2000 to 3000 destroyed; put it at 1000, and you have 10,000 houseless heads; many shops were burned, and as there is no insurance, hundreds of men who were last night prosperous have now only the labor of their hands to look to for support, in a country where the hardest labor of strong men barely earns food and clothes enough to sustain life. This fire has leveled half a mile square of a populous city. Houqua told me he had men ready to pull down the street which lined the western wall of the city, and that he had promised the occupants, if he was obliged to do it, to build their houses new at his own expense. The authorities seem subdued from their usual insolence by this awful calamity, and have not opposed the entrance of foreigners into the usually sacred walls of the city. I went this P. M. with Hathaway, mounted the wall, and walked on the top of it for half a mile, during which we met with civility, for the first time in all my residence in China; or rather, we did not meet with a single insult — a miracle. We descended from the wall, which is perhaps ten feet thick and eighteen feet high, by steps which led into the midst of the ruins, which were blazing close to the wall; we were trying to penetrate over the rubbish into the interior of the city, when a petty mandarin turned us back civilly and without insult.

"I have been so constantly on the move that my feet are as sore as if I had been on a long journey, and my eyes swelled and bloodshot, from ashes and want of sleep. Do not mention my name in connection with Houqua's; it would seem ostentatious to speak of my intimacy with the old hero, and though it might give me notoriety, I don't care to shine with borrowed light; I shall be content with what share of respect I can command for myself."

Bearing in mind how large a part of my father's

work in after life was devoted to railroads, and how successful he became in their management, it seems the irony of fate to find that his first feeling towards them was one of distrust and dislike. His brother Bennet had written from Boston suggesting the investment in railroads of some funds of my father's of which he had charge there. To this suggestion my father replied : —

CANTON, January 9, 1836.

MY DEAR BENNET, — The principal object of the present is to request that you will by no means invest any funds of mine in railway stocks, and to advise you to keep clear of them. I have good reasons to believe, from all I can learn of the English railways, that ours will prove a failure after the first few years ; the wear and tear proves ruinous. At any rate, keep clear of them. Three ships going this week. I am very well, and quite busy.

Ever yours most affectionately,
J. M. FORBES.

Towards the end of this his second and last residence in China my father spent some time in Macao in a house taken by himself and Francis Hathaway ; but as this was a small one, Dr. and Mrs. Colledge, friends whom he had made there, lent him their house for a farewell fancy ball which he proposed giving in acknowledgment of the many hospitalities he had received. The following is his account of it, written at the time : —

"September 12th, 1836. I undertook to invite some Portuguese, and have made a mess of it; quarreled with half the town. I to-day called on the governor; he and his suite will come, also some English army officers. I have eighty-four on my list of accepted. I am to have a green satin frock coat ornamented with green cording, white satin tights, white Spanish boots, a hat and feather, simply a crown hat looped up on one side. Both men and ladies have been most obliging; one looks after the decorations of the house, another the lighting, etc. . . . .

"At the ball the first who entered was a Turk in full costume, looking quite a character; then a German student, then a lady in court dress; nearly all the gentlemen in coats, which I at once asked them to change for white jackets. As the room filled, the effect was most brilliant; several ladies came as nuns, as Swiss peasants, Spanish ladies, etc., all very much dressed and ornamented. I soon lost all tremor, and entered into the full enjoyment of the thing. One man came dressed as a woman, and I did not find it out for some time. Three captains came in Moorish and Parsee dresses; no one would have detected them, unless from knowledge of their features — they looked and acted their characters perfectly. So did another captain, who came dressed as a 'good old English country gentleman.' Presently Alexander Robertson entered, in full Spanish costume, brilliantly ornamented, and in attendance on a Spanish lady in black hat and feathers and black bodice on a white dress (Mrs. Stewart). Then came a Jack Tar in company with an Englishman dressed in trousers representing the stripes and a jacket of stars intended to mean the Yankee flag; then an Arab, a Turk, and a Greek. All seemed in good-humor, and just filled the rooms enough. There were about forty plain dresses, and thirty or more fancy ones. After hot coffee we began dancing. The lady highest in point of rank was Mrs. Elliot, wife of one of the British superintendents; but she had rather discouraged my party, and came in a plain dress, so I led out Mrs. Daniel for the first dance; she had taken a strong part in my favor, and indeed, with one or two others, had fairly carried the thing through. She was dressed fancifully, in something between Swiss and Spanish, and as usual looked pretty. At twelve we supped at small tables in the veranda. I led in Mrs. Elliot. Captain Elliott got up in a chair, and made a long speech about me and my party, and then proposed my health, with cheers, which seemed much out of place among ladies. In due time I got up and thanked all present for the honor they had done me in accepting my invitations, etc., and finally proposed as a toast, 'The bright eyes of Macao.' When supper was over we had a few songs, then dancing and waltzing until nearly three A. M. I never saw so brilliant a party anywhere, not even at the garrison fancy ball at Gibraltar. It could not have gone better, and Inglis (of Dent & Co.) is already insisting on another when the weather gets cooler.

" 16th. Now for the disagreeable part of the ball. It is very likely to lead to some ball practice of an unpleasant nature. I asked a Portuguese gentleman (Sr. R——) to name to me a few Portuguese who were proper persons to be asked if I chose; well, he sent me a list of twenty-three people, from which I crossed off three garrison officers and sent him notes for the rest, informing him that the gentlemen outnumbered the ladies already very much, and that I had therefore omitted a few of the bachelors on his list. I employed his clerk to write the invitations, and he sent them to Captain Lonero, with the list containing the crossed-off ones. The crosses were laid to R.'s account, as he does not speak to the other. My navy friend and his wife immediately sent a refusal, and none of the list accepted. The morning after the party, I found on my table a note from the gentleman, asking an explanation of my conduct, and since then I have been carrying on a pistol and dagger sort of correspondence. The officers are vaporing and talking of satisfaction, and the captain writes letters of dangerous consequences if I refuse to give up R.'s name as accessory to the crucifixion. In my first letter, I made all the concessions and apologies that I intended to, and as it now stands, I have told my peppery friend that I alone am responsible for my own omissions and invitations. I am staying at home now in momentary expectation of a visit from some of the garrison officers. This is not very pleasant, it keeps me from going to Canton. I

don't think it will come to anything — am pretty
much decided not to risk my life against any of
the creatures. I shall not go out, unless quite convinced that my reputation would suffer by refusing."

My father waited all day for his not forthcoming
challenger, and then returned to Canton and work,
and on the 5th of the following November I find
him in Macao again, and writing : —

" Yesterday was a fine bright day, and with De-
lano I started for the Lappa, a hilly island half a
mile from Macao. We went at eleven, walked
about a couple of miles to the top of a high hill,
and there in the sun and breeze upon the ' bonnie
Highland heather ' it was delicious ; a splendid
view on all sides, and then the wild rugged loneli-
ness of the spot surrounded by heath-covered hills,
so different from Canton, and indeed from all tropi-
cal scenery. I could easily have imagined myself
on one of our own barren hills, for there were no
trees, except a few stunted pines, contrasting well
with the brown grass. We gathered some wild-
flowers, and some running evergreen and fern, and
heather for Mrs. Sturgis, and had some good runs
over the hilltops, and drank out of a leaf from a
pure stream of clear water, and then laid down in
the sun for a couple of hours."

This period of my father's life, which ended in
December, 1836, embraced that of the giving up
by the East India Company of their monopoly of
the English trade with China. This led to a large

influx of Englishmen, to the forming of a club, the Union, of which he was a member, and much sociability and festivity not before existing; under the strain of which British official reserve seems to have broken down entirely, as appears from the following extract: —

"Sometimes we raced our boats on the way to the baseball grounds, then played leap-frog along the dikes towards the upland. In out-of-door sports the Englishman has perforce to drop his insular dignity and become democratic, and he never does it by halves. Often we found ourselves holding, or jumping over, the head of a high dignitary of the company's service in India, who, when at home, held power of life and death over thousands of natives; and perhaps when the game was organized for ball the same official would be found 'tending out' in his turn or getting pelted by the hard ball as he tried to run in, for it was then the fashion to throw at the runner, and if hit he was out for that inning. I think we had no quarrels, and that the best spirit prevailed between the American and foreign residents. The Laird of Innes was not, I think, a member, but some of Jardine & Co. were, and the whole effect of the club was civilizing."

In looking back, in 1884, to his mercantile experience in China, my father speaks of the strict honor of the Chinese merchant, and sums up with, "I never saw in any country such a high average of fair dealing as there." When his agreed term was expiring, though it was at the busy time of the

year, he could not of course consent to stay longer.
He writes : —

"So, after making arrangements with Mr. Green
for a moderate share, I think three sixteenths, of
Russell & Co.'s business for three years while attending to its interests in the United States, I took
passage for home in the Luconia, Captain Charles
Pearson. . . . The afternoon of our sailing comes
back to me, with my sensations as I paced the deck,
just as clearly as if it were yesterday, and I recall
the very tune I was humming — nearly sixty years
since; it was Moore's

'There's a bower of roses by Bendemeer's stream,
  And the nightingale sings round it all the day long.'"

The Luconia's run was fast (120 days), and without incident, till she was nearing New York, when
my father writes in his journal : —

"Four days since, I was reading in the cabin,
when, about four P. M., I heard a fall on deck;
then down came some one saying a man had fallen
from the mast and was killed. I went up to see
what I could do, being less flustered than the rest.
I found it was a poor boy, the favorite of all on
board. My old friend Brown was holding him in
his arms and trying to bring him to. . . . The boy
was the son of a country physician, and being in
delicate health, a sea voyage had been necessary
after he had prepared for college. He could not
afford to pay for his passage, and had shipped as a
sailor boy; he had been ill several times, and when

we sailed was dangerously so. I then got interested for him, used to go and see him and try to keep up his spirits, and when he was well enough to read lent him books. He got well, and was perfectly recovered and grown very stout, with every prospect of being home in a week, when this unaccountable accident happened; it was nearly calm, and he was in the mizzen top, where any lubber can go without danger. He was a gentle, kindly boy, and must have been dearly loved at home. . . . Poor fellow, I came nearer shedding more tears for him than I have before for many years. I was much touched, too, to find that his clothes were coarse as any of the crew's, and that he had spent his little earnings in buying at Canton a couple of pair of velvet slippers and a box of gay fans, presents, no doubt, for his father and mother. . . . Four o'clock P. M. was appointed for the funeral; I dragged myself to the deck; the sky was black, with every indication of an approaching gale; the ship was plunging swiftly on; every blast seemed louder than the last. The crew were collected at the gangway. The body, sewed up in a sheet, with shot at the feet to sink it, was placed on a board which rested on the gunwale, and covered with the American flag. Captain Pearson read the Church of England service to as sober a set of men as I ever laid eyes on, not a few brushing away a tear now and then. At the sentence, 'We commit his body to the deep,' the flag was removed, and his messmates raised the board till the body plunged into the sea, and we sped swiftly on our way."

A few days later, after an exasperating interval of contrary winds, my father landed in New York (March, 1837), and as to what followed he writes: —

"The Providence steamer was then the only short way of reaching home, and the next forenoon found me snugly harbored at my aunt James Perkins's, in Pearl Street, where my wife, perhaps by accident, met me after an absence of a little over three years."

CHAPTER V

DURING the latter part of my father's stay in China my uncle Bennet had seen to building for him on Milton Hill the cottage which, with some additions, is now occupied by my brother Malcolm; and here he found my mother already established.

My father had left China in December, 1836, when no warning of any commercial storm had reached Russell & Co. He did not anticipate having more to do than to attend quietly to the interests of the firm in the United States, and expected therefore to take life more easily than had been possible for him in Canton.

But this was not to be. When he landed in New York, in March, 1837, he found the business world in wild confusion. The three great banking-houses in London, Wiggins, Wilson, and Wilde (familiarly remembered as the three W's), through whom the greater part of the Chinese-American business had been done, had failed, and only Baring Bros. and the Browns stood firm. He found that Russell & Co. had drawn bills for over £400,000 sterling on the three broken bankers, and that these bills had at once to be provided for; a matter simple enough had the Chinese goods represented by the bills, and on their way to the United States to sundry correspondents of Russell & Co., continued to hold the values which ruled at the time of their shipment; but these had fallen during the panic to such a point as to make it impossible for weak correspondents, and impolitic for tricky ones, to make prompt remittances to London to take up the dishonored bills. One of these latter did refuse to do this and caused much trouble, but most of the houses for whom the shipments had been made did whatever was needed to sustain their own and Russell & Co.'s credit, notably, as my father says in 1884, in looking back to this time, that of "the square, unpretending Tom Wigglesworth;" and the storm was successfully weathered.

Russell & Co.'s affairs, however, were not his only care at this period. During the panic his brother Bennet, too, had suffered, and at his own request had gone once more to China to take my father's place in Russell & Co.

One of his brother's business difficulties had to do with some nail works in Farrandsville, Pa., and thither in the spring of 1838 my father took a trip, accompanied by Mr. Russell, of Plymouth, on whom he had called for advice as an expert in the business.

I give part of a letter written by him during this trip, as it may bring home to the minds of those of my readers who feel aggrieved when, on any forced journey, a Pullman car is denied them, what such an

undertaking was in the days of their grandfathers.
He writes, in April, 1838 : —

FARRANDSVILLE HOTEL.

. . . " Landed day before yesterday at Lewiston
at eight A. M.; went right to a livery stable ; could
get a carry-all and pair of horses for $10, but they
would only travel four miles an hour. Went to
another, found a ruffianly looking fellow whose man
would drive five miles an hour; told him to hitch
on two pretty, little, spirited horses, who soon
started off with your humble servant, Mr. Russell,
and a way passenger to go two miles, with an Irish
eighteen-year-old to drive. We two in the hind
seat of a carry-all, very like our veteran, only I
could not get up the top to keep off the sun ; most
luckily. Glorious day; found Pat was for prancing
along; forbade this; got down first hill pretty
well, but Mr. R. scary. Was telling him of my
fall from Kate (in Boston) just as we crowned the
second hill; says I, ' She threw me so far as to clear
her, or else — Hullo ! driver, mind your hand ! '
Kick ! kick ! Pat frightened, pulled his left rein ;
both horses went up on a four-foot steep bank, and
over went carry-all, without my having power to
stir from my seat. I scrambled out of the road
unhurt, except my umbrella knocked into pi — ' te
poor plack crow ; ' sprang to the horses' heads, and
with the aid of passers-by and the driver, who had
kept his feet and the reins, stopped the kicking
horses and righted the carry-all, which was turned

bottom up, not a strap broken, not a bone, my two companions rubbing their shins, I unscathed, the driver exulting over his unbroken leathers, and I in a gale at the comicality of the whole thing, especially Mr. R.'s fright and distress, though hardly bruised at all. 'Noo,' says Pat, 'get ye in; no fear noo; I'll warrant ye safe.' Mr. R. would not set foot in that again, would go back to Lewiston. After consultation we agreed to walk down the mountain and see how the horses went, etc.; then I got in and took care, sitting in front, that Pat should not let horses get excited again, and with some difficulty I controlled him, and Mr. R.'s fears gradually subsided. Glorious day and splendid scenery, mountains, river, brook, rocks, and trees, giant trees such as I never saw before; wild roads like those in Berkshire specked with riders in saddle, men and women in groups, going up to a plain, log-hut, Methodist church; not a vehicle in the way but ours; and at the church the grouping was fine, of horses tied under the forest trees, and the plain old church, and plain old country-looking people. Stopped at the post-office to borrow a wafer, and at the next (Pattie's Mills) put my letter in. At twelve, or one P. M., found a nice house kept by a Boston man; his daughters tend the table dressed in black silk gowns and looking quite 'genteel,' but modest withal. Heard much of the iron works from Mr. Coverly, a shrewd Yankee who has made his fortune here, as he told us, 'though,' says he, 'God made me and my brothers just the poor,

broken-down, weakly looking critters that you see
I am.' Heard that our horses were celebrated as
being the most vicious in the country. Through a
beautiful country, and much tribulation, we passed
first Pennsylvania Valley, fertile and picturesque;
then the mountain, which was on fire not far from
us, if smoke told true; and finally reached Belfonte
(read Cooper's 'Pioneer' for a description of this
valley), a most dirty village, finely placed on one of
the most perfect spots I ever saw. At five P. M.
went to a tavern and asked where was a livery stable
— only one in the place — tried to make the man
start off and get twelve miles on our way to-night,
but the innkeeper gave him a wink on hearing Mr.
R. talking to me about the danger of night travel,
and so would not go till morning, and wanted $11;
whereas our pay from first post, at $10, was ex-
orbitant for thirty miles. Offered him $10, and
start at this hour in the A. M. Let him go, after
telling him that I was aware that I must expect
Scripture rule, 'When saw ye a stranger and took
him not in,' but I would not be bled too much if I
had to walk. Sent for W. Manly, brother of a man
at the works, now in the shoe business at Belfonte,
shook hands with him, told him I must have a
carry-all to start early next A. M., and would pay
$10, etc., — said he 'd try. Came in and told us
he had borrowed a carry-all left there for sale and a
horse to go with his three-year-old colt, neither ever
before in double harness. (Mem. Never hire carry-
alls left for sale, and especially eschew old blood

mares — rather walk.) Poor Mr. R. remonstrated against going over the hills in this plight, but I told him I would not submit to the livery stable keeper's charges, after once sending him off, if it cost double money and risk. Woke before day, dressed and mustered up Manly, determined to succeed, and such a team as we had ! A flashy carry-all, a lanky gray three-year-old colt, and a white, very old, and spirited blood mare, each carrying the head as far as possible from the other. Found Manly afraid of them, so insisted on driving myself, and well it was I did. 'All aboard !' — Mr. R. trembling — 'All aboard !' (Mem. Heard that yesterday's team smashed a carry-all the last time they were here and had to be ridden back.) Started on the jump, hauling Colty along. Soon brought her to bearings and gradually made them know my voice a little (lucky) ; got along well enough for eleven miles over a decent road sprinkled with stumps and holes (my driving much admired), everybody we met on horseback. Stopped at a Dutch inn and had a long argument on politics with an old Dutch farmer ; did not hope to convert him, only wanted a little fun ; Mr. R. quite indignant at the old fellow's putting Washington and Jackson together ; I told him W. was a real Federalist and bank man, and he ought not to praise him. (Mem. May tame a tiger, find a silent woman, catch the sea-serpent, but convince a Dutchman, never !) A mile farther met a train of covered wagons, men with rifles, women and children walking, bound West. A little farther on, Manly sang out, 'Hold hard!' 'Wo-o-o!' says I, pulling up just in time to avoid another capsize. Fore wheel, starboard side, just on the axletree; stopped half an hour, got a staple from a farmhouse and drove it in half way. 'There,' says Manly, 'that 'll go forever!' The white critter pranced, and off we went again. Came to a long hill; then says Manly, 'Let them go down lively, Mr. F.' 'No,' says I, 'that won't do here.' Just then they began to go it, and I to hold on, both horses prancing, Whitey kicking like a devil right against the dasher. 'Turn them up that bank,' says M. 'Wo-o-o!' says I, holding hard, 'I 've had enough of banks!' So after a while I stopped them in the road, instead of turning over again; got out, and lengthened the traces so as to bring the horses farther from the carriage. The two men walked, and I drove down the hill, horses still very restive. Near the bottom the staple came out and wheel nearly off again. 'Better look at the other wheels,' said I. 'They are all right, I 'll secure,' said Manly, a harum-scarum dog. 'Look,' says I. 'Hollo! here 's another linch-pin gone.' 'I do believe,' says he, 'that skillful livery man took 'em out.' 'Fix it,' says I. 'Boy, where is there a smith?' 'A little piece on.' So on we went, they walking, I watching my wheel, which varied from one to six inches on the axle; found the smith and set him to work making pins. That nearly done, I thought I would take a look at all the fixtures of the carry-all. 'Hollo —

no wonder the horses kicked!' The bolt by which the pole holds back the carry-all was gone, and the jamming of the pole between two small pieces of wood was all that kept us from the horses' heels; the next hill would have fixed us. In two hours the new bolt pins were made, and off we went. Our only trouble now was, that at every ascent the tired horses would stop. Whitey began to act, and one of us got out and led them again, and jumped in without stopping. Dined at Lockhaven, found G. B. Manly. Crossed the river and started for Farrandsville along the towpath (river on one side, ditch on the other) twelve feet high and twelve feet wide at the top. Frequent stops, coaxings, whippings, and starts. At one of these, as we were starting pretty quick, and I holding in, I found the horses steering right for the river, off the track, which was here a little wider than usual, say twenty feet. In vain I pulled the other rein, then by roaring 'Wo-o-o!' stopped the horses just on the edge. My right rein had caught in the runner by a buckle, and by pulling both to hold, I was steering into the river. Arrived here at four P. M. Looked at the works, slept soundly, and from a bright heavenly day woke up to this snowstorm."

I am sorry not to find any account of my father's return trip, but, strange to say, it must have been safely accomplished. Looking back on this period he writes : —

"The care of R. B. F.'s affairs and my work for

Russell & Co., with the sales of consignments from China, gave me little leisure for two or three years, but were a very valuable training in American business. My direct relations with Houqua continued after my return from China."

As to these relations I give extracts here from two of Houqua's letters to my father : —

CANTON, May 4, 1837.

MY YOUNG FRIEND, — It is several weeks since I have called on an amanuensis to pen for me a letter to you, and I do so now to show you that notwithstanding my age and the many cares which oppress me, I bear you in mind. Before you receive this you will probably have been at home more than six months. I count on seeing you again, probably before another year is ended, and shall be most glad to welcome you back. . . . You must recollect that I have given *you* authority to manage my business, and I do not wish you to delegate it to any one unless you should come back to China, and then you must leave the power in the hands of the consignees of the property, or if they should not be trustworthy, in those of some other safe house. . . . Mr. Green has reminded me several times that I promised to sit for my portrait for you, but as yet I have had no leisure.

Pray don't neglect to write to me,

I remain, your friend,

HOUQUA.

THE SAME TO THE SAME.

CANTON, *August* 10, 1838.

MY YOUNG FRIEND, — I have received your letter of March 3. By the Levant I make you a considerable consignment of tea and silk piece goods, which I have had on hand for some time, and cannot sell here. I wish you to consult Mr. Cushing about the sale of this consignment and to follow his advice. Remember, *security is my first object:* I desire to run no unnecessary risks, and want, if possible, to have the accounts closed early. . . . It gives me much pleasure to hear of your good health, though you say nothing of your son's. You know it is an ambition common to my countrymen to have many sons, and I confess I feel inclined to congratulate my friends when I hear that they are contributing their quota to posterity in this way. My grandson sends his regards, to which, my dear friend, I add my own most sincerely,

HOUQUA.

It was in the interval between the dates of these letters of Houqua that an event occurred which was the first to startle all New England out of the indifference about slavery; and (with what followed it) it strongly affected my father's after life. This was the murder of Elijah P. Lovejoy,[1] a clergyman who had tried printing a newspaper at St. Louis, in which he condemned the burning of a negro. For this offense his press had been destroyed. He

[1] At Alton, November 7, 1837.

had retreated to the Illinois side of the Mississippi and managed to set up another press, which shared the fate of the first. He scraped together enough money to set up a third. But this was too much for the Missouri mob, who this time crossed the river in force, killed Lovejoy, and burned up press, building, and all. This aroused Boston at last. An indignation meeting was proposed by Dr. Channing, but so strong was the hold of slavery in those days that the use of Faneuil Hall was granted only after much urging. The meeting was held, but the upholders of slavery were to the fore in great numbers; they made so much noise that it seemed doubtful whether the meeting would indorse Lovejoy or his murderers, when a young man climbed to the platform, and, with a voice which never afterwards failed of holding his audience, made a speech which turned the tide completely. Of it my father says : —

"I was present by chance and heard Wendell Phillips, then almost unknown, break out in his great speech, perhaps the best he ever made, denouncing the murder. I had never before heard his name, and few people outside of his class in college knew him as a man of talent. Up to that time I had been neutral or indifferent on the subject of slavery. That speech changed my whole feeling with regard to it, though the bigotry and pigheadedness of the abolitionists prevented my acting with them."

To return to the calmer atmosphere of my father's

agency for Houqua in Boston; I need only add that, as time went on, it did not stop at Chinese and other merchandise, but embraced general investments in this country. I find him saying, when recalling that period: —

"I had saved up the moderate competency which I had brought home from China, and was owning ships and doing a commission business with good credit, based upon what I had done in that country and upon somewhat exaggerated ideas on the part of my correspondents, due to my having the management of about half a million of my friend Houqua's money. This, at his especial request, was held in my own name, though the ownership was indicated in my books by the initials A. S. I., which meant American Stock Investment. This account was kept carefully unmixed with my own investments, although I made it a rule never to buy anything for it which I was not also buying for myself."

Then he goes on to speak of different fine ships in which he was interested in those days, and adds: —

"These were then called clippers, although a few years later, when for California we built yachts of 1500 to 2500 tons, they would have been called clumps."

With regard to one of these ships, the Acbar, I find the following instructions given by him to her captain, Philip Dumaresq, when she was about to leave Boston for Canton in 1839. I insert these in full as illustrative of the methods of business in those days, and of my father's careful forethought:

"CAPT. P. DUMARESQ, — On making the coast of China, please have a letter to Mr. R. B. F. ready, stating what cargo and funds you have on board, and that unless there is some extraordinary inducement to buy teas, your object is to employ the ship either in some freighting business in the East (cotton being your first object if there is a fair prospect), or, if nothing can be got except rice, in taking freight to this part of the world. Tell him where you mean to anchor, and ask information by return boat as to the state of affairs,[1] and advice as to taking your ship to Lintin, and taking very quietly a pilot at once, or waiting among the islands, if anything secret is to be done, until you can see him and concert measures. Give him all the information you can as to the markets, ships, etc. When you are boarded by a Fast Boat, if they lead you to believe that the Americans are at Canton and will agree at once to carry up a letter, anchor in some out-of-the-way place, and send the boat up with such letters only as are marked to be put up, for it would not be safe to risk others: make the Fast Boat man's pay depend on his keeping your arrival secret and on bringing you an answer within a stipulated time. If upon cross-examining the Fast Boat men you have any doubt about the Americans being at Canton and you can ascertain that the Lintin, Captain Gilman, is still outside, send one of your mates to the Lintin. Tell

---

[1] War between England and China was expected when these instructions were made out. — ED.

him, without letting out where he comes from, to find out where Mr. Forbes is and to forward to him your letter as quickly as possible. If you cannot satisfy yourself that the Lintin is outside, send your mate to Macao with like orders and cautions. Keep back all letters and papers, except such as you have orders about, until you get advice from Canton that they may be delivered without injury to us. The reason for thus trying to keep your arrival secret may be either, that it is an object, from any cause, to buy at once to extent of your funds, with the market to yourself; or it *may* be that the negotiations of the English with the Chinese are just at such a point, that if it were known to the former that an American ship was going up they would give her warning that she went up with the risk of being kept in (an informal notice it would be, but still might be embarrassing); or it may be that if they had nearly decided to commence a blockade, they might reason, Here is an American ship going in and it is a good time to begin: when if they did not know of any vessel going up, a day or two's delay on their part might turn the scale in favor of the voyage — by letting you slip in lawfully. In case no China boat came near you, you would have to go either on to Macao Roads or to Lintin, and then keep your own counsel and your letters until you could act advisedly.

"In writing R. B. F. it would be well to give him a copy of our other instructions to you about cargo, and to authorize him if necessary to act

upon them promptly without awaiting a reference
to you.

"As it is possible you may on arrival, or afterwards, be below Canton, while that port is in a state
of blockade, we would in these *private* instructions
give you our ideas with regard to the risks we shall
be willing to run.

"1st. If you can at any time get into port before the blockade, it might be very important for
you to wait until the time allowed by the blockading squadron to come off with cargo had expired,
in order to get teas down in consequence of other
vessels being off. Again, you might be able by
a false start for sea from Macao Roads to return
(after a blockade commenced) and get into the
river without much risk. Again, you might perhaps be able to get in back of Macao in some snug
bay, or even run up to Hong Kong (at the end of
Broad way passage), and then by concert meet
cargo boats from Canton. Under such circumstances we should be willing to have you take either
of these steps, provided, after a full knowledge of all
the chances, you and Mr. Forbes agree that the
object, the prospect of gain, was much greater than
the risk. If the British fleet should from any cause
be placed as they were during the war, viz., at or
about Chunpa only, we should think a well-con-
certed run in might be made with but little risk,
and that you might by watching your chance run
out with little or no risk; but if, as is likely, the
Chinese block up the river, or the English take the

forts and send a ship to Whampoa, you would stand no chance of escape. Unless, therefore, there is strong probability of their staying at Chunpa and taking half measures, it would be highly imprudent to run in or stay in. We will only say, however, that we should be willing to take a small risk for the chance of a very great gain, and with this remark shall agree to whatever you and Mr. F. may decide under such circumstances.

" Remember that in case of a blockade the Chinese would pardon your running into the river without a pilot, and secondly that if you had secret notice or strong enough suspicion to warrant such a step, you might (having no notice that could be *proved* upon you) take a good chance and run for the river, with only the risk of being stopped and turned back."

It would seem that war had actually broken out between Great Britain and China when the Acbar arrived off the coast, but that all consequent difficulties were met ; so that this voyage was referred to afterwards as unusually successful.

To return to his Milton life and its amusements. Prominent among these was tree planting, which all through life was one of my father's chief interests and occupations " out of office hours." One of the first things he did after buying " the Briggs lot," on Milton Hill, in 1834, on which during his second voyage to China his cottage was built for

him, was to import about 20,000 trees, of which
white pine and Norway spruce were his favorites, and
so to shut out the bare expanse of Neponset mud-
bank which lay below the place to the north. This
belt of trees, as time went on, made a barrier against
the north and east winds, not only for the cottage,
but for the house, which he afterwards built about
a quarter of a mile to the east of it. The whole
place was very bleak and bare when he bought it,
and the tree and evergreen shrub planting completely transformed it. Indeed, after a time, it became necessary to open views of Boston Bay, and it
was always a struggle for him to cut down any of
these cherished objects, even when he recognized
that one tree hindered the perfection of another's
growth. Later on at Naushon, where Governor
Swain had already made some beginning in tree
planting, my father continued it with great zest,
trying experiments of various sorts to the end of
his life.

Riding was always one of his chief enjoyments.
He looked back fondly to the black mare, named
Di Vernon, which he had bought for my mother,
and the Judge, a three quarters bred chestnut, of
which his brother Bennet gave him the use. My
father's order to the groom, when requiring these
to be saddled, "Saddle the Judge and Di," was, as
he recalls, long remembered. The Judge was left
with him when his brother returned to China in
1837 ; and my father tells how that spirited animal, soon after this, came near breaking his neck

and that of Governor Swain, already a very heavy man. As they were driving into Boston, the Judge ran away with the chaise for a mile at full speed, my father and the governor both holding on to the reins, and contriving to pull him in just as he was on the point of dashing down the Boston side of Meeting-House Hill. The governor alighted and made for a house. My father exclaimed, "Where are you going, governor?" "To get a gun to kill that horse." "Get in, governor, and go on." "Not for ten thousand dollars," said the governor, "will I ever sit behind that horse again." My father winds up with, "Of his (the horse's) career I remember nothing except that, some time after, he ran away with somebody else and broke his neck against an iron fence."

It must have been in the thirties that Johnny Crapaud, the queer little animal already mentioned, came to Naushon, where he was to pass the remainder of his life. Captain Anthony, of New Bedford, on a voyage to Havre, saw Johnny there, carrying a rider twice his own size, took pity on him, brought him home, and presented him to Governor Swain. Johnny was the incarnation of intelligence and mischief, could open gates and let all the horses into the cornfields, and was withal the only steed I ever heard of which the governor's wife, my quiet Quaker aunt Lydia, would mount. He suited her exactly, for she could knit tranquilly on his back.

I may as well say here that he was translated in

1864, at no one knows exactly what age, but certainly over thirty-five. He disappeared one day, and though all the swamps at his end of the island were searched, his small body was never found.[1]

[1] I give here his epitaph, in which my father took great delight, written by the Rev. John Weiss; perhaps one of the cleverest of the contributions to the "Island Book," — a book wherein were inscribed all names of family and guests at Naushon, with such verses and skits as the poetry or wit of the visitors afforded : —

This Page
Is dedicated to the Memory of
Johnny Crapaud:
Who emigrated from Havre, France,
In disgust
At carrying a rider twice as large
As himself.
He left
An overgrown Civilization
To offer his services,
Like Lafayette,
To
Young America.
Fortunate that he looked upon
Naushon
As a stable place of residence,
For there all the good
Little people of the mainland go.
Also
Light-weighted Clergymen
And light-witted Women.
Hard as the latter are to bear,
Johnny Crapaud
Bore them with his native gayety.
But he loved best
To trot out the little people;
And light Clergymen.
This he did for nearly thirty years
Under two beneficent régimes.
How many
Pale cheeks and dull eyes he trotted
Into glow and gladness,
Whisking his inefficient tail,

Johnny's portrait still adorns the walls at the mansion house at Naushon.

Every hair of which
Could be numbered without the assistance
Of Providence:
It was a tail that might have been
Told.
His color was a russet-brown:
Though he was a little heavy by
The head,
His eye twinkled with private reflections
Which he had the sense never
To impart.
Like all persons who have
Made up their mind,
He was rather hard to turn;
And has been known
To Carry a Clergyman Contemptuously
Through the underbrush,
As if Nature were superior
To Grace.
He could open gates
And thus extend his area of freedom:
And was not always
Found in his appropriate pasture:
Thus singularly sympathizing
With mankind.
Of late
He had become enfeebled;
So that when one day
He attempted to reach his grand
Climb-act-trick,
He turned a summerset and
Went down the hill:
For his tail
Was futile to arrest him.
He has been going down ever since.
His last ride he gave to
The little grandson,
Whose father is at the Country's front.
To be set upon
In this way
Was an honor to a foreign pony:
And no doubt he felt that his

At Milton, on the 15th of November, 1838, my
twin sisters, Alice and Ellen, were born, and on the

Crib was full.

At length

Sometime in the month of

August, 1864,

Though all the gates were shut,

He disappeared.

Search

Was made for him

In the supposition that feeling his

End approach

He went to meet it:

Thus

Delicately saving the expenses of

A burial,

And adroitly prolonging the period

Of mourning among those

Who so often felt themselves

Above him.

His friends

Are all the good little people who

Have grown up able to

Recollect

And appreciate his

Mute and honest service:

And at least one

Clergyman.

No doubt

As a happy recognition of

That service,

He

Who had taken so many to ride

Was at last carried off in

A Chariot:

Poached like the patriarch.

May he find many

Clergymen

In the place whither he has gone:

And innumerable Orthodox children

To render happy

Who have hitherto been deemed

Damned.

20th of December, 1839, I find my father writing to his brother in China : —

" With care I hope to see them robust children; yet they are remarkable already for a thousand valuable qualities of heart and head; one ought to be named Prodigy and the other Phenomenon! They sit at table, stand, almost walk alone, say a few words, or something like words, and in fine are getting to be very charming. . . . . I'm getting quite in love with the dear little souls."

In 1840 my brother William was born; and in the following spring my parents went to Philadelphia to see my mother's brother, William Hathaway. He was taken very ill a week after their arrival, and my father says in his notes : —

" I had to resume my post as nurse for the second time in a smallpox case. This time the trial was short and sharp, for in about a fortnight we laid his remains in the Laurel Hill cemetery, afterwards transferring them to Naushon. He was only twenty-eight years old, and was the most attractive man I ever came in contact with; manly, handsome, magnetic; he sang well, rode, hunted, did everything well, and was the universal favorite of all who knew him, men and women. I have always felt that if he had lived until the rebellion

And as he has not remaned,
May at least
His tail
Resume its lost hairs
Now
Hairs of glory.

he must have played a great part in military life,
for which he had a marked turn."

When, years afterwards, my uncle's body was
removed to Naushon, my father, who had been sud-
denly obliged to take a voyage to England, wrote
from on board the steamship Canada: —

" I only regret that I could not be with you
when consigning them to their last resting-place in
the bright forest which he loved so well, and where,
if I ever wasted a thought upon the disposition of
my shell when the spirit has left it, I should choose
my own to be placed; although I may as well say
here, that for myself I have no feeling on that subject and would rather the poor mortal form should
be forgotten, and only the picture of the inner man,
lighted by such spirit and such affection as my
friends could throw around it, remain for their memory."

I have referred to my father's precautions for our
younger folk at Naushon in the matter of boating.
He himself speaks as follows of the only boating
accident in his own experience, which came near
being a fatal one: —

" Perhaps the nearest I ever came to having to
swim for my life was in 1842, when Commodore
Bennet was out on a trial trip with the new
schooner Ariel, a boat of about 100 tons, destined
for China. It was a blustering summer day, and
we soon found she was over-sparred, or under-bal-
lasted, but having a strong crew, including Fowler,
the Boston pilot, we kept on trying her at some

risk, once nearly going over off the Hardings, outside of Boston Light, in sixty feet of water or more.
Coming in through the narrows we had a strong
head wind with a tide going the other way, which
tripped her up, and the first thing we knew was
seeing the sails in the water and the sea pouring
down the open companion way, filling her. We
scrambled up on her bilge, and then Fowler called
out to me to help save the old gentleman who was
being swept down into the cabin by the rush; we
got hold of his collar and pulled him up among us,
and found it was old Captain Richard Cleveland
(perhaps eighty years old), the father of cousin
Sarah Cleveland's husband, and a cousin of our
President Cleveland. He was a very plucky old
man, and had been capsized a little while before on
Jamaica Pond (besides many other adventures since
told in a book), and took it very coolly. We had a
boat towing astern, but by bad luck her painter was
fastened to leeward and the belaying - pin was
already under water out of reach. R. B. F., with
his usual presence of mind, walked out on the main
boom, got into the boat and began cutting the hard
painter with a little penknife, sawing away at it as
our vessel sank. We watched him with eager eyes,
for our lives depended on its not breaking and on
its continuing to cut fast enough. I had (as usual)
a good jackknife, which I opened and held ready in
my mouth while steadying myself to run or swim
out to him if his knife gave out; but he had the
line out just as the water began to rise over our

shoes where we stood on the Ariel's side, still nearly dry. He pulled the boat in rapidly by the end of the painter, and we all got on board without any serious wetting, except Captain Cleveland. The captain and crew of the vessel, however, who were forward letting go the anchor, got a panic when they saw her sinking for fear the whirlpool would suck them in, as is the traditional danger of sinking ships, so they jumped overboard to escape being drowned, while the vessel sank with hardly a ripple or a whirl, the whirlpool danger being one of the many popular chimeras which annually destroy a certain number of valuable lives. Here too came in an illustration of the value of coolness in danger. When we went over, the yacht Breeze, steered by old Captain William Sturgis, was close by us to windward, with a party of friends. The captain somehow for once lost his head and did the wrong thing, and did not get down to us until we were safe on our boat, nor in time to save one of the crew. These were rescued by the captain of a fisherman, half a mile off when he saw us go over, who jumped into the little boat which was towing astern and reached us in time to pick up some of them. I was glad to find that danger had not paralyzed me, and I had made up my mind that as one boat might not hold us all, some of us younger ones had only to get overboard and hold on to the little boat until relief came up. As we sailed up the harbor another yacht, I think Winchester's Northern Light, hailed us, and asked if the Ariel was still down the harbor. The commodore, R. B. F., jumped up on the taffrail and with a very pregnant gesture, pointing to the bottom, said, "Yes, very far down!' We got ashore and back to our friends on Milton Hill without their having seen the accident, it was all so quick, although they had been watching us. The Ariel was raised, her spars reduced, and she went out to China, proving a very safe and fast boat. She was modeled, and half owned, by old Joe Lee, and was very long for her beam, and very sharp."

I find that in April, 1843, Daniel Webster, then Secretary of State, sent a circular to China merchants asking for suggestions from them in view of the public mission about to start for China, "for the purpose of cultivating friendly relations with that empire." My father was deputed to draw up the answer which was signed by the merchants of Boston engaged in that trade, and sent in due course to the proper quarter. This document seems to an outsider to cover all possible points, but as it runs to a "Seventhly" and "Finally" I refrain from giving it here.

About this time I find my father giving his views to a relative in the matter of expenditure by men engaged in trade. I think it best to give what he wrote, though I have already referred briefly to his opinion on the subject:—

"There is one point on which I think I can convince you that you are wrong.

"You say that where a man is engaged in trade there are no means of computing his income, or what amount it would be prudent for him to spend. Now I think there is a way of judging the future by the past. My trade operations since I began business when a boy in Canton, or, if you take a fairer test, since I returned from China, in 1837, have not averaged over six per cent. interest on the amount invested, if you *take out* the first lucky hit of the Acbar by being out during the China war, and the very nice tea speculation to England that was made for me at the same time. Without these two operations I am sure my profits have not been over six per cent., and I am inclined to think that *with them* they would not be much over six. And yet you and others have thought my adventures have been at least as profitable as the average of commercial operations; and they have certainly been undertaken with some advantages over other people in having good friends in China. But the truth is that competition is so sharp here that money must be made either by the most penurious saving in fitting ships or storing goods, etc., etc., or by being constantly on the lookout and giving up body and soul to managing business. . . . Moreover, it is my firm conviction that for twenty years past the average interest gained on the whole capital engaged in the China trade has not exceeded six per cent.

"Mr. Cabot always said that from 1820 to 1830, P. & Co. would have made more money if they had put their property out at interest than they did in the China trade, and I believe him; and we can see that since 1830 he cannot have realized much over six per cent., taking into view the Levant's bad voyage.

"In short, if you are going to keep in trade, I would rather take six per cent. interest on your money than the profit you will make.

"Theoretically, you are right in saying that a man in trade has no fixed income, but in practice I think you will see from the above data that if he calls his income six per cent., and spends it, laying by the profits over six per cent. of one or more successful years to meet the losses of the bad year, which comes in this country every two or three years, he will spend as much as is consistent with keeping his principal unimpaired."

My father, after speaking in his notes of the imprudence of a merchant, when reckoning on making more than six per cent.,[1] in the long run, on his invested capital, goes on to say : —

"In looking over some old letter books running from 1837 to 1846, I note fluctuations in the rate of interest, which sometimes for pretty long periods ran as high as thirteen per cent. per annum. At one time I could not pass Colonel T. H. Perkins's six months' note, with my indorsement, at a lower rate than eighteen per cent. per annum."

He speaks of some not very good ventures which he made at this period (1843–1848) and of his joining in building, under Ericsson's auspices, the steam-

---

[1] My father's "six per cent." at the period of which he was speaking would have to be translated now into four per cent. or less.

ship Massachusetts, of about 750 tons, one of the
first Atlantic steamships; which proved, however, too
small for that service and was sold to the United
States and did good work in the Mexican war.

Up to this time he had taken no active part in
politics, but he writes as to this : —

" I see that I spent something in politics, as a
passive member of the Whig party, until March 7,
1850, when I left it.   Among other similar outlays
was my contribution to the Webster fund, which
really was largely influential in preventing Webster's reaching the presidency by putting him in
the position of a candidate subsidized by rich men.
Political subscriptions were in those days on a small
scale and would make a very poor show compared
with modern ones."

About this time my father first became interested
in railroads.   I have already given his letter to his
brother Bennet, stating his opinion of their prospects in the United States at an earlier date.   Looking back in 1884, he refers to the gradual growth
of the American railroad system, up to about 5000
miles of track in 1846, and then says : —

" My judgment was sound in 1836 when I kept
out of railroads, but how I came to get in in 1846,
ten years later, may be worth telling."

He continues, referring to a relative who, though
absolutely trustworthy, was not a brilliant man of
business : —

" I was stupid enough to dream that he might
earn a salary by being made a figure-head in a rail-

road, which I supposed to be a nominal place like
the presidency of insurance companies, then generally given to honest and reliable, though unsuccessful, merchants, — while the secretaries did the
work. About the early days of 1846, having this
absurd idea in my head I was led to take an interest, perhaps a tenth, in buying of the State of
Michigan its quarter-built road, at seventy cents on
the dollar, my copartners being John E. Thayer,
Williams *et al.*, of Boston, John C. Green, George
Griswold *et al.*, of New York, Erastus Corning
and a few others, of Albany, and above all J.
W. Brooks a young engineer, then in charge of a
section of the New York Central, I think from
Utica to Syracuse. Little did I dream of the load
I was taking when I accepted the office of presi-
dent."

But he had put his hand to the plough, and after
that there could be no leaving it in the furrow. In
his notes he goes on to tell of the wonderful capacity of Mr. Brooks, and how under his general
management this 140 miles of state railroad, " built
on strap iron and lengthwise timbers, and, though
still young, nearly worn out then," soon became,
in spite of the stupidest and fiercest opposition on
the part of those most to be benefited by it, a
thoroughly well equipped line, and a model for railroad management, which was then throughout the
country in the crudest possible state. And then,
speaking of his own and his brother directors' absolute unconsciousness of the coming conversion,

within a few decades, of a swamp on Lake Michigan into a populous city, he writes (1884) : —

" Like a young bear, with all my troubles before me, I had plunged into the railroad vortex, and on June the 11th, 1847, I find by my letter books that I was at Milwaukee with the other Michigan Central directors, we having decided to take our road around the lake to Chicago, instead of trusting to New Buffalo and water carriage on the lake for our western outlet. It was on this trip that W. B. Ogden drove us about Chicago and tried to coax us into rapid action by offering us land in that city, for which he was the selling agent, at low prices. The land below the harbor on the lake was then a sand drift and might have been bought very low, but the cheapest purchases would have been the wet prairie lands within a mile of the hotel where we stopped, which were offered us at $1.25 per acre. Sheltered by our absurd prejudices against land we were proof against Ogden's seductions, and I do not think any of us ever bought a foot of land in Chicago for ourselves while the road was in course of construction. My hotel bill of $125 would have bought 100 acres, now worth $8,000,000 to $12,000,000."

The ordinary routine of mercantile and railroad interests was now broken in upon by the Irish famine, of which he writes in his notes : " In 1847 came the great Irish famine, the stories about which were more pitiful than those of any other such calamity, partly, perhaps, because we heard them

so directly from the Irish around us, who themselves contributed all they could to relieve their
relations in the old country;" and tells how the
idea came to him of borrowing the Jamestown
from the United States government, how she loaded
up in Boston, and under the command of his brother was sent with her cargo to relieve the distress
in Ireland, and returned to the United States, to
find another ship, borrowed by New York for the
same purpose, only half loaded; to all which I do no
more than refer, as the history has been given at
length by my uncle Bennet in his book of " Personal Reminiscences," already mentioned.

It must have been soon after the Irish famine
that my father was requested by one of his New
York correspondents, a most conservative man, to
join him in making an advance to an English company working some iron property at Mount Savage,
in Maryland, to enable them to complete their blast
furnaces. This was made, other advances had to
follow, the English company failed, and the business became one of my father's most perplexing
problems for long afterwards. Within my own
recollection it was a constant source of irritation to
him; he had to be going to Mount Savage at all
seasons of the year; and when after many years a
good man of business was found able and willing
to take this old man of the sea off his neck there
was a general family rejoicing. He refers at length
in his notes to this " episode in my business life,"
as he lightly calls it. Giving an account of one of

the journeys taken in the interest of this enterprise, he writes: " We made arrangements for getting from Mount Savage to Cumberland on a hand car in the night. We had a most exciting slide, very fast, in the dark, nearly running over dogs, pigs, and men, by good luck getting without an accident into Cumberland, where I established myself in coat and shawl in the baggage car for the night."   And of another, —

" I was once called up to Mount Savage rather late in the fall, and in passing through New York I stopped to see the celebrated Dr. ——, who was a crank on the subject of treating diseases of the throat with nitrate of silver. After poking his probes far down my throat and examining the condition of things, he said, ' There is nothing for it but to cut off both tonsils in your throat.' I asked how long it would take. ' Five minutes.' I told him to go ahead; whereupon he cut off both tonsils, each as big as the end of my finger, and then stopped the bleeding with nitrate of silver, and packed me off to the train. He had not thought to tell me, what I found to be the case, that my throat was so tender that I could not get anything down for twenty-four hours, so I had to make the journey on an empty stomach, after getting through the needful business."

There is nothing else in the history of Mount Savage which I think likely to interest or amuse the general reader. But, on the other hand, I cannot refrain from giving the following letters which

I have chanced upon, among my father's papers, as they present a side of his character — his strong love of a good practical joke — which is not brought out in his graver correspondence. The occasion which provoked the letters was this. His cousin, Dr. Edward Robbins, of Boston, a man with the warmest of hearts, but a patience which had its distinct limits, had learnt that Mr. Corning, of Albany, had a herd of very fine milch cows; and my father had agreed to join him in buying some of these animals. Dr. Robbins, however, contrary to my father's advice, had insisted on inquiring if there were no young unmarried German laborer in the neighborhood of Albany whom he could hire permanently and who could begin work by fetching on the cows. He had deputed my father to make the inquiry. This was made, and my father had received from New York a genuine letter from a Mr. Whitehouse strongly recommending one William Reynolds, " a good farming man with a wife and four small children." My father had seen at once that this did not answer the good doctor's description of what he wanted; but he could not resist sending on the letter to him, and writing at its foot, " Answered as follows: 'Send Mr. Reynolds along at once with his wife and children. Let them go straight to the house of Dr. E. H. Robbins, Summer Street, who is in great distress for exactly this family.'" Promptly had come the following screed from his cousin :—

J. M. F., — Who the devil is Mr. Whitehouse?
Write him that there are more women and children
in these parts than food; that you have no use for
such folks.   A German emigrant, worth five dollars
a month, is not a man and wife and five children.
Mr. Whitehouse be buttered !   E. H. R.

June 3, 1848.

Then my father, seeing the way in which the
genuine letter had been received, gave himself up
to the joke and concocted the following letter (of
which there is a rough copy in his own handwrit-
ing), and sent it to some correspondent in Utica to
copy out, sign with the name "James S. White,"
and post back to himself in Milton : —

UTICA, *June* 2, 1848.

To MR. JOHN M. FORBES, Milton, Mass.

Dear Sir, — When in Albany Mr. Corning informed me that German labor was in demand in
Boston, and that you had sent to him for one or
more men.

We are overstocked with it here, and thinking it
doubtful whether Mr. Corning could furnish what
you want, I have helped and encouraged two or
three families to return to Boston and have given
them letters of introduction to you.   They cannot
get over $8 to $10 per month here, and I feel confident from what Mr. Corning said that if you don't
want them you can easily provide them with places
at better rates, and that their families can find em-

ployment in your factories, which they cannot do here.

When will you make a dividend on the Michigan R. R., — in July or January?

Yours truly, JAMES S. WHITE.

N. B.—I have also furnished a poor Irish family named Gallagher with funds to reach Boston. The father, who has seen better days, is a good farmer, and would make a very trusty and intelligent superintendent, as foreman of a large farm, though unable to work himself, owing to an accident to one of his arms. His sons are stout lads, and his daughters are willing to go into service. I have lent them $11, and if you employ them I wish you would try to get it for me; also the Mullers' $8, Rucker $6, and Schmidt $6.

Yours, J. S. W.

This, when received from Utica, my father forwarded to Dr. Robbins, who swallowed it all and replied as follows : —

MY DEAR J. M. F., — What an infernal set of correspondents you have; I shall be very careful how I join you again in any speculation; the simple request to have the German sent with the cows ought not to have imposed upon me, or even you, the whole German nation, or the surplus Irish population of western New York.

If this is the way Michigan stockholders use you, deliver me from such friends; if any of them do come, I shall immediately enter a complaint to the city government (saving always one simple German man), to have them seized and taken to Deer Island, to be provided for, and Mr. Whitehouse, of New York, and Mr. White, of Utica, called upon to respond with suitable bonds to the city against the parties becoming paupers to be supported by the city; as for the cattle (the cows) I shall take my cow, and deliver yours, promising never again to enter into any cattle speculations with you; there is too long a tail to your conduct.

Yours truly,   E. H. R.

Boston, *June* 5, 1848.

Then followed a steady stream of letters of recommendation, which, as I find from my father's indorsement on the bundle of real and fictitious documents, gradually brought home to his cousin's mind the fact that no crowd of immigrants, German or Irish, was on its way to him to be transferred to Deer Island. My father notes that the doctor bore no malice, and that they continued the best of friends.

CHAPTER VI

THE letter books of this period (1848) show that the difficulties of railroad construction, and the questions of financial engineering incident to it, were taking more and more of my father's time.

In the midst of this came the discovery of the California gold fields, which set everybody crazy. He promptly availed himself of the new opening for merchandise, and by his advice a relative went out to San Francisco and started there as a commission merchant. When settled there, he asked my father for the benefit of his experience in this business, and received the following reply. It seems worth preserving for the same reasons that led me to print the instructions to Captain Dumaresq, ten years earlier.

MILTON, June 17, 1849.

MY DEAR ——: I will, as you request, touch upon some of the important points for a commission merchant to aim at.

First. As to correspondence. Always look back to previous letters before sitting down to write; then try to give to each constituent a continuation of the history of his business, studying as much conciseness as is consistent with exactness and method. In quoting prices before actual sales take place, be careful not to lead to too great expectations as to net results. If you name a price on arrival and don't get it, they are very apt to complain because you did not sell on arrival. On the other hand, if you name too low a price, owners are apt to hear other letters quoting higher rates. I suggest, therefore, great caution in quoting prices except from actual sales, and taking care to make at the same time any remarks that are applicable to the matter, such as the expense of landing, measuring, weighing, etc., all which will be high ; and it will probably be good policy, if custom has not too firmly fixed it, to make people pay all these charges exactly as they stand you in, so that your commission shall be net. Many people would grumble at a high nominal commission, who would be perfectly satisfied if you charged them a moderate commission and put among charges the actual expense to you of handling the goods, even if the sum of the charges is higher than in the other case. Then instead of employing clerks, you may find it good policy to have a weigher, a measurer, a surveyor of lumber, etc. Custom may very likely have settled all this. As to market advices, try to give actual sales and other facts, and be cautious how you give such encouragement as to the future as will lead people to think you are urging consignments. Give all the facts you can, and all the circumstances which bear upon the future : such as the tide of emigration, the effect of plentifulness of gold in causing free expenditure, the temporary overstock which may at the time cause dullness; but I would not venture many predictions as to future prices, except where you are very sure you are right. Give facts, and let those who are to run the risk speculate upon them. Of course to me and other private friends no such reserve may be needed, but I refer to general letters: you thus avoid the appearance of extravagance, and induce people to rely upon your judgment.

Second. As to sales and accounts. Always, where it is left to you, sell promptly, unless there are very strong reasons for holding. Everybody who has had foreign business gets disgusted with the long delays before they get their returns with squared accounts; besides this feeling, there is always expense incurred by holding and loss of interest, and it takes considerable rise to pay for holding goods long. As a general rule, therefore, sell early and make prompt returns. Most of those who have gone into so wild a trade as that to California are speculative people and will be glad of their money back in good time. Of course, there will be great fluctuation in California, and great room for judgment about holding, and my own impression is that it may be best to hold shiploads of goods till the digging season is entirely over and the overland emigrants from the Western States come down to the coast: sailors' and other labor will then be more cheap.

Third. Be very careful how you give one house information as to the business of others intrusted to you. Even those who like to get such information distrust those who give it. Even a sale that everybody knows had better be mentioned in general terms, rather than especially referred to as "a sale made by you of the C.'s cargo." When you have sold nearly all a consignment, close the rest, even at a low price, in order to send promptly the sales and proceeds, closed to a point. I have often had a letter reach Forbes, Forbes & Co., London, with large remittances in sixty-day bills, and have received accounts made within twenty-four or forty-eight hours, showing the discount of the bills on London, the purchase and remittance of bills on Bengal, and the whole closed to a cent, and an account current returned. This system is beautiful, and any American that can combine this English method and precision with Yankee energy will command all the business he can do. Really good commission houses are very rare, and I know of only two or three in the world. Mr. William Cary I consider as good as any other. The custom as to giving credit may be well established before you get there, but it will be more or less modified as trade increases. There never was such a chance for a community to get on without credit, and you may rely upon it that the shorter you can make the credit, even to having sales made strictly for cash, the better for you in the long run. Commission houses generally like sales on credit because they give them a chance to charge a guarantee commission, but people will be all the more ready to pay a large commission if there is no discount for cash to be added to it. Besides this, if you give credit where none is needed, as in California, it leads to competition and inflation. Each house gradually, for the sake of making sales, will sell on longer credit to weaker customers, and the risk of guarantee keeps on increasing, while the rate is stationary or decreasing as houses multiply. Use all your influence, therefore, to establish a cash system. Don't try to make money out of storage, etc., etc. The charges of this sort will be enormous, and you had better fortify yourselves against the complaints which will follow by charging others what you pay, and telling them so. If you undertake to own or hire warehouses and make a profit out of them, you cannot add much to the enormous prices you will have to pay. I should say, therefore: go for making all charges on goods as simple and small as possible, and trust to doing a large business and laying the foundation for its long continuance, rather than trying to make the most out of what is sent to you at first.

Very truly yours,   J. M. F.

Nota Bene. — Always try to keep ahead of your work so as never to be obliged to write hastily or carelessly, as I too often do. Do as I say, and not as I too often do.

N. B. — The great art of making bargains is to find out other people's ultimatum without letting out yours, and this can be done with most people by letting them talk.

His relative acted on this advice to some purpose, and I am glad to say with successful results.

It was at this time that my father built and sailed those clipper ships to which he referred as by comparison reducing the fast ships of an earlier day to "clumps." They earned for a time $40 a ton freight for the passage round the Horn to San Francisco. So every inch was of value, and after the sailing of one of them my father speaks of his having been "laid up some days at Naushon with leeches on his head," and adds, "My wife always calls it my 'box fever,' as my mind was running on finding small boxes to fill up the chinks under the ship's decks."

As to this California trade, I find a letter of my father's, dated January 4, 1850, to the Hon. Daniel Webster, complaining of the dog in the manger inaction of the postal authorities, who would neither themselves carry promptly the mercantile correspondence on which the fate of many million dollars' worth of merchandise depended, nor any longer allow the express companies to do the work. The letter inclosed memorials on the subject to each house of Congress.

In 1852, during the discussions that preceded the memorable expedition of Commodore Perry to Japan, my father writes, under date of the 28th of February, to Mr. William Appleton, a member of Congress:

From a Crayon by Cheney about 1851

" The newspapers reiterate the charge that our government are fitting out a fleet to coerce the Japanese into commercial intercourse. . . . The course of these Japanese expeditions is a stereotyped one. The ships of war appear, and the local mandarins are made responsible for driving them off; and, failing to persuade them to go, the poor wretches draw a knife across their throats or go to the executioner; and this tragedy is repeated until the foreigners see the impossibility of gaining either glory or trade, and withdraw after getting, without pay, all the supplies which the land affords.

" If we have shipwrecked sailors in captivity, then one or two vessels of war can accomplish all that is to be done, viz., make their demands and get any men given up that are there, and can make the government and the mandarins fully aware of the trouble they bring upon themselves by keeping our people prisoners in future; but as to forcing a commercial intercourse, I do not believe any man of sense who has been in China will admit the probability of accomplishing anything without pretty much such a war as John Bull got up with China.

" A smaller force may butcher thousands of men in petticoats and sink their arks, and the officers may call their Chinese junks 'men of war' and sing pæans over their glorious victory, but the glory will be all the Navy will get except fresh beef and vegetables; and the conservative Whig government will have the discredit of an unsuccessful intervention in the affairs of a people whom even John Bull has been ashamed to attack."

In the early spring of this same year (1852) my father took his first trip to Florida for the benefit of his health. He wrote to my brother from Enterprise, under date of March 26: —

MY DEAR WILLIE, — It is now your turn to have a line; but as I have been pacing the sandy beach by the light of the moon and stars until 10.30 P. M., you must be content with a scratch. The night is a lovely one — a light breeze over the lake, but hardly enough to make a wavelet on the shore; thermometer 60 to 70; sky and stars like those of the tropics, and all the elasticity, too, of the sea air; for we are only about eighteen miles from the Atlantic.

This afternoon, after dinner, we took my sailboat, the Mary, and with a gentle breeze sailed over to Fort Mellen to see the Indian captives brought in by General Hopkins and his scouting party. We found them all assembled in a large rough room, and quite a scene it was! First, there was a poor suffering young woman who had been shot with seven buckshot on the thigh, and the bone broken: she lay in the midst on a rude litter, upon which she had been brought 120 miles through swamps and bushes between two ponies; she showed no signs of pain, and hardly appeared to observe anything. Then a family of a mother and five children, from one and a half years to twelve — the three youngest, bright-eyed little imps, entirely bare except a cotton handkerchief tied around the neck and hanging behind — quite an original way of clothing a youngster. Then one or two other women, and two or three older children about thirteen to fifteen; and finally a warrior lying in a corner, with a rope around his neck, which was held by a sentinel with a loaded gun in his hand — his legs and feet were bare to the thighs. The elder ones looked dull and rather stupid; the children bright and happy. They were caught, a week ago to-night, out of their boundary; made prisoners on charge of being cattle stealers; but whether they are outlaw Indians, who do not acknowledge Billy Bowlegs, or whether they are a party of the Seminole nation, is the question. If the latter, we may have the whole tribe down upon the settlements for vengeance; but I hope these are certain outlaws whom Billy would like to have us catch and send West. The most singular part of the whole was the troop of undisciplined volunteer woodmen who brought them in — amongst whom one or two were sober — the major was lying drunk on the floor! I was introduced to General Hopkins, a rough farmer-looking man, who might remind one a little of Peter Blake,[1] also a Captain Jarnegan, who is at the bottom of all the trouble, having taken two prisoners a month or more ago, one of whom, a woman, hung herself. He was a rough-looking man, who is said to be the best Indian hunter

[1] The family fishman at Milton.

in Florida, and is, I fear, a mischievous fellow.
He tells me it means war, and that these are Bow-
leg Indians. It may lead to war, but I think it
is his fault. The rest of the troop were a hard-
looking, hard-drinking set, and the horses, having
had no corn for a week, looked almost starved.
The men obeyed no orders, and were swearing and
drinking and almost fighting. The steamboat was
at anchor waiting for them, and after seeing enough
of the Indians and playing with the children and
giving them some small change, I prepared to start,
when General Hopkins asked me to take his Indians
on board the steamer; so I took my man Pablo,
and took the whole eleven or twelve on board. It
was lucky I was there with my roomy boat, as the
poor woman would have suffered in a canoe, and as
it was, she groaned dreadfully as they laid her
down, and looked wistfully at the water. If you
could have been magnetized to see me with my
cargo, and pouring water into the mouth of the
wounded woman, you would have thought of R.
Crusoe and his Island.

I got them safely on board the steamer, and then
got my party and made sail for home, taking a
little cruise to enjoy the beautiful sunset and the
delicious warm breeze. It was one of those soft
sunsets, with long feathering pink and crimson
clouds, such as is seldom seen out of the tropics.
It was eight before we got home, and now the mosquitoes are killing me, so good-night. Dr. Bryant
thinks the woman will die.

28th *March*.

One of our invalids died on Friday, and the other is just going now, and both bodies are to go up with us in the steamer!

Yesterday we took another sail up river, and I hit three alligators and killed one; they were lying out on the banks and swimming round with their heads out of water, just as you see frogs in a pond.

Tuesday we caught a chameleon of a beautiful light green, but he soon changed to a dull brown. Dr. Wyman [1] has him in spirits: he also has my alligator all dissected, and means to have him set up at full length in Cambridge.

Yesterday Mr. Schley came in from his camp, having killed six deer; the Indian troubles scare the folks here, and so he gives up hunting for this year, and my chance for a deer hunt is done. Mr. Schley has been living out in a tent most of the time for three months, with only one blanket.

My father recalls no notable event in his mercantile life during the years immediately succeeding this first trip to Florida, except, perhaps, his joining Messrs. John and Loring Cunningham in sending the clipper ship Flying Childers to Cronstadt, whence she brought away " the last cargo of Russian goods before the blockade was established by the English and French at the time of the Crimean War," and thereby made quite a profitable trip.

Captain White, who commanded her, told on his

---

[1] Professor Jeffries Wyman, **of Harvard** University.

return a good story of the gallant but rather bombastic admiral in command of the blockading squadron, who had hailed him as he ran out, and wished to know what there was to prevent his "slapping down" with a dozen English frigates into Cronstadt? "Well," the captain had replied, "you can slap them down easy enough, but whether you can slap them back again is a question." And he used to add, with a dry chuckle, "The admiral did not try it."

My father speaks of his having been at this time "undoubtedly very busy with the Michigan Central Railroad, and also with the small roads which then formed the embryo of the Chicago, Burlington and Quincy," and goes on to tell of his "very trying enterprise of building the Hannibal and St. Joseph road, to connect the Mississippi and Missouri rivers."

In 1855 he took his first trip to England, partly on business and partly for pleasure. He writes to my brothers William and Malcolm : —

BRUNSWICK HOTEL, Jermyn Street, London, *May* 17, 1855.

Chilly northeast storm, but trying to clear up. I brought my story up to Liverpool in a letter to the girls. Such confusion on board! Anchored in the river. The tide rises so much that vessels cannot stay at the wharf, so they have built immense stone basins with gates towards the river. When tide is high, open come the gates, and ships pass in and out; then, being shut up, the docks remain full of water and the ships far above the river. Common tides rise seventeen feet. Well, you never saw such confusion ; 200 passengers, each about four trunks — 800, and two custom-house officers to examine all in a little crowded place on deck. After several hours, got my trunks passed, and E. C. his, and we went on board boat to go ashore. Remembered a forlorn woman on the steamer with a small child, a little like our Sarah ; my conscience smote me for not having helped her, so I told E. C. I would meet him on shore, went back to the Pacific, found her sitting in the same cold place with her child, waiting for her turn ; got a description of her trunks, etc., and went on deck and hunted them up, lugged them down myself, and put her and her things in charge of the officer, and as she could take care of herself thenceforward, rushed back to the boat just in time to rejoin C. ; felt not a little relieved. Landed in the moist chilly atmosphere. Drove to hotel, leaving our baggage to follow with the crowd. Ordered dinner for two ; fat landlady, waiter in gloves. Presently a plated dish and cover, larger than you ever saw, was put before us, and under it about half an ox. Ordered a Hansom cab, and what's more got into one. We drove furiously along the streets, and everybody stared. I thought it must be the only one in Liverpool. Imagine a red bodied-chaise, with driver perched up behind and overhead, reins passing above our heads, a lanky horse, and we going like mad Drove about town (Sunday), and then out to Greenbank ; did not stop ; saw some rather pretty houses, but they have prison-looking brick walls, and everything here (and indeed all over England) looks and is damp. Home at nine P. M.; baggage not come, but just before train started, at 9.20, got it, and embarked for Birmingham; carriages instead of cars; landed at 1.20 A. M.; fine hotel. Up at seven A. M.; drove out to a gunsmith's, William Greener, to make myself a present of a gun; back in time for train at nine o'clock. Railroad one hour, and then took a fly, — so called because it does n't fly, being a heavy closed carry-all; hired it for the day, and started for Warwick Castle, one of the old feudal castles, built 800 or 1000 years ago. Eight hundred years! — and no finer building made yet. Has man improved much in that time? I hope so. . . .

It was a fine sunny day, though chilly and with passing clouds. Took train at Leamington at six, for London. Tuesday, drove to Baring's. The city seems like Boston twenty times bigger and with a river through it, and with lots of old palaces and churches sprinkled about; the common houses and streets much like Boston, crooked and up and down hill, crowded, all of the streets like Washington Street on a busy day. Found Mr. Ashburner and Beckwith, who took us to see Windsor Castle and Park, and a fine old country place, "Gilwood;" a lawn with good trees and a park. Windsor Park was made by the Norman kings, who destroyed two thousand villages to make hunting grounds sixteen miles across; now open to the public for drives and walks. Lot of poor, wet, tame-looking deer like uncomfortable sheep, smaller than our deer and tamer than Naushon sheep.

We took at the station an open carriage with a postilion in tights and spurs; home by rail, and dined at Mr. Ashburner's club. Home, the spiritualist, here, and is engaged days ahead with the fashionable people, who have got hold of him through the Lawrences.

Second day in London. . . . Went to House of Commons. You enter a fine old hall built by William the Conqueror, lofty and gothic. The new houses are not much, and the members, with their hats on, look ordinary enough; the speaker and clerk sat in their wigs; stayed five minutes. The wealth and magnificence of London is incalculable, but this climate is perfectly intolerable, raining every five minutes, and chilly and cold. Read "Bleak House:" the opening account of Lady Deadlock and the country seat seems like a description of all the weather here. On Wednesday, Mr. Edward Baring takes us to the great Derby race, fifteen miles off. He offered to take us in his mother's carriage. We take a hamper of provisions and sit all day; see Dickens's description of the Fat Boy. And now, darlings, with love to all, I must say good-by.

While in England my father must have made the personal acquaintance of Nassau Senior, the political economist and drafter of the modern English poor-law, formerly Professor of Political Economy

at Oxford, with whom he had already been in business correspondence for some years. They had
some discussions on the burning question of the
day, — as is clear from the letter which follows. It
is curious to note how little the nearness of the
coming storm was realized, — though the hand of
the writer was pretty carefully held on the public
pulse. He at least felt as Lowell afterwards said : —

> " Ef you want peace, the thing you 've gut to du
> Is jes to show you 're up to fightin' tu."

TO NASSAU WILLIAM SENIOR.

STEAMSHIP AMERICA, *July* 3, 1855.

MY DEAR SIR, — I have read your article in the
" Edinburgh " with much interest, and still more
with astonishment at your intimate acquaintance
with American affairs. . . .

There is one error or misconception into which
you have fallen in regard to the existing opposition
to the Fugitive Slave Law, and especially to the
excitement in Boston last year upon the surrender
of Burns. You ascribe it all to Mrs. Stowe's book,
and in this you do injustice to the progress which
sound opinions had made, even in the conservative
portions of the North, before her book appeared.

It is notorious that after Webster made his 7th
March, 1850, speech, which carried the Fugitive
Bill and its kindred measures, he would not have
had the vote of one third of his own party for any
office in the gift of the people of his adopted State,
Massachusetts. Immediately after the passage of

the Bill I was present at the following conversation between a Southerner and a conservative Boston merchant : —

Southerner. "Now, my friend, we shall have quiet ! The South has got her rights, and there is an end of agitation."

Northern Merch^t. " You are all wrong. Agitation has only begun, unless your people avoid exercising their rights and use them simply as a bugbear to keep their slaves at home ; for the new law will never be enforced except at such cost that it will be far cheaper for the master to let his slaves run."

Southerner. " Then the Union is dissolved. The law must be executed in good faith and made to work practically, or we leave you."

Northerner. "Good-by, then! the sooner you set your house in order the better, for our people will never allow that law to be executed except in isolated cases ! "

The above, I am sure, gives a correct view of the opinions of those who know the state of public feeling at the North, — and the result had been in accordance with those opinions even before Mrs. Stowe's book appeared. Even those at the North who approved of the law expected to see it merely held *in terrorem* over the blacks, as a preventive of escape. . . .

True the book of Mrs. Stowe had been stimulating the masses throughout the country, but the Nebraska iniquity, just then perpetrated, took away the balance-wheel which had existed, and was the immediate cause of the tremendous excitement which pervaded the usually quiet town of Boston on 2d June, 1854. . . .

In looking over my files of American papers I see that Massachusetts has passed a bill " for the protection of personal liberty," which it is supposed will render the Fugitive Bill entirely nugatory within her borders. It is much criticised by the conservative press as radical and dangerous, but I have not the least fear of any mischief coming from it; if it really goes too far, our people will correct it in time to avoid revolution. I have not seen it, but will get it and send it to you herewith. . . .

The real danger will come, if ever, when the North, strong and growing, shall wake up to find itself bound through corruption and fraud to the will of the aristocratic minority. Then the North may insist upon being put back where they were, even at the cost of revolution. The Southern politicians have undoubtedly been aiming at securing enough new slave States to give them a majority in the Senate, which would then become practically a House of Lords, with a veto on all legislation and with a claim to a large share of the patronage of government.

Apart from the moral question, and on the mere lower ground of expediency and statesmanship, can there be a doubt in any sane mind that the safety of the North and of the Union consists in a firm resistance to the further extension of slavery or the increase of slave States beyond what the Constitution in its strictest, clearest sense calls for ?

Early in the fall of 1855 the Barings (acting, as it seemed, for Louis Napoleon, though this was never acknowledged) began to feel the way towards the purchases of wheat and flour which later in the year were undertaken for their account by J. M. Forbes & Co. This appears from the following letter of September 22, 1855, from my father to his cousin, Mr. Russell Sturgis, who was then a partner in Baring Bros. & Co.

My dear Sturgis, — . . . I notice that you are somewhat disturbed at the idea of buying our bread-stuffs at high prices, but it is an ill wind that blows nobody good, and it will stimulate us here. I only hope you will not send us large amounts of stocks to sell. . . . Our crops are but just coming to market and have hardly begun to have their effect on commerce. Upon our Michigan Central road, for instance, the receipts of wheat and flour are far behind last year, while our receipts generally are twenty-five to thirty per cent. additional. This is partly owing to the wet weather at the harvest, making much of the Michigan wheat unsafe to grind or ship until very thoroughly dry, and the lakes and canal will probably close with very large supplies of grain left in the country, although from this time forward all the avenues of transportation will be fully occupied. There are various ridiculous stories about the governments of Europe sending here to buy bread. If the French government really wanted to help fill the bellies of their people, they could do it easier than by buying wheat. Let them employ Philippe's head cook to make Johnny-cakes fashionable and palatable, and to mix about the same proportion of Indian meal with their wheaten bread that we often do here from pre-ference; open public bakeries and confectioneries on this plan in the principal cities, and instead of flour or wheat, import Indian and other cheaper meals to eke out the French wheat crop. If the French nation could be taught to eat from economy as large a proportion of Indian meal as my family eat from choice and for health, millions of dollars might be saved and lots of hungry bellies filled. As it is, I suppose we must put up flour here, and thus force our own people to eat our own coarse grains; and in this way I believe we can keep you all comfortable until next harvest brings you round. . . .   Always yours,

                                        J. M. F.

My father, referring to the transaction which fol-lowed, says: " Prices were still low here, but it re-quired good management to conceal the ownership of the breadstuffs and to give the operations the appearance of private commercial speculations. . . . Our secret was so well kept that nobody dreamed of any government being behind us, and some of the agents we employed to buy suffered very seri-ously by going on buying on their own account after our order stopped." Writing in 1884 of this transaction, and without reference to his books, he says that the purchases of provisions may have amounted to considerably over $5,000,000, and that this fact and the shipment of the whole of them to France left no doubt in his mind that they were for the French government; and he adds: "I am not sure whether the operation proved a good one for the emperor, but it certainly helped to tide over the danger of a hard famine in France."

It was in order to get through the extra work thus caused that he took into his office Charles Russell Lowell, of whom more will be seen later on. At their first interview in New York he was strongly attracted to him, and, as will be seen, the attraction continued and increased till the day of Lowell's death.

In March, 1856, the press of work caused by the shipments of breadstuffs having abated, my father was about to take a trip to Florida and Cuba with my brother Malcolm, then a small boy. Finding that Lowell's doctor wished him to go abroad for his health, he proposed that he should join them, and they made the trip together, Lowell going afterwards in a sailing ship to Europe from New Orleans. They visited the "Carolina" sugar plantation near Cienfuegos in Cuba, the picture of which, though it was a humane plantation, with the whip seldom used, was always a very painful one, as it rose in my father's mind in after years. It was on his return through South Carolina from this trip that he made the acquaintance of Mr. Hamilton Cowper, having first heard of him from the lady of

a house in which he had been staying, who had
been rescued years before, with her daughter, then
a baby, by Mr. Cowper at great risk to himself,
from the wreck of the steamer Pulaski. This gallantry naturally inclined my father to make friends
with him, and the pleasant relations then established continued after his return home.

During the political campaign of the following
autumn (1856), which ended in the election of
Buchanan to the presidency, my father wrote to Mr.
Cowper, with the pretext of asking his opinion as
to the possible employment of Chinese in Florida,
but chiefly, as he says in his notes, "with the view
of learning whether the all-absorbing question of
the day was still so far short of being a 'burning'
one as to admit of two men of the North and South
respectively, conservative and presumably patriotic,
approaching the subject with cool minds and arriving at some practicable compromise which might be
recommended to their friends on either side."

To this letter, he received just after the election,
the following reply : —

J. HAMILTON COWPER TO J. M. FORBES.

NEAR DARIEN, November 6, 1856.

MY DEAR SIR, — Your letter of September 18
reached my residence soon after my departure on a
visit to the up country, which will, I hope, be a
sufficient explanation of the long delay in my answer to it.

I have read and considered attentively the scheme

of your Chinese correspondent to establish a colony
of laborers from that country in Florida. My present impressions are that it is not feasible. I am
not sufficiently informed as to the amount of work
that the Chinese are capable of performing to enable me to compare the result of their labor with
that of the negro slave; but I suspect, with the
disadvantages of enhanced wages, and the absence
of compulsory labor, that the balance will be in
favor of negro labor. In employing a large number of Irish and negroes on the Brunswick Canal,
I obtained more work from the latter than the
former, at a much smaller cost. I know too little
of the laws of Florida to say whether the introduction of free Chinese would in any respect be an in-
fraction of them; but I believe it would not, and I
believe also that a strong prejudice would be created
against such a colony. Enlightened patriotism will
revolt at the introduction of an inferior race of free
men; and local prejudice will suspect an attempt to
attack the institution of slavery. The success of
such an enterprise will depend on keeping the col-
onists together, and at low wages. In a country
like this, in which labor is in demand and well paid,
this will I think be impossible. Contracts for a
term of time may be made, but they would not be
respected or enforced. The intelligent and useful
will soon abandon the colony in search of higher
wages and a more independent position; and the
enterprise will be left to drag on with the drones.
Many years ago, W. Trumbull brought over a col-

ony of Minorcans to Smyrna (south of St. Augustine), the members of which were indented for a term of service. The establishment was soon broken up in consequence of the infidelity of the laborers to their contracts.

I thank you for the communication of *Cecil* on the exciting question of the day. It is written with great elegance and ability, and he enforces with great strength his own views. I demur to two of his positions, which demurrer, if sound, is fatal to his conclusions. First, I deny that Congress has any constitutional right to say to a future sovereign State that it shall be curtailed of a power possessed by other States, viz.: to decide for itself whether it shall or shall not establish slavery. The union of the States is of equals and not of inferiors. I deny the power of Congress to exclude a part of the Union from equal participation in common property. Secondly, I deny that a majority has a right to govern irrespective of the Constitution, and of the rights secured by the great principles of justice. An *ex parte* assertion of constitutional right is no ground for the enforcement of majority prejudices. This subject is a delicate one for discussion between the North and the South, and I usually avoid it as unprofitable. There is one practical view which should be clearly presented to the whole country, which is, the unavoidable result of any attempt to enforce the Northern views on the subject of the exclusion of slavery from the Territories. Be assured, my dear sir, that a dissolution of the Union is inevitable whenever the free-soil principles of the North shall in any instance be enforced. If that principle be dearer to the North than the Union, let it avail itself of its numerical superiority and enforce it; but let it not deceive itself into the belief that any fear of consequences will deter the Southern States from meeting the issue. I love the Union, and rank among the conservatives of the South, but I am prepared for a dissolution of our government rather than yield a *right which is essential to the very existence of the South.* The result of the recent election of president is unknown to me. If in favor of Mr. Buchanan, I shall breathe more freely, as Mr. Fremont's success will, I apprehend, be the knell of the Union. I rejoice that sectional feelings have still no influence in private relations, and that I still hold my Northern friends with the feelings of respect with which I am,

Yours most truly,

J. HAMILTON COWPER.

This letter must have convinced my father that it was impossible for his correspondent and himself to arrive at any point near an agreement on the vexed question, and his reply which follows could only have been written with the view of showing clearly and once for all the standpoint of the North and West, from which no bullying or cajoling could make them budge, viz.: that slavery had at least to be content with what it had got in the way of territory, and must not " ask for more."

(Private.) BOSTON, *December* 4, 1856.

MY DEAR SIR, — Your favor of the 6th ulto.
reached me in due course and I am much obliged
for your valuable information and suggestions in
regard to Chinese labor in Florida, which will probably nip that scheme in the bud or reduce it to a
very safe experiment.

I thank you too for your frankness in regard to
the great question of the day. You say truly that
it is too delicate for profitable discussion among
friends, but this makes it only the more important
that the real state of public opinion, outside of
partisan politics, should be better known than it is.

I had supposed that there existed a party of great
latent strength at the South who value the Union
much more than they do the extension of the institution of slavery, and who would put forth their
strength whenever any real danger came. Knowing
how far you are above being influenced by any
desire for office, or for any popular extravagance, I
take it as the very worst indication of the coming
storm to find that you are not on that side of the
question. Regretting deeply that it is so, I thank
you for the warning, which coming on top of the
election of Mr. Buchanan assures me that we are
doomed to continued agitation until 1860, and then
to the first real experiment of the strength of our
confederacy. You have thrown a gloomy shadow
over the hopes I had entertained of help for the

Union from the conservatism of the South; but it is far better to know the truth, and I owe it to you in return to tell you what seems to me the state of public opinion here. Upon the only real point of difference suggested by you, — which indeed is the only real issue between the North and South, viz.: the constitutionality of the principle of the Jefferson Proviso, — there is hardly any division of opinion at the North excepting among the partisans of squatter sovereignty; and the experience in Kansas has, I think, reduced the advocates of this doctrine to a small minority. We are then all united here in the opinion that either Congress or the squatters (some looking to one and some to the other) have a clear right to prohibit slavery in the territories from the moment that settlement begins. We have been brought up in the faith that this was settled constitutional doctrine, held as it has been by all the men we are accustomed to look upon as great authorities at the North, and by many of your own best men, and confirmed too by the adoption of the Ordinance of 1787, at the very time when the Constitutional Convention was in session, as also by the adoption of the Missouri compromise when Mr. Calhoun was a member of the Cabinet.

But it is not my purpose to argue. I only mean to state the almost universal conviction at the North that the restriction of slavery is as clearly within the constitutional rights of the majority as any of our admitted and daily exercised rights; and the only real difference of opinion here is as to the expediency of exercising that right. Mr. Webster, with a respectable body of Whigs and a large body of Democrats, was, in 1850, against exercising that right unnecessarily; but it is a very solemn conviction that there is, as nearly as possible, unanimity here, since the repeal of the Missouri compromise, in favor of exercising that (real or supposed) right at all hazards whenever practically necessary to prevent the extension of slavery into territories now free.

Beyond and above all this, the conviction is being daily forced upon the North that the designs of the South do not stop with introducing slavery into our own territories, but that the question to be settled in Kansas is whether the whole power of the confederacy shall be exercised for buying or conquering all the territory and islands north of Panama for the mere extension of your institution. Some of your more bold and ultra men plainly avow this intention so far as Cuba, Mexico, and Central America are concerned; and the Cincinnati platform is certainly so framed as to warrant this apprehension on the part of the North.

Mr. Buchanan, if aided by the conservative men of the South, may allay the apprehension that the South seek anything more than the assertion of their (supposed or real) right to take their slaves into our own territories, but even if he does succeed thus far, it is my belief that the issue has been so sharply defined to be a struggle for political power between the North and South, that it is too late to change it until one or the other side yield, or until we separate and begin again on a new basis. I believe that the public mind in the non-slaveholding States has been in a state of revolution for some years, but of active change since the passage of the Nebraska Bill, and that the change will go on during the next four years in a progressive ratio, until in 1860 there will be not the ghost of a chance for any man's getting an electoral vote in the North and West who is not sharply opposed to the extension of slavery at home and abroad; and, moreover, that it will take all the strength of the moderate men of the North to draw the line there — to keep within the Republican platform of 1856.

It is hard for you to appreciate justly our position here without knowing more of the parties who rule the North than you can know through the expression given us by the press, the pulpit, and the rostrum.

I will try to sketch the elements that now move the Northern mind. The abolitionists [1] have never had much direct influence, and they have been losing ground for several years; they may be thrown entirely out of account. The conservative men of both political parties have hitherto believed that they could occupy a common ground with those of the South in advocating the policy of letting slavery alone where it existed, and still retain their

---

[1] This refers to their power as a separate organization. My father, as has been seen, though opposed to their extreme views as to the destruction of the Union, was yet much influenced by them. — Ed.

proper influence with the masses; but the issue at last made of slavery extension leaves them no choice between opposition to it and political annihilation. They have very extensively joined the Fremont party, and unless the issue can be changed they must continue to go there, until the remainder who take the Southern side becomes so small as just conveniently to fill the federal offices and the easy-chairs of their drawing-rooms and clubs. But it is the masses, the democracy (call it by what name we may), which must rule; and they are hopelessly against the Southern policy, whether it be called the extension of slavery, or the establishment of a balance of power between the two sections.

Buchanan owes his Northern success to the Fillmore diversion, and to the name of Democrat which in certain slow-moving regions, like parts of Pennsylvania, still retained its power, under the representations of his partisans that he was for popular sovereignty (squatter) and for free Kansas. But, my dear sir, depend upon it the Northern democracy can never again be depended upon for a Southern alliance. Fifteen or twenty years ago the abolition men and women were mobbed everywhere, and their lives endangered and their halls burned; now the mob are all the other way, but it is not that they have become abolitionists. The wrong of slavery preached to them from the pulpit, the waste and inexpediency of slavery reiterated to them by the press, doubtless weigh with the masses, but all other influences sink into insignificance compared with that brought to bear for two years past, and especially during the past four months from the stump and by the tremendous machinery of the campaign press, to convince the laboring classes here of the aristocratic nature of the institution of slavery; of the small number of slaveholders compared with the white population North and South, and of the coming issue being whether this small class (supposed to rule the South) shall own half the Senate and shall use the national arm to extend their institution at home and abroad.

So long as there is a pretext, a color, for holding up to the people such an issue, there can be but one result.

The masses in all countries can be roused upon two points, their nation's interests and their own prejudices; and if there is anything in this country fixed, it is the prejudice against aught which has the appearance even of aristocracy. Are you entirely free from danger from this prejudice at home?

Unless then some strange and almost impossible change takes place in Mr. Buchanan's policy from that of his predecessor, you may count upon the popular vote of 1860 being against the increase of Southern power with as much certainty as you could upon its being thrown against the reëstablishment in our territories of the feudal institutions of the Middle Ages. I have said far more than I intended, but I have not that power of condensation which you so happily possess.

I cordially respond to your hope that difference
of opinion as to public policy may never interfere
with friendly private relations between individuals
of the North and South, and am with great respect,

Yours very truly,   J. M. FORBES.

P. S. — In reading over what I have hastily written I see that I have omitted to explain what I
mean by the danger from Mr. Buchanan's election.
Any attempt on his part to strengthen the South
immediately or prospectively in the Senate, by foreign acquisitions of territory or otherwise, will only
precipitate the crisis and increase the agitation.
The only hope of safety for the Union seems to me
to be for the South now, when they apparently have
the power through their own President, and can do
so without sacrifice of their pride, to recede from
their position in regard to slavery extension, and
from their struggle for that fatal chimera "the
balance of power." Let it give up this, and by its
compact union it will always have more than its fair
share of the government; then by taking ground
on which the conservatives of the North can stand
with them (and still retain their due influence at
home), the true interests of the whole country may
be secured by putting down radical and dangerous
experiments in government, and by avoiding those
foreign wars which our turbulent spirits, North and
South, will always be only too ready to engage in
against the despotisms of the Old World.

Yours truly,   J. M. F.

To turn now from politics to home matters. It may be remembered that some years previous to this winter (1856–57) my father had joined my mother's uncle, Mr. Swain, in buying the island of Naushon, Mr. Swain assuming the duties of host, or as it was jokingly called, " governor," of the island, and my parents spending a month of their long vacation every year as his guests. Mr. Swain's increasing disabilities now made it desirable to reverse these positions of host and guest; and the control of the island was consequently handed over to my father. The " Governor " charged him in a pathetic letter, dated 2d December, 1856, to preserve " that simplicity which is after all the great charm of such a place," and urged that " the secret of enjoyment for those who visited the island had been the feeling that the hospitalities of the place were dispensed without being a tax upon the family, no labored attempts at entertainment either at the table or elsewhere, but people left to enjoy themselves in the most simple way." From this time the island became my parents' summer and autumn home. I think it will have appeared from what I have told of their life there that they entirely sympathized with the views of their relative, and carried them out as host and hostess in letter and spirit, so long as this was practicable.

With the view of insuring easy access to the island my father got his brother Bennet to model for him the schooner Azalea and supervise the building of her. He speaks of her as being needed

for " a family carry-all in those days when we had
no railway to Wood's Hole and only a tri-weekly
steamer between New Bedford and Naushon." She
entirely answered her purpose and did good service
in both work and play for more than a score of
years.

For the ten years preceding the time at which we
have arrived, my father's business in ships and merchandise had been gradually decreasing, and its
management largely delegated to others. His own
personal interest had become centred in the growing railroad systems of the West. His work was
mainly devoted to the Michigan Central, and to the
enterprise already, in 1856, known by its permanent
title of the Chicago, Burlington and Quincy Railroad, with which, from its first small beginnings as
a feeder of the older line, he had been so intimately
connected. This change, no doubt, was partly due
to the altered conditions of trade with the East,
caused by the introduction of steamships. As yet
the ocean telegraph, which was soon to do away
with the old-fashioned China merchant, had not
come. But men were already dreaming of it, and
experimenting with it.

There were two reasons which conspired together, as time went on, to involve my father more
in railroads and less in the shipping business. In
the first place, railroads, in their early days, had a
tendency towards financial bogs, and he was always
being called on to help them out. Once interested
in any affair, it was one of his marked traits, when

that particular bit of business was in a bad place,
never to rest until by dint of hard tugging he had
pulled it out. The other reason may be made
clear by what a partner in his old firm in China
said of him: "Mr. Forbes never seemed to me a
man of acquisitiveness, but very distinctly one of
constructiveness. His wealth was only an incident. I have seen many occasions when much more
money might have been made by him in some business transaction but for this dominant passion for
building up things. The good, also, which he anti-
cipated for workmen and settlers through opening
up the country always weighed much with him."

His views, at that time, as to the future of the
Chicago, Burlington and Quincy Railroad, may be
seen in the following reply to queries addressed to
him by his correspondent in Calcutta, Mr. George
Ashburner: —

MILTON, January 19, 1857.

MY DEAR MR. ASHBURNER, — ... You ask what
permanent advantage the Chicago, Burlington and
Quincy has over other roads to the Mississippi?

It runs through the very finest country in the
State and in a very direct line, has two feeders from
the West, no hurtful competition yet, good outlets
East, efficient officers and an honest president who
wants to get rid of the office, and never sought it,
and a local traffic which must, I think, always give
it a fair business even if its through traffic dimin-
ishes. It has not been built very economically,
having paid high prices for labor and iron, and

some high shaves in selling its bonds, as you can
testify ; but it has been run by honest and very intelligent men, simply and purely for the interest of
the stockholders, and not for any town, village,
other railroad, or individual. It has been, up to
this time, managed by people having a large interest in it, and what mistakes or extravagances
they have committed have been honest ones, growing out of their being too full of work to attend to
details as much as our New England Yankees do ;
and against this rather lavish expense I put the
advantage of having it planned and managed by
large minds who looked ahead, and knew the great
interests they had to care for.

Now, it is not to be denied that, in that flat country, others may at a time of cheap money and iron,
come alongside of it and build a cheaper road that
could diminish its profits, but with so wide a field
open as those prairies give I should think railroad
enterprise would naturally take other unoccupied
fields for years to come. Still there lies its danger.
Of course it has others, like all railroads, from
change of management, dishonest financial management, etc., but it has passed safely through the
infantile diseases of railroads, and its chance seems
to me good for the future. It is not cursed with
branches. . . .

So much for the intrinsic advantages of the railroad ; now as to its comparative ones. I have not
the means of judging, as it requires infinite time
and trouble to dig deep into the bowels of a cor-

poration ; I can only say that the other roads there may have a country nearly as good, and a location nearly as good, but some have a complication of doubtful branches, some zigzag to meet local interests, some have been built by *contractors* who were directors, and pronounced on the proper execution of their own work ! And as to the others, it is hard to say how far honesty and intelligence have directed them. Some may be cheaper and better than this; but I am too old to go into the investigation of their merits, preferring, until this line gets much higher and others lower, to stick to the one that I know has had certain positive advantages over the majority of roads, by being located, planned, and built by the right sort of men, and also the advantage of proving by its results from month to month, that the projectors only underrated the pecuniary results of their work. True, they also underrated its cost; but that is a chronic complaint about railroads ! . . .

Very truly yours,   J. M. FORBES.

No note of warning is sounded in this letter to Mr. Ashburner of the coming financial panic of 1857. I suspect the truth was that, busy in altering the mansion house at Naushon, and on the thousand details incident to his occupation of the island, he did not follow the business world with quite the same keen sight as was habitual to him. Possibly too, intent, up to 1856, on the management of the Michigan Central, he did not see that overbuilding

of railroads was going on throughout the West,
— tying up capital in non-paying and ill-advised
adventures and bringing on the crash, of which
an account is given in the following chapter.

CHAPTER VII

THE year 1857 seems to have opened quietly for
my father. I find him writing, in April, to Mr.
Edward Cunningham, one of the partners in Russell & Co., who was about to return home from
China, and discussing the sale of " blacks and cheap
greens " (teas), the new minister to England, and
French and English operations in China. He writes
in his notes, "I had left the Michigan Central
presidency, and though still a director, I considered
myself on the retired list and remained quietly at
Naushon all summer, hardly attending at all to the
railroad."

The following letter from Mr. William Sturgis,
directed to him at Naushon, shows that at the beginning of September he could not have been contemplating any excitements apart from those to be
looked for on the island : —

BOSTON, September 5, 1857.

MY DEAR FORBES, — On my return from that
centre of " Devildom," New York city, I found
your kind note inviting me to a hunt on the 22d

inst., and time was when I should have accepted it as eagerly as the governor would a challenge to a game at all-fours, — at which he is usually sure to be beaten, — but now, alas, though the spirit is willing and more than willing, the flesh, especially the lower extremities, cannot be relied upon, and I dare not make the attempt.

Do not think I am deterred by apprehensions of broken limbs or a bruised body under your guidance. Any one who has followed you as I have, carrying a heavy gun on a wild colt dashing at full speed through dense woods, and over that so-called trotting-course full of holes, stumps, scrub oaks, and tangled briars, and escaped a smash-up, may feel assured that fate has destined him for some other end than a broken neck by such means.

You say that you have "made a thorough reform, clearing out all the old break-neck horses and substituting well-bred and well-broken animals." I am bound to think that you believe what you say, but I got an idea of what you consider a "well-bred and well-broken" animal from a description I have had, and a sketch I have seen, of an occurrence that took place a few months since, which would satisfy the most incredulous that he would be as safe in driving one of your reform horses as he would be in a wagon harnessed to a fresh caught mustang stallion in the middle of a Western prairie.

You refer to the elder Mr. Quincy; now that won't do, my dear fellow. You cannot make a stool-pigeon of the venerable gentleman; even his certificate would not neutralize the stubborn fact above alluded to.

Seriously, though, I should very much like to gratify the Governor — God bless him — by joining the hunt, and gratify myself by meeting the old set of sportsmen once more, yet I dare not venture to undertake that which requires more physical powers than any one can expect to possess at seventy-six. I must, therefore, content myself with again thanking you for the invitation and assuring you that I am faithfully yours,

WM. STURGIS.

The financial panic, " more extensive than that of 1837 and equally sharp while it lasted," as my father says of it in his notes, must have struck Boston about the middle of the month, for I find the following to Mr. Edward Cunningham, then in Europe, on his way home from China: —

BOSTON, *September* 28, 1857.

MY DEAR EDWARD, — We are in such a crisis here as only those who went through 1837 can conceive of. J. K. Mills & Co. and many stronger houses have gone, and other large ones on Milk Street only exist by sufferance, and many large manufacturing companies are in the same straits.

New York Central Railroad has run down from 87 to 55, and Michigan Central from 95 to 45, while the weaker concerns are clear out of sight — Erie 10, Southern Michigan 10–15.

Having taken in sail, not expecting a storm, but out of pure laziness, I am very easy unless other people swamp me ; but I don't believe W. Appleton's note indorsed by W. Sturgis would bring $100,000 here within forty-eight hours, at three per cent. per month, — such is the panic.

. . . Tell B. the Chicago, Burlington and Quincy Railroad seems very snug for a month or two to come, and Joy is sanguine that it will do a fine business when the crops begin to move east.

Yours always,   J. M. F.

It is clear that he had not then the least expectation of meeting his correspondent on the other side of the Atlantic. But he was not long to remain " on the retired list."

Early in October he was called up from Naushon and urgently requested to go to London to get a loan of two million dollars, which might prevent the Michigan Central Railroad becoming bankrupt. As to the policy which had brought the road face to face with such a dilemma, he writes in his notes : " Somehow the directors had taken the view that the high rates for money in the street were only temporary ; and so for the needful construction and other outlays they had allowed the company to incur a heavy floating debt instead of selling stock and bonds to meet their outlays." But the crisis had to be met, and he could not refuse to go ; so, taking his two eldest daughters with him, he started for London by the next steamer. He soon accomplished his object, obtaining the needed loan from the Barings, though, as was inevitable in time of panic, on very onerous terms.

During this English visit he made a trip with his daughters to France, where his stay was saddened by the sickness and death, in Paris, of a cousin, Charles Hathaway, of whom my father was very fond. He was with him at the end, and he had to see to things for the widow before leaving. While in Paris he discovered that the great efficiency of Louis Napoleon's police could be turned to good account. He heard by chance that Mr. E. Cunningham must have got wind of the panic in the United States, and that he was hurrying home through France that very day, not dreaming of his own presence in Paris. My father went to the Police Bureau, and managed to have him arrested as he was embarking for England; and thus was able to satisfy him, when they met the next morning, that he had attended to his affairs before leaving Boston, and that there was no need for his giving up a particularly pleasant European tour, which he had been enjoying when the news of the panic had struck him.

My father and his daughters returned to New York by the American steamship Atlantic, commanded by his friend, Captain Eldridge. They had reckoned on opening the house at Naushon and eating their Thanksgiving dinner there, but just as they were about to leave Milton for New Bedford he got an urgent telegram from General Fremont, the Republican candidate whom Buchanan had defeated at

the late election, begging him to meet him in Boston
about some affairs very important to the General.
So my father sent part of the family ahead to catch
the steamer from New Bedford to Naushon, and
went to Boston himself.   As soon as he was free of
the Fremont business, he whisked off the rest of
the party, and, catching at New Bedford "a rickety
fishing-smack bound towards the Vineyard," landed
at the island, where, as he says, in spite of cold
weather and a smoky chimney, they managed to
have a very jolly visit.

Soon after this, the Michigan Central passed into
New York hands, and my father sold out his interest
in it "at only a moderate profit on the investment
to pay for some ten years' hard and responsible work
without pay."[1] But he had gained experience which
was invaluable to himself and the Chicago, Burlington and Quincy Railroad, then in rapid course of
development.

The railroad panic had, it would appear, shaken
the confidence of the Barings in American credit
generally, for I find that my father wrote in March,
1858, to their Boston agent, Mr. S. G. Ward, showing, with regard to the credits which he still found
it convenient to have from them, in view of his
Chinese shipments, that he had seldom used more
than half their amount, and adding that he had
never had at one time more than half of what he
was actually worth, invested in merchandise.   What
he wrote satisfied his London friends that in mer-

[1] Except a complimentary gift at parting. — ED.

cantile matters he was what he claimed to be, "ultra conservative."

But it was neither commerce nor railroads that now occupied the chief place in his thoughts. Politics were rapidly becoming his absorbing interest. Prior to 1850 he had been a subscribing but not active member of the Whig party, the leaders of which in Boston were among his social friends; but the time came when he found this no longer possible. He writes in his notes: —

"When Webster made his great speech, on the 7th of March, 1850, supporting the Fugitive Slave Law, and indorsing all the compromises by which we surrendered to the slave-owners, the scales fell from my eyes, and I gave up the Whig party and acted in my quiet way with the Republicans, then called 'Free-Soilers.'"

Apparently his withdrawal from the Whig party and his reasons for withdrawal caused only hilarity among his friends (the Whig leaders), for in mentioning that they continued to come to the deer hunts at Naushon he adds, as to the talk on those occasions: —

"Our discussions were frequent upon politics, but were good-natured; and I especially remember the roar of laughter which followed my very innocent question, 'What are you going to do about the Wilmot Proviso?' (against extending slavery into territories then free). 'Why,' shouted they, 'the Wilmot Proviso! You will never hear of it again; but look for it among the old flags and torn posters of the campaign; it has served its purpose, like them, for the time, but will now disappear.' They were *practical* politicians and really believed so."

But long before Buchanan's election in 1856 my father's friends among " practical politicians " must have begun to suspect that the principle represented by the Wilmot Proviso was not going to be put away among the old " campaign flags and torn posters; " and now that the political cauldron had come to show unmistakable signs of boiling over, they must have been convinced that it was making a very live issue indeed. What my father thought of the situation will appear from the following letter to one of the partners in Russell & Co., then in Paris : —

J. M. FORBES TO N. M. BECKWITH.

MILTON, *January* 17, 1858.

MY DEAR BECKWITH, — . . . I suppose you get out of the papers all our politics. They are, in a nutshell : James Buchanan, or rather James Platform, having sold himself to the South, has blundered right and left, and especially has played into the hands of Douglas, who will make capital enough out of squatter sovereignty to divide the North at the next election, and will quietly turn to the South and say to their old file leaders, " That old fool Buchanan was spoiling your game; Kansas was gone, and he was ruining the Democratic party at the North for an abstraction; your only allies are the Northern Democrats: you know me to be just as deeply pro-slavery as any man can be who can get a show of hands at the North ; vote for me and you get the power four years longer, and with the help of official patronage, and using the land-stealing mania adroitly, and above all by returning from bullying to the traditional policy of the South, viz., *political* management, you can continue to divide the North and retain power indefinitely, or at any rate until, with Northern men and money, you have gained all the territory you want; and then you can try bullying again, and either govern or dissolve the Union."

Such, I fear, is the programme, and to my eye the "situation" looks worse than it has any time since the Nebraska villainy was planned. Douglas has retrieved his position, lost by that folly, and from his superior boldness is the most dangerous opponent free principles can have. Of course, we shall fight him to the last !

My father had supported Fremont at the previous election, but was very doubtful as to whether his speculative tendencies and consequent unsavory hangers-on did not disqualify him as leader in that which was to come. At the same time he recognized that " Seward was too much of a hack, McLean too old, Sumner too theoretical and egotistic," and doubted whether " Commodore Paulding was man enough, even if the South would consent to persecute him till he became a hero in the eyes of the North." Then again, though he sympathized in a great measure with the Abolitionists, amongst whom he had many friends and relatives, he could not, as a true patriot, longing for the keeping of the peace, help seeing their rashness and trying to keep them within bounds. Thus, to Wendell Phillips and others, prior to one of their Abolitionist meetings in Boston, he gave the following advice: —

"You had better use your influence to defer, if not give up entirely, the meeting. The Boston Republicans have not hardened enough to stand the test. The Bell-Everetts and Democrats, touched in their pockets, are in a highly irritated state. At the night meeting the Abolitionists vindicated their right to speak, and the community is with them now, as having both been persecuted and shown pluck after it. Let them be content to wait. At that night meeting it is reported that large numbers of Abolitionists went armed with deadly weapons. If they have another, there is every probability that the young broadcloth rowdies and the Ann Street men will also go armed. Suppose a collision takes place and serious consequences come, the pro-slavery party, if successful, may consider the present to their Southern allies of a few Abolition lives as a peace offering that will help the Union and their pockets. On the other hand, if the Abolitionists succeed and some fatal consequences occur, it will turn the tide of sympathy from them. Their success is very doubtful, — mischief very imminent. They had better be content with their success or their draw-game as it now stands, and wait.

"Their policy is, towards the Republicans, to let *them* fight the pro-slavery men; just as our policy in this time of excitement is to let the Union men of the South fight the fire-eaters. Let the extremes keep out of it as much as possible."

The following letter to his son will show that in the midst of all this political turmoil my father did not forget the good of his family: —

Tuesday, 29 *January*, [1858,] MILTON.

MY DEAR ——: I am very sorry to hear from your mother that there is some doubt whether you can remain in college, unless you study more successfully during the short remnant of the term, or use up your vacation.

Now, my dear boy, do try for the rest of the term to make such an impression upon your teachers as will help to remove the memory of past deficiencies.

Consider what a miserable thing it will be to begin life by a failure! What a bad augury for your future fortunes!

You may think it is only because you have no taste for study that you succeed so ill, but you must remember that in the beginnings of *all* work you must sacrifice taste to duty and principle. All the real work of life goes hard until you have accustomed yourself to do it manfully, without considering your inclinations, and then work often becomes a pleasure, and always forms the basis of true happiness or content.

It may seem to you too late now to begin, but it is not so. Take hold with a will; make your teachers feel that you have a disposition to retrieve; and you will find they will make allowances for you on account of your accident, and you may still begin the term with a fair reputation.

Perhaps I have done wrongly in not saying this to you earlier, but I hate to be always before you as a monitor. I want to be in your mind as your best friend, ready to promote all innocent enjoyments and to look lightly on your faults; but I do want to see you act a man's part in this world, and to do so you must make great sacrifices of your taste and inclination. Do not make the dreadful mistake of thinking it is the circumstances of the present that control you, and that at some future time you will change.

The present is all that belongs to you. Now, I have the means to give you an education that will always (if properly used now) put you on a higher level than the mass; put you among the workers with the head instead of the hands. *Now* you have youth, and health, and kind friends to encourage you. All this may change at any moment.

> " Your hand will never be stronger,
>   Nor wanted as *now to-day.*"

Ever your affectionate   FATHER.

To return to the political situation. Among its great perplexities there was, for him personally, an additional complication. His railroad interests had led him into building, as has been said, the Hannibal and St. Joseph line, the stock of which stood in the name of three trustees, of whom he was chairman and manager. He therefore was responsible to all the stockholders of the road for its prudent conduct. This road ran through the heart of Missouri, a bitterly pro-slavery country; and however indignant my father might be at the claims and conduct of the South, he yet, so long as he represented other people's property, could not, in justice to them, proclaim in the market-place his distaste for pro-slavery methods. On the other hand, the railroad was the direct connecting link of Kansas with the East, and over it, supplied with money and Sharps' rifles, which he had helped to provide, came the free men from Massachusetts, bent on preventing the dreaded institution of slavery from gaining a foothold on that disputed ground. The latest compromise with the South had thrown the responsibility of slavery or freedom in Kansas on the voters, and the pro-slavery Missourians were contesting the election, revolvers in hand. The Free-Soil party were the men responsible for the Kansas immigration, and with them my father worked quietly all through that time, until at last, as he says in his notes, " The rebellion broke out, and I was glad to be able to join the party of freedom and to have the *chance* to raise the money needed for supplying uniforms to the first loyal regiment which General Frank Blair raised in Missouri."

To those born in times when people accept all

such stories very much as ancient history, perhaps the following letters will not bring the thrill that they are likely to rouse in such of us as have lived through the period described; but "lest we forget" the suffering, struggles, and inspiration of the time preceding the war, as well as the war itself, I give them.

S. G. HOWE TO J. M. FORBES.

NEW YORK, February 5, 1859.

MY DEAR SIR, — A friend requests me to write a line to you introducing Captain John Brown of Kansas.

I have carefully watched the movements of Brown for two years and have considerable personal knowledge of him. He is of the stuff of which martyrs are made. He is of the Puritan order militant. He is called fighting Brown, because under his natural and unaffected simplicity and modesty there is an irresistible propensity to war upon injustice and wrong. He is cool, fearless, keen, and ready with all his mental and bodily powers in the most sudden and imminent dangers. If you would like to talk with him *upon the square*, and hear what he has to say about what might perhaps seem at first to be treason, he will be glad to talk with you.

So far as one man can answer for another whom he has not known very long and intimately, I can answer for Brown's honesty of purpose.

Faithfully yours,		S. G. HOWE.

THE SAME TO THE SAME.

BOSTON, *May* 9, 1859.

MY DEAR SIR, — Captain Brown (old J. B.) is here. If any one desires to get the thirty-two hundred and fifty dollars' reward offered for his apprehension by the governor of Missouri and the President of the United States, he has only to go to the hotel in Beach Street, and try to take the old fellow.

He is a character, I assure you ; and if you are disposed to have a conversation with him, he will call at your house, or your office, as you may appoint. He knows more about the question of practical emancipation than any one whom I have seen.

Faithfully yours,   S. G. HOWE.

My father gives in his notes the following account of the visit from John Brown. The statements as to numbers and position, recalled nearly thirty years after the events, do not always accord with those in the printed records. I give them as they stand : —

"When I received the last of Dr. Howe's letters, I was busy in town, and wished to show the captain to the rest of my family ; so I invited him and Mr. Frank Sanborn out to Milton to tea, and one rainy night they appeared. We summoned such neighbors as we could easily reach, among them William Hunt, and had a most interesting evening, and indeed night ; for, the storm continuing, we kept them over and sat up talking until after midnight.

"Captain Brown was a grim, farmer-like looking man, with a long gray beard and glittering, gray-blue eyes which seemed to me to have a little touch of insanity about them. I did all I could to draw the old man out and make him talk, first politics and then about his adventures in Kansas. He repelled, almost with scorn, my suggestion that firmness at the ballot-box by the North and West might avert the storm; and said it had passed the stage of ballots, and nothing but bayonets and bullets could settle it now. He had been visiting Europe, partly on wool business, — for he had been and perhaps was still a wool buyer or broker, — and had seen a good deal of the European armies, then in open war, and made many shrewd comparisons between their methods and ours, talking like a man who had made war his study as well as practice. Leading him back into Kansas by asking him about the battle of Ossawatomie he replied, in his jerky way of throwing out his words, 'That was n't any battle! 't was all on one side;' and then he told me that on that day he had been roused by having his son killed by the Missouri border ruffians, and another son dragged at their horses' heels all day in the sun, until he was nearly frantic; he had raised a small force (I think only thirty) to watch the invaders, and perhaps get a chance to strike a blow at them. Waiting on the edge of a large swamp, through which he could at any time retreat, he saw the enemy coming along careless and confident. 'How many, Captain Brown?' 'Wal, they *said* there was 270 of them.' When they were within close shooting distance, his little band poured in a volley which threw them all in a huddle, and they completely lost their heads, while he repeated the attack. At last they realized how small the Free-Soil force was and made a serious attempt to attack it, and then Captain Brown just scuttled off through the swamp without much or any loss. 'How many did you kill?' we asked. 'Wal, they said we *hurt* seventy of 'em.' 'But you had some real fights with them, captain?' He reflected a moment, and then told us of the battle of Black Jack. When Major, or Colonel, Henry Clay Pate came against him with twenty-eight well-armed men, fitted out at the East on purpose, he marched nine to oppose them, and chose a well-covered clump of black jacks, while they advanced on the open prairie, until they were within easy reach of their long-range rifles; then he opened fire from his ambuscade, and picked them off until they surrendered. 'They could n't do nothing else,' he modestly said, 'for we were under cover, and had only lost two or three, while they could neither advance or retreat, for you could see a guse's head' (not goose's) '300 yards.' So with his remaining four or five men he marched what was left of the enemy back captives with their well-burnished arms, one of which I remember was a very fine revolver presented to Henry Clay Pate by his neighbors, when setting off on his expedition.

"The captain had to go to town by the earliest

train, so I saw no more of him after that night; indeed did not hear much of him until his outbreak at Harper's Ferry, to which I had contributed $100 or so, supposing it to be merely for use in Kansas. When our parlor girl got up early, to open the house, she was startled by finding the grim old soldier sitting bolt upright in the front entry, fast asleep; and when her light awoke him, he sprang up and put his hand into his breast-pocket, where I have no doubt his habit of danger led him to carry a revolver."

By an odd chance the very next day Governor Stewart, the pro-slavery governor of Missouri (who had set the price of $3250 on John Brown's head), "appeared on railroad business, and he too passed the night at Milton, little dreaming who had preceded him in my guest room. Some six months later came John Brown's capture at Harper's Ferry, his surrender to Robert E. Lee, and then his execution.[1] This was really almost the turning-point of our own rebellion, but we hardly appreciated the consequences then."

It was at this time that my father made the acquaintance of John A. Andrew, so soon to become famous as the great war-governor of Massachusetts, but then only "a leading young lawyer in Boston," employed to defend one of Brown's adherents.

It was nearly a year later, in November, 1860, when Lincoln was chosen president. My father

[1] On December 2, 1859.

writes in his notes: "I had never taken any recognized part in public affairs, and I cannot now remember why I was made one of the electors at large and so had a hand in electing him president. Perhaps it was because the Free-Soil party wished to ally themselves here with the business men that they chose me for that position. I still have somewhere, as a relic, the pen with which I signed the certificate of our election of Lincoln, about the beginning of 1861."

What my father thought of the coming president's self-reliance, before he came in personal contact with him, will appear from the following letter to Mr. Senior: —

J. M. FORBES TO NASSAU WILLIAM SENIOR.

Boston, June 18, 1860.

My dear Mr. Senior, — Thinking you may be interested in the antecedents of our promised ruler Lincoln, I send through my bookseller a copy of his speeches (and Douglas's) during their great fight for the Illinois senatorship — which form his chief record.

From such of them as I have read I get the idea that he is an earnest, rough, quick-witted man, — persistent and determined, half educated, but self-reliant and self-taught. These speeches, made before Seward's, show that Lincoln originated in these latter days the utterance of the "irrepressible conflict," — and what is more, stuck to it manfully. Those who know him assure me that he is honest and straightforward and owned by no clique of hackneyed politicians.

Seward was killed by his association with the politicians who joined in the plundering of the last New York legislature, and by his speech in the Senate ignoring the irrepressible conflict and smoothing over his supposed radicalism.

The first evil lost him the confidence of the right sort of men, not because they believed him corrupt, but from the bad company he had been in and would probably be in again! His latter-day conservatism conciliated his enemies, who would not, however, vote for him, happen what might; and cooled the zeal of his radical supporters, and especially of the country people. I think on the whole the actual nominee will run better and be quite as likely to administer well when in. We shall elect him, I think, triumphantly, by the people; and avoid that abominable expedient, an election by the House, — filled as it is with so large a proportion of mere politicians. There is some danger that we shall be disgusted with a repetition of the log-cabin and hard-cider style of campaigning which was so successful in the Harrison election, but this is a minor evil compared with either having Douglas, with his filibustering crew, or a set of Albany wire-pullers under a Republican administration. . . .

Although you say nothing about it, I still hope you will come out this summer and take care of your young prince and see our heir apparent!

Yours very truly,   J. M. FORBES.

In October of this year came the death of my eldest sister, a very lovely girl only twenty-one years old. I have already spoken of the tender love given to sons and daughters by my father. This break in the home circle gave him a deep wound, and was partly the cause of his undertaking the inordinate work during the civil war, which fills a large space in the following chapters.

Fragments of the war-cloud were already beginning to fly across the Atlantic and to attract the attention of observers in the Old World. The widow of Alexis de Tocqueville,[1] in writing to my father in November, 1860, says : —

" At last, returned home to quiet and repose, I feel more courageous, more curious, and I venture to ask you to tell me the probable result of this new conflict between the Republicans and the Democrats. You are a most volcanic people, and when one fancies you are in a dead calm, out bursts a tremendous storm."

It was indeed a " tremendous storm " that was now impending. In meeting it my father was for quick and vigorous measures. A very different policy was that of Mr. Seward, the coming chief of Mr. Lincoln's cabinet, for whom and for whose political methods my father had long had an antipathy.

In closing this chapter, I give an extract from one of Charles Sumner's letters, which showed that

---

[1] My father cared for her American investments, as he had done for those of her husband. — ED.

he shared his correspondent's feelings in this matter : —

WASHINGTON, 13 *January*, 1861.

MY DEAR FORBES, — . . . I think you will agree with me in regretting the tone of Seward's speech. He read it to me last Tuesday, and I *protested* most earnestly against every word of compromise, concession, or offer to the traitors. I wish to try the strength of the government now. Surely it is not worth having, on the condition that any one State may at any time break it up. If this is the rule, it were better to know it now, and govern ourselves accordingly. We must not postpone this question until still greater interests will depend upon it. Besides, what kind of concession can we offer? Ignoble will it be in us to concede beyond the Constitution, which of itself embodies all that our fathers would concede.

The South calls Seward's speech a " cheat." It is unsatisfactory, except to a very few. Even Cameron, of Pennsylvania, told me that he regretted he should " so let down the party."

If the North will be firm, our future will be bright. For God's sake, let there be no wavering. . . .

Good-by! Ever sincerely yours,

CHARLES SUMNER.

CHAPTER VIII

WE have now arrived at the beginning of those five years the high pressure of which must have equaled that of any other fifteen of my father's life, those, namely, which covered the war of the Rebellion and the beginning of reconstruction. The reader will find the selections from the notes and letters exactly as these stand ; though in some cases time has rendered a different verdict from that given, off-hand, by a man to whose eager temperament and fiery energy the course of events seemed often embarrassed by unnecessary and absolutely intolerable delays. Whatever may be thought of my father's views, I am clear, at any rate, that to soften or withhold the distinct expression of his opinions would be to rob the writer of his individuality, and to sin against historical truth.

"The war," writes my father in his notes, "virtually began, for me, with what was called the 'Peace Congress,' of February, 1861.

"In January, Virginia asked the other States to send delegates to a congress for the purpose of devising means to avert the civil war then threatening. This was pretty generally responded to at the

North, and resulted in the meeting of what was called the Peace Congress at Washington in the early part of February, 1861. It was unauthorized by law and entirely informal, and simply a conference of men of the different States. Each State was represented by as many delegates as it had members of Congress, our Massachusetts contingent being thirteen (I think), all nominated by Governor Andrew, under authority from the legislature. Of my colleagues on the Massachusetts delegation I recall the names of George S. Boutwell, J. Z. Goodrich, F. N. Crowninshield, T. P. Chandler, and B. F. Waters, of Marblehead, as having been the most active.

"We started, nearly all together, about February 10, with the political horizon everywhere darkly lowering. My wife and daughter Mary accompanied me, and, through the kindness of Captain W. H. Swift, I had secured an asylum for them with Baron Stoeckel, the Russian ambassador, to be availed of in case the rebels pushed into Washington, an event which seemed as probable as it really was easy of accomplishment, had the rebels been half as smart as we thought them.

"At Philadelphia we took a special train provided for us and other delegates, among whom I remember General John E. Wool, of the United States army, from New York, who astonished us by the boldness of his prediction that in case the rebels proceeded to actual violence, one hundred thousand men would spring to arms from the North and West, sweeping all before them. Mr. S. M. Felton, the president of the Philadelphia, Wilmington and Baltimore road, joined us, and taking me aside proceeded to show me his plans for meeting the designs of the rebels against the long bridges we were passing over, which he had discovered through his detectives. These were simply to take steamers at the north bank of the Susquehanna (where his line was safe) and send troops around to Annapolis and Washington by water. It is noteworthy that when, in April, General Butler reached Philadelphia, and found these very bridges burned, and Baltimore practically an enemy's city, Felton had great difficulty, with the help of Admiral Dupont, in showing the general that the Annapolis plan was the true one. Once adopted, Butler always assumed to himself the credit of the discovery. Mr. Felton at the same time confidentially informed me of the plot which he had discovered to attack President Lincoln on his way through Baltimore, and intrusted to me a message to W. H. Seward in regard to it, and to the mode of defeating it, by sending Mr. Lincoln through incog., after cutting the telegraph wires; all which was exactly carried into effect about a month later. From Philadelphia I telegraphed G. W. Brown, the mayor of Baltimore, and his partner, F. W. Brune (my old friend), that I would stay the night there to discuss the state of affairs with them. That night Mayor Brown came to Barnum's Hotel and spent the evening with me. Though full of local Baltimore feeling, I found him in the main loyal and well disposed, and promising to do all in his power to keep the peace in Baltimore; and I have never doubted his sincerity. When our troops were attacked in the streets on the 19th of April, he put himself at their head, and did everything he could personally to protect them. He did not realize the full magnitude of the crisis, but to the extent of his light he was sound and honest. I remember asking his opinion about one expedient which was then under discussion, and especially advocated by the Blairs; it was for the United States to purchase the slaves and colonize them in Central America and the West Indies. His answer was that Maryland wanted every black she had, and more; and that the large body of free blacks in his city were among the best of their laboring population, with less rioting, less drunkenness, and fewer paupers than any other class! Later, Seward had Brown imprisoned at Fort Warren, where I visited him; and when released had him for a day or two at Milton.

"The next morning we went on to Washington, and took possession of comfortable rooms on the 14th Street side of Willard's Hotel, in the large hall of which the Peace Congress was in session. The alarm was so general that the city was not crowded and was especially bare of ladies from abroad.

"We soon plunged into our work, our advent having very much the effect of a bombshell explosion. Before our arrival the talk had been chiefly

of compromise, and some progress seemed to have
been made in preparing the way for a surrender
by the North on the basis of the Crittenden Resolutions, so-called from Senator Crittenden, who introduced them into the Senate. They practically
surrendered the ground which the North and West
had taken against the extension of slavery, and
gave up the advanced position for freedom which
had been gained after long years of conflict, and
which was represented by the election of Lincoln.
In the convention were Seddon, of Virginia, and
Ruffin, of North Carolina, who afterwards were
prominent in the secession ranks, the first as secretary of war, the other, I think, firing the first gun
against Sumter. I am not sure about this, but Ruffin was distinguished as having given us one of our
best anti-slavery weapons. When judge, he had
carried the claims of the slave-owners to their legitimate extreme, and decided that logically the system
of slavery gave the master the supreme right *to use,
to punish*, and if he thought necessary to *kill* his
slave.[1]

"We who went to see what chance there was of
any real peace, soon found that the Southerners in
the convention were ready to *receive any concessions from us* 'in the hope that it might do some
good,' but to commit themselves to nothing.

---

[1] The allusion is to the case of State *v.* Mann, 2 Devereux's Reports, 263 (1829), an indictment for assault and battery upon a hired
slave. This opinion became widely known by Mrs. Stowe's citation
of it in her *Key to Uncle Tom's Cabin*. — ED.

" When we asked the border States, ' Suppose the North concedes what you ask, will you join them in forcing the South to obey the laws? ' ' No,' was the reply, ' but we should hope that such concessions would lead to a settlement, and we will do all we peaceably can to bring this about.' It was simply asking the majority to yield unconditionally to the minority all the great principles for which we had contested.

" It was plain to us then, as it is now, that such concessions would have merely demoralized the North, and have led to more unreasonable demands. Our only policy was then to stand firm, and as the 4th of March was approaching, when the weak old Buchanan and his Cabinet would go out, to make all the time we could in the Peace Convention, and avert as long as possible the onslaught of the better prepared South which was plainly impending. Our first move in the congress thus set them back from the prompt compromise which was proposed. We had been called to consider what remedies could be found for the alleged grievances of the South. So the Massachusetts delegates introduced a resolution calling upon the representatives of the border States, who had asked us to meet them, for ' a statement of the grievances which we were asked to redress.' This led to long debates, and some of us who had not the gift of speaking, and could read the reports of the convention in print, turned our thoughts naturally to other modes of saving the Union.

" One of these schemes soon suggested itself.

Some little time after our arrival, I met quite a large party at dinner, who I remember were much animated by the report of General Dix's telegram, just then published, to the collector of Pensacola, — 'If any man tries to haul down the American flag, shoot him on the spot.' Sent to a post completely in the hands of the rebels, and unsupported by any force, it was rather a cheap piece of patriotic eloquence ; but it answered its purpose, for the day, of showing the right spirit in one of Buchanan's Cabinet, and it has since helped to put General Dix into the governor's chair of New York. At the same dinner W. H. Aspinwall, who, though not on the delegation of his State (New York), was an interested and very influential visitor to the Capitol, took me aside and told me of a late conversation with General Scott — then at the head of our army — in which Scott had confided to him the great straits to which Major Anderson and the garrison of Fort Sumter were already reduced, the small supplies of ammunition and provisions, and the impossibility of so small a force making any successful resistance in case of attack. They were in fact dependent from day to day upon the Charleston market for their meat. We both agreed that it was an easy thing to reinforce Fort Sumter, and we there decided to call on General Scott after elaborating our plans, and propose to undertake it, — Aspinwall having already told me that Lieutenant Fox, an able and experienced naval officer, was ready to lead the enterprise, and was confident of success. I may here mention that I had not before this heard of the man who so soon afterwards, as assistant secretary of the navy, was to play one of the most effective though least showy parts in the great struggle then impending.

" The plan, which we agreed upon, was a double one, so as to have two chances. First: we proposed to buy a moderate-sized freighting vessel, put on board of her as stores the articles of most pressing necessity, and to have her enter Charleston, which port was still open, seeking a cotton freight; but as she passed the fort she was to run under its guns, either going in or out as the best chance offered. Nobody but the captain was to know our plans, and the consignees were to be first-class secessionists, with whom the Boston owner was to begin a correspondence at once, so as to divert suspicion. The mails were still open to Major Anderson, and some time after this Lieutenant Fox paid him a visit under secret orders from Washington. In this way everything but men could be thrown in, and by giving Major Anderson notice of our intention and establishing a signal, he would have been ready to protect the ship and land her stores, and it was even thought that part of the ship's crew might enlist after reaching there, and thus add to the little garrison.

" Plan No. 2 was to fit out one or more propellers ostensibly for Japan, load them with stores, and let each take in tow a couple of coasting schooners loaded below and on deck with Manila hemp, one on each side of the propeller, thus protecting her from shot, excepting those fired directly in front. Fox and a couple of hundred soldiers were to be added at the last moment. His experience in the navy convinced him that the untried gunners in the rebel batteries, firing at a moving object, would not disable either of them, and he stood ready to lead with the reinforcing troops. Subsequent experience in the Potomac and elsewhere proved that the chances were very slight of any disaster; but if the danger had been far greater the exigency fully warranted the experiment. The steam frigate Powhatan was to convoy them down to the entrance of Charleston Harbor, or as far as her draught of water would permit, serving as a transport for the troops until transferred to the little propellers. They were to be bought, and sent at once to the Delaware Breakwater, and the schooners were to sail down at once to Charleston bar, they requiring very little time for preparing cargoes of hemp.

"By appointment with General Scott, Mr. Aspinwall and I called upon him on the evening of February the 7th, and we remained with him until after midnight. As we developed our plans the general's spirits seemed to rise, and when we had finished he marched up and down his office, crying out, ' Ça ira, ça ira ! ' It was agreed that Aspinwall should start the next morning for Philadelphia, where he knew of some propellers, inspect them and see what they were fit for, and learn their price, while I was to write to G. B. Upton, in Boston, and prepare him on receipt of a telegram to go ahead. At this time all the telegraph offices in Washington were filled with ' secesh,' so I had arranged with Governor Andrew, before leaving Boston, a commercial cipher code under which, using cotton bales and other terms to cover our political meaning, I could, through J. M. Forbes & Co., communicate with him without danger of our plans leaking out. Aspinwall and I left the good old general and his aide, Colonel Keyes, after midnight, in full faith that when I saw the general the next day I should get the final authority to go ahead, and we returned to the hotel, he to prepare for starting in the early train for Philadelphia, and I to write my letters for the morning mail. I had selected G. B. Upton, then in his prime, as the most active and efficient agent to do the business in Boston, and it was agreed that nobody outside the general's office, except ourselves, Upton, and Fox, was to be admitted to our councils. The captains of the vessels were to be carefully selected, and were not to be informed of our plans until the last moment. I spent the best part of the night in arranging the telegraphic ciphers to meet the new conditions, and in writing to Upton instructions which were at once to be carried into effect when he should receive my telegram ; and the next day (I think at about ten A. M.) I went by appointment to General Scott's headquarters. To my infinite disgust I found him closeted with Captain Ward of the navy (afterward killed on the Potomac), who had somehow got wind of an intended movement, and claimed that it ought to be intrusted to the navy. As Toucey was at the head of the Navy Department, and his loyalty was more than doubtful, and moreover as secrecy and promptness were totally incompatible with red tape and naval etiquette, I saw at once that the game was up, and I told Colonel Keyes that it would be worse than useless for us to go on with our scheme in combination with the navy, as suggested. Aspinwall and I had offered, for the sake of secrecy (the *sine quâ non* of success in such an enterprise), to find the needful funds or credit, if fully authorized by General Scott to go ahead, and to trust to being reimbursed by government; but we considered it indispensable that the whole control of the details and preliminary arrangements should be left with us. So our promising scheme fell through, and thus ended one of the efforts of a peace commissioner to save the Union!

"Later, about April 10th, 1861, Mr. Fox persuaded President Lincoln to let him undertake a similar project in the steamer Baltic; but partly through Seward's double-faced diplomacy, and partly from being postponed till quite too late, it had little chance of success. The rebel batteries had been immensely increased around the fort, and the rebels got notice of the intended movement, and opened fire before Fox and his transports arrived there. The Powhatan was, I think by Seward's interference, diverted from, or certainly delayed in, joining the expedition, and a gale of wind destroyed what little

chance of success remained. Fort Sumter fell, and
when the gale abated Fox had the melancholy satisfaction of receiving on board the Baltic Major
Anderson and his garrison, who had been obliged
to make terms of surrender! Had the 20th of
February, 1861, opened with the news that a sufficient garrison, well supplied with powder and provisions, had been thrown into Fort Sumter, it might
have changed the history of the war.

"While the Peace Congress was slowly talking
against time, and coming to no conclusions, Washington was, of course, the focus of the greatest
excitement. Rebel State after State was seceding,
a rebel Congress was sitting at Montgomery, in Alabama, and the North was waiting for the inau-
guration of Lincoln before making any movement.
Governor Andrew was taking active measures to
organize and equip his militia. Seward was pro-
phesying that in sixty days the trouble would be
over, and was negotiating with the rebels, and
promising that Fort Sumter should not be rein-
forced. We in Washington were prepared each
morning to see the rebel flags flying in that city,
the Treasury sacked, and Congress, still in session,
broken up.

"Scott had less than one thousand men under
him. Among other dangers was one of form which
at one time looked threatening. Breckinridge, the
Vice-President, was a well-known rebel, and Jeff
Davis still retained his seat in the Senate, with
some other similar villains. On a certain day in

February it was the duty of the Vice-President, as
president of the Senate, to march down at the head
of that body from their chamber to the House of
Representatives, carrying with them the electoral
votes which had previously been deposited with
them for that purpose. Until these votes had been
opened in the presence of Congress, and counted,
and the result declared, Lincoln could not become
the President under the forms of the Constitution;
and in case this form could be prevented, it was
thought possible that the rebels might claim that
Buchanan and his Cabinet still held power. It was
rumored that there was a plot to seize the ballots
in the long and narrow halls through which the
Senate passed nearly the whole length of the Capitol; and with the traitor Breckinridge as the bearer
of these ballots it would have been easy to play into
the hands of the conspirators. Various plans were
discussed for protecting ourselves against this danger (one, I remember, being to fill the vacant spaces
in the Capitol with trusty men specially sent on
from the North); but the rebels were much nearer
than the loyal States; Washington, and even the
Capitol under a rebel Vice-President, was full of
traitors, and such a plan involving so many men
was likely to be discovered, and might easily have
been turned against us by substituting the Baltimore and Washington roughs, or even the Virginia
militia, who were right across the river, for our
Northern allies; so it was given up. Another expedient on which we did rely somewhat was this:

Captain W. H. Franklin, of Pennsylvania, a loyal
and efficient West Point officer (afterwards major-
general), was in charge of the Capitol extension,
and had under him over one hundred mechanics,
many of them Northern men. He had lately called
on me in response to an introductory letter from
Captain W. H. Swift. As a last resource, I had a
free conference with him, and he agreed to be on
hand early with his workmen on the day of count-
ing the votes, and to make sure that no body of
conspirators was collecting in the halls or corridors
of the Capitol, with every inch of which he and
his men were familiar. The day passed without
disturbance, and my story is only interesting as
showing one of the many alarms of the period.

"Just before the 4th of March our Peace Congress adjourned. It had met with all sorts of criticisms, and little praise. The 'Tribune,' I think,
called it a convocation of old hens sitting on a nest
of eggs, some of which would hatch out vipers,
while most were addled. The rebels of all hues,
from copper-colored to deep black, abused the Massachusetts delegation without stint, laying upon us
the blame of defeating all chance of peace. When
my old friend Erastus Corning, during the war,
charged upon my devoted head the whole sin of
bringing on the war, which he said I might have
averted by influencing to compromise the Massachusetts delegation, I begged him to give me a certificate to that effect, promising to have it framed
handsomely and handed down as an heirloom for

my descendants to boast of! Corning was a strong Democrat, and the leader of the New York delegation."

Mr. Charles Sedgwick's [1] comment on the convention is as follows : —

"It is supposed that your convention will proceed to save the country at two o'clock precisely, and will immediately proceed in a body to the Patent Office and patent the process. It is supposed that it will sell well in Mexico and Central America."

It is a twice-told tale, — that of the opening of the war. The rush of feeling through the North can only be understood when one realizes that for years the people of that section had been forced by political divisions at home to accept compromise after compromise with the slave power, which like the horse-leech's daughter was ever crying, "Give, give !" The sight of leaders perpetually knocking under to their opponents, and all for political cold scraps and bare bones, is not one that makes any people's temper the milder ; and the incessant kicks (undoubtedly invited by the Northern concessions) which all Southern newspapers and speakers felt at liberty to administer, openly to their enemies, covertly to their allies, at the North, had bred a spirit of bitterness scarcely to be conceived of in these days when our orators "sprinkle battlefields with rose-water."

No wonder, then, that the news of a Southern

[1] Representative from New York State.

attack on a United States fortress had only to be flashed through the North to fuse all differences and set ablaze the fire so long smouldering. Many Northern people had no clear conception of the evils of slavery, nor were all aware that this inherited curse was at the bottom of the strife, but all understood an attack on the Union.

I find among my father's papers an article which appeared in the " Louisville Courier " just after the first battle of Bull Run. When it is recollected that it was one of many similar in character, it can be readily conceived what sort of feeling articles such as this excited in the North. We trust that we can laugh at such effusions now; then the effect was serious enough.

" This has been called a fratricidal war by some, by others an irrepressible conflict between freedom and slavery. We respectfully take issue with the authors of both these ideas. We are not the brothers of the Yankees, and the slavery question is merely a pretext, not the cause of the war. The true irrepressible conflict lies fundamentally in the hereditary hostility, the sacred animosity, the eternal antagonism between the two races engaged.

" The Norman cavalier cannot brook the vulgar familiarity of the Saxon Yankee, while the latter is continually devising some plan to bring down his aristocratic neighbor to his own detested level. Thus was the contest waged in the old United States. So long as Dickinson doughfaces were to be bought, and Cochrane cowards to be frightened, so long was the Union tolerable to Southern men; but when, owing to divisions in our ranks, the Yankee hirelings placed one of their own spawn over us, political connection became unendurable, and separation necessary to preserve our self-respect.

"As our Norman kinsmen in England, always a minority, have ruled their Saxon countrymen in political vassalage up to the present day, so have we, the 'slave oligarchs,' governed the Yankees until within a twelvemonth. We framed the Constitution, for seventy years moulded the policy of the government, and placed our own men, or 'Northern men with Southern principles,' in power.

"On the 6th of November, 1860, the Puritans emancipated themselves, and are now in violent insurrection against their former owners. This insane holiday freak will not last long, however, for, dastards in fight, and incapable of self-government, they will inevitably again fall under the control of the superior race. A few more Bull Run thrashings will bring them once more under the yoke as docile as the most loyal of our Ethiopian 'chattels.'"

To return to my father's notes as to what was happening in Massachusetts : —

"At this time Governor Andrew was getting his four thousand soldiers overcoats, which was considered as taking a great responsibility. I need not say that I encouraged him in this, and every other measure of prompt preparation, and when the call for troops came on Monday, the 14th of April, by telegraph, it will be remembered that he was the first to respond, and that on Tuesday he had already collected in Boston three or four regiments reasonably well prepared to march, and not merely a paper force.

"On the 12th or 13th of April, when we heard of the actual attack going on against Fort Sumter, I had under my charge a steamer bound for China, which had been disabled in a gale off Hatteras, and had reached Norfolk with her rudder crippled. I, of course, considered Norfolk an enemy's port, and at once telegraphed Captain Morris (agent of the underwriters) to go thither without delay from New York and get the vessel out at all hazards, which he did; taking her into Baltimore, however, which, as it was on the point of rising up for the rebels, I considered little better than Norfolk. So my partner, E. J. Hale, went to Baltimore; and somehow he got her out of that port on the morning of the 19th of April, the day they were firing on our troops in the streets of that city."

It was to this action that Wendell Phillips, in one of his invectives in 1867, referred as follows : —

"If this government had been as wise as the merchant in his counting-room we should have saved to the treasury $2,000,000,000; and two hundred thousand men who are sleeping in honorable graves would now be living. A merchant in our city had a vessel at Norfolk, Va., when the war broke out, and the first thing he did was to telegraph, 'Bring my ship north of Mason and Dixon's line.' And they brought her. He saved his vessel. But the Secretary of the Navy heard the first gun, and he thought of his office, of red tape, of somebody doing this, and the other body doing that, and he left $3,000,000 worth of ships there and the Confederacy took them. Now, I call that merchant a statesman; and I call that Secretary of the Navy a fool."

To return to the "merchant's" memories of those times : —

" When Sumter was fired upon I was already in close *rapport* with Governor Andrew, going to the state house daily and acting as adviser, or clerk, or better still as physician by carrying off the governor to dine, a ceremony he was ready to postpone until midnight, unless some friend captured him for this purpose. While waiting for him one day I heard an insatiate office-seeker insist on having five minutes. ' My time,' said Governor Andrew, ' is taken up every moment (looking at his watch) until midnight.' ' Say five minutes after twelve to-night,' said the enemy, ' and I 'll wait.'

" Perhaps my connection with vessels and railroads led the governor to put into my hands the first arrangements for moving the troops South, for which we were expecting orders. The course pursued in making these arrangements shows how small an amount of red tape was needed, at a pinch, in those early days of the war. The letters from General Scott to the governor had indicated an all-rail route to Baltimore for the two regiments destined for the relief of Fortress Monroe. But I remembered well President Felton's warning as to the intentions of the rebels to burn his bridges, and I saw the danger of any delay in garrisoning Fortress Monroe, then held by old Colonel Dimmick with only a couple of small companies of regulars of about sixty men each, — hardly enough to man the gates, much less the ramparts. Seeing the importance of using water conveyance I took my brother, Captain Forbes, into my counsels, and drove with him to the chart store for a large chart of the coast of the Chesapeake (which nearly filled the cab), then to the state house, to show the governor the absurdity of trusting to hiring steamers in a half rebel city like Baltimore, even if we got the troops through to that place without interruption. He was beset by crowds on all sides. After studying the map and General Scott's letter, and hearing our arguments, he quickly said, 'We will take the responsibility and send them direct by water.' So we made all arrangements to send this important reinforcement by sea, one regiment from Boston direct, the other from Fall River. I had first, however, passed on to Colonel Keyes, who was superintending the movement of troops at General Scott's headquarters in New York, President Felton's suggestion as to the water route."

"TELEGRAM.

"Boston, *April* 16, 1861.

"Colonel Keyes, General Scott's Headquarters, N. Y.:

"Pray examine chart of the Chesapeake. Consider availability of Annapolis for rendezvous of our Massachusetts troops bound for Washington.

"J. M. Forbes.

"General Butler's claim to be the originator of this plan is told elsewhere.

"Then followed telegrams for transport: —

"Boston, *April* 16, 1861.

"To Colonel Borden or Boat Agent, Fall River:

"On what terms will you send eight hundred Massachusetts volunteers hence by rail, and by your regular steamers, to Fort Monroe, Old Point Comfort? How much more, if required, thence to Annapolis or Washington, government warranting against war risk — you find rations? Considerable camp equipage included. Leave here to-morrow morning. Answer immediately.

"J. M. Forbes.

"Massachusetts was so quick in collecting her quota, that the troops were waiting several hours in Boston before any actual orders came to dispatch them.

"Tuesday, April 16th, was a stormy easterly day, and I had stayed in town for a dinner party (probably at Horace Gray's, in Summer Street). I had already got the terms of one of the Baltimore steamers (the S. R. Spaulding); but we had given up any expectation of orders for that day, — it being after four P. M., — when I felt a hand on my shoulder as I sat writing in my little den at the City Exchange, and heard Colonel Henry Lee's voice — he was then on Governor Andrew's staff — saying, ' The orders have come, we must send off the first troops to-night.' I sprang to the window to see what the weather was, and said at once, ' It is too late to start to-night in this storm.' I sent, however, a messenger to Colonel Borden by the five P. M. train, and then hunted up George B. Upton, and got him started out to hurry up the Spaulding, then lying in Boston. Having completed the arrangements with the Fall River steamer, State of Maine, as far as was possible that night, I went to the dinner party.

" I find the following telegram of the next day in my book : —

" Boston, *April* 17, 1861.

" To Colonel Borden, or Boat Agent, Fall River:
" Letter received. Seen Crowninshield. Four hundred and fifty men leave at two o'clock. Want State of Maine ready on terms proposed. Men will take cooked bread and meat. Put in other things, including salt provisions for a week, and hard bread at actual cost — balance to be landed. Will she be ready ?   J. M. Forbes.

"FALL RIVER, *April* 17, 1861.

" To J. M. FORBES, Boston :

" Will get the boat ready probably before morning. Will do it as soon as possible. Are now
coaling her.   RICHARD BORDEN.

"BOSTON, *April* 17, 1861.

" To COLONEL BORDEN, Fall River:

" We send the four hundred men at two. Count
upon your hurrying up. Must go right on board
and start to-night, even at some extra cost. Massachusetts must keep up her end, and you are the man
to do it.   J. M. FORBES.

"FALL RIVER, *April* 17, 1861.

" To J. M. FORBES, Boston :

" I hope to get the State of Maine ready to go
this evening.   RICHARD BORDEN.

" That afternoon (Wednesday the 17th), we got
off one regiment by the Spaulding, and, by an extra
train, the other for Fall River, where it was shipped
by the State of Maine, with my old friend, Captain
Oliver Eldridge (formerly commander of the clipper
Coquette), put in charge.[1]   Another regiment was
sent by land route, marching in fine order through
New York, where it produced a great effect in giving confidence and spirit to the people by such a
show of promptness.

[1] Captain Eldridge says in a letter dated November, 1898 : " A
telegram came, asking me to take command of the State of Maine,
but not until long afterwards did I know that Mr. Forbes had suggested that I should be chosen for the duty." — ED.

"In one particular of this relief of Fortress Monroe red tape was allowed to prevail, and might well have caused the failure of the expedition. That Wednesday morning, while the troops were getting ready to take the Fall River train, I occupied myself at the governor's room in drawing up instructions to Captain Eldridge about the voyage, urging haste, and suggesting certain precautions as to having guns loaded, and looking out for interruptions when he approached the Chesapeake, where the rebels, by an armed steamer from Richmond, might easily intercept them. I had got the orders into shape when unluckily one of the governor's aides, who was somewhat of a martinet, and a student in military affairs, intercepted me. 'What!' said he, 'put our troops under the orders of the transport captain! It is against all military rule, and will never do. It is utterly irregular! The orders must go to the colonel of the regiment.' This colonel happened to be an entirely inexperienced militia officer, while Captain Eldridge was one of the finest sailors who ever trod a deck, true as steel, and full of courage and decision. It was all sound red tape doctrine that had been spoken; I could only wish that that aide had been in some hotter place; and though it went against my stomach, with my customary flexibility I gave up my common-sense plan, and accordingly addressed the orders to the militia colonel. Mark the result. Captain Eldridge steamed to New York to coal up, with only 450 men aboard, a number much below the steamer's real capacity, when the rough water disturbed some of their imaginations. A council of war was called, and the country doctor who acted as surgeon gave the sage opinion that the steamer was overloaded. So she waited further orders in New York. On my arrival in town I was greeted with a telegram from Colonel Borden, giving me this news. This time the red tape was cut roughly, in the unmistakable terms of the governor's order through me : —

" BOSTON, April 18, 1861.

" COLONEL BORDEN, 70 West Street, New York :

" Have seen governor and adjutant-general. No further orders for Colonel Packard. Push steamer on without stopping. Massachusetts must be first on the ground. Telegraph when she passes Sandy Hook ; also weather.   J. M. FORBES.

" The State of Maine continued on her way, arriving at the fort the next morning, to the great joy of Colonel Dimmick, a fine old West Point soldier, who, it is said, almost shed tears on seeing the reinforcements pour in upon his ill-defended post, — the most strategic point on our whole coast, commanding as it did the entrance to Baltimore, Washington, and Richmond.

" The Spaulding, from Boston, arrived safely, after the State of Maine. Captain Eldridge related that while disembarking his troops the Virginia planters expressed great indignation at seeing the sacred soil thus trampled upon by ' Lincoln's hirelings,' and told him, with ominous shakings of the head, that they would never go back home. 'No,' replied Eldridge; 'we like the looks of the country down here, and we never intend to let it go.'

"After unnecessary delay, one of the regiments was put on board the frigate Powhatan, and reached the navy yard, Portsmouth, opposite Norfolk, after dark, and just too late to prevent the scuttling of the frigate Merrimac."

Work at high pressure continued for my father. He took the part of deputy commissary of Massachusetts, as will be shown by the following letters and notes. The first is amusing, from Governor Andrew's terse indorsement. Time was precious just then.

(Private.)   BOSTON, *April* 23, 1861.

TO HIS EXCELLENCY, JOHN A. ANDREW:

My dear Sir, — To give you an idea of the time it will take to get *good* hard bread for shipping: I should think for a month's supply to our Massachusetts troops now in the field it would need at least three days from the time the order was given to do it properly — possibly more.

Other things can be had quicker, but I should like, if you think proper, to have an order by the bearer to provide *a month's* supply of hard bread for 4000 men. By the time this is ready you will have plenty of troops here and an order for them, and with the bread can send other things to match. . . .

I don't want to interfere with the duties of your commissary-general *that is to be,* but some things take time, and bread ought to be ordered to-day.

You cannot be too careful in getting a working *business man* for the commissariat. It will save the State thousands of dollars, and save *us* our credit when accounts come to be settled after the enthusiasm boils past.

Yours,   J. M. FORBES.

At your Excellency's request the Committee on the Militia have considered the within proposition. We unanimously recommend that Mr. Forbes be authorized to purchase forthwith provisions for 4000 for thirty days, more or less, and that arrangements be made to forward them promptly.

HUGH W. GREENE,
JOHN I. BAKER,
OAKES AMES,
Committee on Militia.

Let it be done.   J. A. ANDREW.

The notes continue : —

" I find among my files a curious illustration of the enthusiasm with which the first troops going South were regarded by their fellow-citizens, and the almost motherly thought taken by the authorities for their comfort. Here is an extract from a letter dated April 27th, 1861, addressed to the adjutant-general by a committee on behalf of the 'Occupants of Quincy Market,' who had learned

that a private firm had offered to furnish a shipload
of ice for the troops, and proposed 'to furnish a
quantity of fresh meats to be packed in said ice,
for the benefit of said troops.' This must have
been referred to me by the governor, for I find that
on the 2d of May, in advising him of my having
got the refusal (at $1000 for a month) of a vessel
to take about 300 tons of ice to Fort Monroe and
Washington, I let him know that I could pack the
provisions on it and would so arrange it, if he said
'Go ahead;' and that he said this accordingly on
the flyleaf of my letter, only suggesting that the
market men should 'give part in vegetables instead
of meat.' His next note to me is so characteristic
that I cannot refrain from giving it entire : —

"COMMONWEALTH OF MASSACHUSETTS.
"Executive Department. Council Chamber.
"BOSTON, *May* 20, 1861.

"MY DEAR SIR, — I wish you would have some
of Baker's chocolate sent on the Pembroke for our
troops at Fort Monroe. Some ask for it, and would
regard this change as a luxury and an advantage.
"Yours faithfully,   J. A. ANDREW.
"And a few dried apples.

"It need scarcely be observed that in all such
matters we very soon came down to hardpan.

"My duties as quartermaster soon became unnecessary, as the governor succeeded in getting the
services of Colonel E. D. Brigham for this sort of

work, but I found abundant occupation in buying ships and doing what I could in the way of helping to give the proper direction to public opinion. About this time I suggested the expediency of buying a couple of steamers for transporting our troops, and (the legislature not being in session and no money appropriated for such naval operations) we raised a subscription among the Boston merchants for half the needful amount and the banks advanced the other half to the governor; and so in partnership with the State we bought the steamers Cambridge and Pembroke, borrowed guns from the navy yard, and fitted them up as transports. The railroads were at this time broken up between Philadelphia and Washington, hardly a mail going, and telegraphing very uncertain; and for a while the merchants of Boston and New York coöperated with the commanders of the navy yards in both places, and did a good deal towards pushing the outfit of vessels from the navy yards. I think I may have had some sort of authority at this time from headquarters, but am sure I met ready help from Commodore Hudson, who was then at the head of the Charlestown Navy Yard, and sometimes stretched the red tape rather largely."

As an illustration of an emergency of those days which had to be dealt with on the spur of the moment, I give my father's instructions to the captain of the Cambridge while she was still in the service of the State of Massachusetts: —

Boston, *July* 13, 1861.

Captain Matthews, Steamer Cambridge, Hyannis:

Dear Sir, — Commodore Hudson sends Lieutenant Stevens by this train to represent the government on board Cambridge, and take charge of any warlike operations, but he will doubtless consult with you about the cruise generally.

You will receive a new twelve-pound rifle by the train, with ammunition; also some preserved meats.

Then get, if you can and think best, ten to twenty good men for the cruise.

Follow Lieutenant Stevens's orders, if he comes. If he misses from any cause, get somehow, by purchase or otherwise, enough coal for a cruise of five or six days with what you have got, and run out about northeast and cruise on the north edge of the Gulf in search of privateers — take the responsibility *carefully,* of hailing vessels, and if you find one that you *feel sure* is a privateer or pirate, take her, or *better still sink her,* but be sure you are right before you fire.

I have little doubt the lieutenant will reach you. I have a telegram from Secretary Welles authorizing me to send you on a two or three days' cruise after the privateer. The best chance for catching her will be at the northeast, on the track of vessels bound to New York from Europe. She was last seen Monday night, about one hundred miles southeast from Nantucket; has had light southerly winds since. She is a full-rigged brig, of about 200 tons, formerly the Echo, slaver, has been showing

French flag, has cotton foresail and top-gallant sails, hemp trysail. Has three jibs and staysail, about seventy men, Captain Coxetter, First Lieutenant Postell, said to be formerly of Texan navy, one eighteen-pound pivot gun, four thirty-two or twenty-four, and all old guns, no rifled cannon.

There have been two revenue cutters sent from here and United States sloop Vincennes, also several vessels from New York, all intending to cruise to eastward of Nantucket. Your best chance will therefore be further north. The Secretary's directions are to cruise for two or three days, but if you get any information which leads you to hope for success, you must cruise longer.

We shall have troops to send by you about Thursday. Return to Boston after your cruise. I have telegraphed Captain John Eldridge to engage coal and men for you at Hyannis conditionally. See newspapers for particulars about pirates.

Yours,   J. M. FORBES.

As an illustration of the great dislike my father felt for those who affected cheap newspaper notoriety, I give his directions, written while he was practically in charge of Massachusetts naval affairs, to W. P. Lee, apparently commanding the Massachusetts steamship Pembroke : —

July 13, 1861.

In a *quiet* way the Pembroke should hail vessels, and warn them, and get information as to the Jeff Davis. See description of her in my letter book.

If you meet with a pirate, you have a right to take her, provided you are *sure*, but let us have no swaggering *à la* C——. If anybody on board writes bragging letters that get into the papers, I will use my influence to get him on the *outside* of her. If she can really do something, she will get talked of enough, but talk alone is of no good.

No harm in a little deviation from the straight track. Remember there are many cruisers out after pirates besides yourselves. Try to telegraph us from Fort Monroe, when we may expect you, and look out for telegraph hence viâ Baltimore.

Don't waste your new shells — twenty-four pounds.

Truly yours,   J. M. FORBES.

To return to my father's memories of this early part of the war : —

" I however only acted as secretary of the navy for Massachusetts for a very short time, as it was entirely irregular for the State to own transports, and indeed only thought of for a temporary expedient. So we soon sold the Cambridge to the United States, and, the Pembroke being too small, sold her to R. B. Forbes and others for China ; and she carried, under John A. Cunningham, the only letter of marque issued during the rebellion.

" My letter books and telegrams show many alarms about rebel privateers on the coast, and others fitting out in Canada. I had to take a lead in overhauling the well or ill founded reports, and sometimes to try and intercept the vessels, but I

find nothing really worth recording. Once, in my
absence, Jack Hale [1] was roused up in the night by
a telegraphic message from Mr. Seward to me suggesting getting the navy yard to send a cruiser to
the St. Lawrence to try and intercept a rebel pirate
thought to be fitting out at Montreal; but there
were only slow old sailing ships available, and I
knew too much of the thirty-mile-wide Gulf of St.
Lawrence to send such vessels on a wild goose
chase; and so confined myself to investigating the
facts through our consuls. In this case I believe it
all grew out of the desire of some Canadian steamship owner to frighten us into buying his vessel in
Canada."

I give a few of my father's letters of this period
mainly as showing his reasons for urging the importance of a volunteer navy, and partly as indicat-
ing the other subjects of public interest which were
engaging his attention : —

J. M. FORBES TO THE " NEW YORK EVENING POST."

A short sentence in the telegraph is suggestive
about Cuba: *No more American ships can get
charters.*

This does not apply to Cuba alone. The loss by
these miserable pirates, in freight and in insurance
premiums, is already ten times what it would cost
to have prevented them by a little forecast on the
part of government.

Next will come a complication with foreign powers

---

[1] E. J. Hale, his partner.

about efficiency of blockade, then encouragement of rebels, and loss of lives and treasure indefinite.

If the government will not act, or Congress, they must be pushed on by the press. Fifty sail of vessels should be got to sea before the 1st of August. Blockading, they will be valuable, and as cruisers; but still more for showing the rebels, and their friends in Europe, that we intend to seal them up.

Governments are always timid about new measures without precedents. Let the press and the people speak, and government must follow; but no time is to be lost. Congress must authorize the needful action.

It is a poor measure, a half measure, to turn this over to the Treasury with their miserable revenue cutters. It belongs to the navy, and should be placed *there*.

J. M. FORBES TO W. H. SEWARD.

BOSTON, *June* 12, 1861.

I have just seen Lothrop Motley (Dutch Republic), who has landed from the steamer this morning, and gives very brilliant accounts of our English relations.

This is all very well while we are strong, and there is a prospect of our whipping the rebels before the next cotton crop; but I have seen letters from well-informed sources, not diplomatic, which have another color.

The aristocratic rulers of England do not like us, and the middle classes want cotton, and our safety lies, while talking smoothly of peace, and believing all we choose of their fair professions, in taking the most vigorous measures to strengthen our navy. . . . We can get some weapons forged for those domestic enemies which will be useful for foreign ones, in case they get hungry for cotton, and try to bully us next fall. I hope you will not relax one iota for all the peace talk. France will act with England if we are caught weak next fall.

J. M. FORBES TO T. DAWES ELIOT.[1]

BOSTON, *July* 4, 1861.

MY DEAR MR. ELIOT, — I have yours of 2d, and note the doubts of Mr. Welles as to the safety of intrusting commissions to our merchant sailors. This is natural at first sight, but a little reflection must convince him that it is entirely unfounded.

During our two wars with England, when most of our merchant ships were of 200 to 400 tons and none above 700, our best commodores and captains came from the merchant service, and showed no inaptitude for carrying frigates into action. Look over Cooper's "Naval History" and see who won the laurels then !

If history were wanting as a guide, we should on general principles come to the same confidence in the skill and gallantry of our merchant sailors. I would make no invidious comparisons with our navy; but the crisis is a great one, and the navy

---

[1] Chairman of the Naval Committee of the House of Representatives. — ED.

can well afford to face the truth. It has glorious men and glorious memories, but they are so closely interwoven with those of our merchant marine that to lower the one it is almost inevitable that you lower the other. If I make a comparison, it is partly in the hope of making suggestions that will tend to raise the navy to its highest point of efficiency.

Let us for a moment examine the training of the two services now. Leaving out the Annapolis school as only just beginning to act upon the very youngest grade of commissioned officers, the youths intended for the navy have been selected at a very early age, with generally very insufficient education, from those families who have political influence, and from those young men who have a prejudice against rough sailor life. Under our system of promotion by seniority these young men live an easy life in the midshipman's mess, the wardroom, or on shore, with little responsibility and little actual work until, at the age of from forty to sixty, they get command of a vessel; they feel that they are in the public service for life, and that the ones that take the best care of their lives and healths are the most sure of the high honors of their profession! Considering their want of early training, of active experience, and of stimulus, it is only surprising that they are on the whole so fine a body of men.

Compare this training with that of our merchant officers. Taken from a class of young men, with somewhat fewer advantages and education, but all having access to our public schools, they are sent to sea to fight their own way up. Those who are capable soon emerge from the mass of common sailors (most of them common sailors for life), and are tried as mates, etc. They are chosen for their daring, their vigilance, their faculty for commanding; and those who prove to have these qualities soon get into command. In nine cases out of ten, the young American-born sailor who is fit for it gets command of a vessel by the time he is twenty-five years old, an age when our naval officers have, as a rule, had but little experience in navigating vessels, and but little responsibility put upon them.

Instead of the little vessels which our heroes of the old wars commanded, you will find these same merchant captains in command of vessels ranging from 700 tons (a small ship now), up to 1500 and 2000 tons, some as large as our seventy-fours, many as large as our first-class frigates! It is idle to talk of such men not being able to manœuvre sloops-of-war or frigates, either in action or in any circumstances where seamanship and daring are needed.

So much for a comparison of the training of the two services; now for one or two suggestions for *raising* the navy. First, let us go on with the naval school and carry its scientific requirements and rigid discipline as high as West Point. To go further back still; I would have the candidates for the school recommended, not by members of Congress, but by the boards of education of the dif-

ferent States, and taken from those who have
proved themselves the best scholars in our public
schools, — at least a majority of them; leaving the
minority to come from those more favored by fortune who use the private schools.

Once in service, I would have our navy actively
employed in surveying foreign seas and making
charts, as the English navy is doing to a considerable extent.   Then let the President have some
discretion to promote those who by gallantry or sci-
ence distinguish themselves. Finally, a more liberal
retiring list, and if possible some higher honors in
the way of titles as a stimulus to our officers.

Perhaps there is not time for the reform of the
service, but it is the time for beginning the organization of our volunteer navy. Do you note that
the only privateer that we know has been taken
has been by sailing brig Perry, though another is
reported by the Niagara? I could say almost or
quite as much in favor of half clipper ships, in
comparison with the ordinary sloop-of-war, as I
have said of our merchant sailors. Until we become converted to European ideas upon standing
armies and navies, we cannot think of giving up
our land or sea militia, and, if we give up privateering, we must have a substitute with all its strength
and more.   Yours truly,

                                 J. M. FORBES.

J. M. FORBES TO MOSES H. GRINNELL.

BOSTON, *July* 6, 1861.

Thank you for your telegram. I wrote you last Sunday in substance as follows : —

We are obliterating party lines, which is all the fashion, especially with the Outs. Why not do so with state lines ? Of all the men who should go abroad, Lothrop Motley would do most credit to the administration. He was shut off by Adams and Burlingame, much to our regret, and to the loss of the country. He is a Republican from the start, a linguist, and the historian of the day. Now that Burlingame has been banished to China, why not send Motley to Vienna ? It would be a delicate matter for Massachusetts to press, as she has two foreign missions, but if the suggestion came from you, upon considerations of public interest, I should think Mr. Seward would not hesitate to appoint him. We have not, outside of London and Sardinia, a very strong representation in Europe, and it does strike me this would strengthen the administration.

If you agree with me, and will push it, you can do it, and I know it will be applauded, as Mr. Irving's appointment, you remember, was universally. It would be a compliment to literature rather than to our State. . . .

I hope to see Congress organize a mercantile navy, and put you at the head of a commission to sit in New York, and see to it. Buy clipper ships, and commission the captains with good rank for the war !

The finding of an efficient " aide " for the over-taxed war-governor of Massachusetts was a matter of importance, and this he enforced on General Scott's mind by the gift of a salmon ; a cod sent, as I guess, with some similar errand, not having arrived in condition to emphasize it. Besides any ulterior object, he had an amused sympathy with the kind old general's affection for a good dinner : —

J. M. FORBES TO LIEUTENANT-GENERAL WINFIELD SCOTT.

BOSTON, July 3, 1861.

MY DEAR SIR, — Your valued note of July 1st is received. It is clear that Neptune owes me a grudge in thus making me the innocent reason of the first failure you ever experienced in entertaining your friends or enemies !

I do not, however, mean to put up with defeat, and so try my own ground, the railroad, and send a salmon alone, as I find there is some reason to fear that his highness, the cod, does not bear transportation, and may hurt the salmon. Possibly, too, his Excellency Governor Andrew's fish may have had the preference in the ice-chest !

I hear that our good governor has turned his face toward Washington. He is killing himself with attention to military details, and if you value him or Massachusetts, I wish you could send him some good army officer to help him organize our last ten thousand men.

This learning the art of war in two months is a serious matter !

With my best wishes and respects.

Yours truly,   J. M. FORBES.

My father's only reference to the first great battle of the war is in some reminiscences of Wendell Phillips, and reads as follows : —

" On the Sunday of the first Bull Run I heard W. H. Channing[1] preach, and made up off-hand a little party for the next day, Monday, at Milton, including James Freeman Clarke, W. H. Channing, and Mr. Phillips. Governor Andrew was ill at Hingham, so that I could not get him ; and I forget who the others were. When they came out they brought out the worst story of Bull Run, looking almost like the capture of Washington. It was a sad feast; Channing almost cried, and all were in the depths except Phillips, who stoutly insisted that it was just what we wanted, and was perhaps the best thing that could have happened; and he was probably right."

The notes continue : —

" I find that on the 9th of July I sent Mr. Eliot my rough draft of the ' Bill for a Volunteer Navy,' which was afterwards carefully drawn up by Mr. R. H. Dana. The bill empowered the government to purchase and arm vessels and give commissions to merchant captains and others on them, to appoint three commissioners of the volunteer navy to organ-

---

[1] Then lately arrived from England.

ize a bureau at Washington to take charge of the new business; and it gave a $3,000,000 appropriation to carry out its provisions. The bill was passed later on, but meanwhile I had been put on a commission, with Commodore Hudson, of the navy yard at Charlestown, and J. C. Delano, of New Bedford, to buy merchant ships for the navy, fit them for sea ready for their armament, and also to nominate from the merchant service captains, and perhaps other officers, to command them. We bought several ships, among which I remember the Fearnot, Captain Faucon."

During his work in ship-buying my father's disgust was extreme to find that a Boston firm had got wind, through some leaky official in the Navy Department, of his intended purchases. He writes of this firm to Assistant Secretary Fox as follows : —

"I think they will cost the department some thousands besides the delay. One vessel that has been, I hear, offered at $25,000 is held firmly at $30,000 and ought to have been bought at $20,000 to $24,000. Others are stimulated by these people to offer at high prices, having first been led to promise —— and —— a commission if they sell to government. Of course, government has thus to pay not for help, but for hindrance. . . . Better far, if Messrs. —— and —— have any claim on the department, authorize us to pay them a commission to help us, conditional on their doing so, than let them exact a commission, practically from us, for hurting our negotiations."

And he says in another letter to Fox of this period : —

" We are still embarrassed by the sharks, who have forestalled us with the vessels we think we must have ; and by a singular coincidence, your naval constructor H. can see very little good in any vessel except those thus forestalled. The others are too large or too small, or too deep or too shoal, and our good friend Commodore Hudson is very shy of going against the established navy dimensions. So in my animosity against the speculators I make scant headway, as I will not see the government fleeced until the emergency becomes greater."

My father recalls in his notes still another form of stealing which he unearthed in the five weeks during which he served on the commission : —

" Feeling the urgency for haste, I had the King Fish [1] thoroughly fitted out by Mr. David A. Green, an experienced merchant and shipowner, with all the substantials of rigging and spars needed for two or three years, and had her towed round to the Charlestown Navy Yard to receive her armament and crew, the receiving ship being full of sailors waiting for vessels. To my disgust, some weeks later I found her still at the navy yard, and upon inquiry I found that nearly all the New Bedford outfitting had been ignored, and new spars, rigging, and other outfit put in. I satisfied myself that somebody around the navy yard got a commission or steal for all this, and though it could not

[1] A new clipper just bought by the commission. — ED.

be proved without a court-martial and perhaps civil
trial, I reported the facts to Mr. Fox, assistant
secretary of the navy, and these, with other similar
occurrences, called his attention to the urgent need
of reform.

"He quietly got Congress to pass a bill providing that thereafter contractors and others furnish-
ing supplies for the navy should become employees
of the department, and subject to court-martial;
and under this new régime he remedied many of
the abuses which had grown up, and came near
getting some very sanctimonious thieves put into
the penitentiary.

"What was done in New England in the way of
buying ships was on rather a small scale, as very
much the larger number were bought in New York
and the other Middle States, through the agency of
a relative of Mr. Welles, an honest and fairly good
business man, who on the whole did his work very
well, although he made the mistake of receiving
a percentage from the shipowners. Neither he nor
the Secretary could see that the commission paid
him by the sellers was really to come out of the
government instead of out of the sellers; so he
made, it was thought, about $100,000, at the cost
of some scandal against Welles and against the administration; but it was done openly and public
opinion was not enough instructed to appreciate
fully the mischief, which was really much greater
than for the government to have paid him a large
commission.

" We of the Massachusetts commission had, of course, asked no charges, except for our actual traveling expenses, and I incline to think that even these were borne by us. In railroad matters, it had always been an axiom that a commission paid by a seller to an employee of the company was the worst form of stealing, for the seller not only added the commission to his price, but it, being a secret arrangement, was liable always to cover bad quality and bad measure. The same holds good of government transactions. Gideon Welles was an honest old Democratic editor, who knew but little of business, and who could not see the point that whatever the seller of the ship paid the agent of the government for buying his ship was not only an addition to the price, but was a bribe to the agent to shut his eyes as to the quality of the thing purchased."

I add a letter from Mr. Fox, from which it would appear that his correspondent was required to be responsible for officers as well as ships : —

G. V. FOX TO J. M. FORBES.

NAVY DEPARTMENT, July 30, 1861.

SIR, — I notice your letter to the Secretary of July 27. I think the Rover better be fitted for a long cruise towards the line, where her steam might enable her to pick up a privateer in calm latitudes. You must send forward nominations for all the officers, or there will be delay. . . . Let us have the officers at once. The department will buy no ships east of New York, except through your board, and any other parties have no countenance from here. If the board jump clear of them, their act will be approved. We mean to have you act unfettered, to the best of your judgment, but I should try to keep inside of 1100 tons. . . .

Very truly yours,　　　　　G. V. Fox.

CHAPTER IX

THE commission for buying ships was dissolved on August 30, 1861, and just before that date my father writes to C. F. Adams, United States minister to London, stating his objection to Seward's proposition to give up privateering. He held that we must keep the right to privateer as a threat, not to be used except in extremity: —

J. M. FORBES TO CHARLES FRANCIS ADAMS.

BOSTON, *August* 12, 1861.

MY DEAR SIR, — I have been hard at work for some weeks upon the organization of the new volunteer navy, and although it will be made an auxiliary, and a very useful one, to the navy, I regret to say I find great difficulties in giving it that efficiency which it ought to have, as a substitute for privateering. I am of course not going to give it up, and am looking to such changes in our law as will doubtless be adopted whenever an emergency really puts us to our trumps; but while it is yet an experiment, I am satisfied that we ought not to give up our right to issue letters of marque unless accompanied by Mr. Marcy's broader principle of exempting all private property on the sea from capture.

Even then I consider the time an unlucky one, and hope that some happy accident or some unreasonable demands on the part of the European powers may enable us to postpone the whole question. I need not, I hope, assure you that I have no disposition to interfere with your duties beyond giving you at the earliest moment the result of my personal observation upon the experiments we are trying now, and which of course has a direct bearing upon the questions which you are perhaps now discussing.

Pray make my best regards to Mrs. Adams and the rest of your family, and believe me,

Truly yours with high respect,

J. M. FORBES.

N. B. — Our hope was (and still is) to make the volunteer navy equally strong for attack — without the barbarism of privateering, but it is by no means so easy a task as we had supposed.

Mr. Adams answered my father's letter of August 12, as follows : —

CHARLES FRANCIS ADAMS TO J. M. FORBES.

LONDON, 30 *August*, 1861.

I do not know that I violate any confidence by telling you that the hope expressed in yours to me has been thus far verified. What the future may bring forth, no man can tell, — but the fact is certain that, now, negotiation is at a standstill.

I hear excellent accounts of your patriotic labors in the cause, and hope the best results from them. The great point now is the blockade. Privateering will come to nothing if that be made effective. If not, I see no end to it. For some of our own people would be as likely to go into it as to carry on the slave trade. The English must abide by the blockade, if it really be one. They will set it aside if they can pick a good flaw in it.

The course of events as seen from here is towards one termination of the struggle, and one only. We cannot afford to go over this ground more than once. The slave question must be settled this time once for all. It is surprising to see the efforts made here to create the belief that our struggle has nothing to do with slavery, but that it is all about a tariff. Even the anti-slavery people have been more or less inclined to give in to this notion.

Of course the measure of emancipation is a most grave one. It must task the capacity of the wisest heads among us. But there is no alternative in my mind between taking it up and absolute submission.

I cannot conceal from myself the fact that as a whole the English are pleased with our misfortunes. There never was any real good will towards us — and the appearance of it of late years was only the effect of their fears of our prosperity and our growing strength. Of course, you will keep these views to yourself. It is not advisable in these days for ministers abroad to be quoted. With best regards for Mrs. F. and your family, I am

Very truly yours,   C. F. ADAMS.

Next in order comes a letter from Mr. Bryant to my father in answer to a sort of fusilade from him expressive of his extreme impatience as to the conduct of the War Department: —

WILLIAM CULLEN BRYANT TO J. M. FORBES.

OFFICE OF THE EVENING POST,
NEW YORK, August 21, 1861.

MY DEAR SIR, — It does not seem to me at all indiscreet or imprudent to make the change in the Cabinet which you suggest. Indeed, I think that Mr. Cameron's retirement would, instead of being impolitic, be the most politic thing that could be done, by way of giving firmness to public opinion and strengthening the administration with the people. The dissatisfaction here is as great as with you, and I hear that at Washington it is expressed by everybody, except Cameron's special friends and favorites, in the strongest terms. If I am rightly informed, there is nothing done by him with the promptness, energy, and decision which the times demand, without his being in a manner forced to it by the other members of the Cabinet, or the President. A man who wants to make a contract with the government for three hundred mules, provided he be a Pennsylvanian, can obtain access to him, when a citizen of East Tennessee, coming as the representative of the numerous Union population of that region, is denied. There are bitter complaints, too, of Cameron's disregard of his appointments and engagements in such cases as that I have mentioned.

Mr. Lincoln must know, I think, that Cameron is worse than nothing in the Cabinet, and a strong representation concerning his unpopularity and unacceptableness, of which he may not know, may lead him to take the important resolution of supplying his place with a better man. I do not think the newspapers are the place to discuss the matter, but I make no secret of my opinion.

I am, dear sir, truly yours,

WM. C. BRYANT.

P. S. — I open my letter to say another word on the subject of yours. It does not appear to me that H. would be the man for the War Department, for the reason that he might give us trouble on the slavery question. Cameron has managed that part of our relations with the seceding States very badly, and I feel H. would do no better. He would do very well in the place of Smith ; but with the exception of making a place for him, it might not be of much consequence whether Smith were retained or not, though he adds no strength to the Cabinet. Some here talk of requiring the dismissal of Seward, but I fear this would be asking more than it is possible to get, and might endanger the success of the scheme for getting rid of Cameron.

W. C. B.

The following letters show that my father was not yet prepared to back the extreme measures of his abolition friends : —

BOSTON, *August* 19, 1861.

. . . . The public need something, or somebody, some word, or some blow, to magnetize them, or else they will be fearfully demoralized in a month. The *word* must be *emancipation,* and war upon slaveholders as such — as a distinct class — as the authors of all the present ills.

Can you not confer with the governor about this? You cannot keep up public interest, much less public enthusiasm, about an abstraction (at least of a worldly and temporal nature), and *Union* is a mere abstraction now; it touches not, and cannot touch, the public heart.

As one blow, I suggest what I vainly suggested last spring, an expedition to land in or about Albemarle Sound, composed mainly of blacks, who would go into the Dismal and other swamps and raise the thousands of refugees there to go out and make sallies and onslaughts upon the enemy; and so make a diversion.

It would at least cause a worse than Bull Run panic. There are plenty of men in Canada, resolute and intelligent refugees, who would enlist in such an enterprise. It cannot, however, be done by private means. Can any other be had, think you?

I have mentioned the matter of expedition to the Dismal Swamp to the governor, but to him only. Please not speak of it to any one else.

J. M. FORBES TO S. G. HOWE.

NAUSHON, *August* 21, 1861.

MY DEAR DOCTOR, — I have yours of the 19th. I confess to being one of that average class which constitutes the majority of our people, who as yet hesitate at the dreadful experiment of insurrection ; if it comes as a necessity, an alternative to the subversion of republican institutions, we should not hesitate a moment. There seem to me three reasons against it at this time, apart from our natural shrinking from a measure of this sort upon humane grounds.

1st. It may unite the border States against us, and check any tendency to division in the cotton States.

2d. It will, if resorted to from anything but obvious, stern necessity, divide the North.

3d. Its success as a weapon against the South is by no means certain. It is, to my mind, — with the light of the past four months' quiet among the blacks, and of John Brown's experience, — very uncertain unless resorted to under favorable circumstances. At present it seems to me worth more as a weapon to hold in reserve to threaten with, than one to strike with.

If resorted to now it would be in a hesitating, uncertain manner by our administration, and from that, if nothing else, would be likely to fail. Once tried, and failed in, a great source of terror to the South and of confidence to the North is lost.

I go therefore for holding it in reserve until

public sentiment, which is the chief motive power behind the administration, drives them to use it decisively. Our people throughout have been ahead of our government, which has followed rather *laggingly:* — it is not a leading, but a following administration. It does not act, even now, readily when first urged by the popular tide. Nothing but the full force of the current starts it. If we could get a good hurricane to help the tide, it might sweep away some of the weaker materials in the Cabinet, and possibly put a leader in their place who would thenceforward draw after him the Cabinet and the people.

Your suggestion, then, even if it were the best thing, seems to me premature. As to urging on the government to vigor, to making serious war with shot and hemp, there would not, there could not, be two opinions with the people. Governor Andrew could give the hint to our Massachusetts papers, and they would all readily sound the trumpet for vigor and for discipline, and the " Evening Post " and such papers would readily help.

As to anything more, or in the direction you suggest, I want to see the demand come from the people, from the democracy, rather than from either the leaders or the abolitionists!

Perhaps the poverty of the South may soon begin to afflict the slaves, and they may lead off. If they do, the responsibility is not ours.

Very truly yours,   JOHN M. FORBES.

The War Department continued to be a cause of anxiety. My father next writes: —

J. M. FORBES TO WILLIAM CULLEN BRYANT.

NAUSHON, August 24, 1861.

Yours of the 21st received. The objection which you suggest to Mr. H. is a very strong one. We need a man in the War Department who, when the right time comes, will not hesitate a moment to assail the weakest point of the enemy. Our Governor Andrew seemed to me to hit the nail on the head when he rebuked Butler for offering to put out any fire in the enemy's camp. The time has come when we can no longer afford to "make war with rose-water," and it was a great mistake in Congress to limit the confiscation of property to that of rebels found in arms against us. All the property of open rebels should be forfeited the first week of the next Congress; this would enable us to proclaim emancipation in the border States with a fixed compensation for all valuable slaves belonging to loyal citizens, without a very large bill for Virginia.

I had hoped that H. was man enough to go in for such a measure and advocate it as a boon to the loyal citizens of Kentucky, Missouri, Maryland, and Delaware, putting it upon the ground of military necessity. If he is not up to this we don't want him; but it is not worth while to try to get rid of Cameron without at the same time making quite sure of a better man. You remember the old story of the trapped fox begging his friend the hawk not to drive off the half-sated swarm of flies only to give place to a new cloud of them — and hungry ones? I wish you would go a step further, and suggest a successor. Is there no one who could take Chase's place, and give him the War? I forget whether I suggested to you James Joy, of Detroit. He would do well for the War, better for the Interior, from his thorough knowledge of the West. Lincoln, Trumbull, Chandler, and all the Western men know him. He is the most able, decided, and plucky man that I know. How would Sherman do for the Treasury, and Chase for War?

As the matter stands now, the effort to displace Cameron will be coupled with one to put in H., and if the latter is not the right man, we had better rub along as we are, until the right man turns up. Governor Andrew has all the moral qualities; but he is perhaps too pronounced an anti-slavery man, and works too much upon details himself, not using other men. He would kill himself in the Cabinet. . . .

The answer came promptly, and is as follows: —

WILLIAM CULLEN BRYANT TO J. M. FORBES.

OFFICE OF THE EVENING POST,
NEW YORK, *August* 27, 1861.

I do not much like the idea of putting Sherman into the Treasury Department. He would make, I think, a better secretary of war. The great objection I have to him in the Treasury Department is that, so far as I understand the matter, he is com-

mitted, as the saying is, to that foolish Morrill tariff.
Yet I am very certain that it would be considered
by the country an immense improvement of the
Cabinet to place him in the War Department. The
country has a high opinion of his energy and resolution and practical character.

Of Governor Andrew I do not know as much as
you do, though I have formed a favorable judgment
of his character and capacity — not a very precise
one, however. . . .

They talk of H. here as they do with you, but I
am persuaded that the disqualification I have mentioned would breed trouble in the end. The dissatisfaction with Cameron seems to grow more and
more vehement every day. His presence taints the
reputation of the whole Cabinet, and I think he
should be ousted at once. I am sorry to say that a
good deal of censure is thrown here upon my good
friend Welles, of the Navy Department. He is too
deliberate for the temper of our commercial men,
who cannot bear to see the pirates of the rebel government capturing our merchant ships one after
another and defying the whole United States navy.
The Sumter and the Jeff Davis seem to have a
charmed existence. Yet it seems to me that new
vigor has of late been infused into the Navy Department, and perhaps we underrated the difficulties of
rescuing the navy from the wretched state in which
that miserable creature Toucey left it. There is a
committee of our financial men at present at Washington, who have gone on to confer with the Presi-

dent, and it is possible that they may bring back a better report of the Navy Department than they expected to be able to make.

Rumor is unfavorably busy with Mr. Seward, but as a counterpoise it is confidently said that a mutual aversion has sprung up between him and Cameron. This may be so. The "Times," I see, does not spare Cameron, nor the "Herald." There is a good deal of talk here about a reconciliation between Weed and Bennett, and a friendly dinner together, and the attacks which the "Herald" is making upon the War and Navy Department, are said to be the result of an understanding between them. Who knows, or who cares much?

I have emptied into this letter substantially all I have to say. There are doubtless men in private life who would fill the War Department as well as any I have mentioned, but the world knows not their merits, and might receive their names with a feeling of disappointment.

P. S. — With regard to visiting Naushon, I should certainly like it, and like to bring my wife. I have another visit to make, however, in another part of Massachusetts; but I shall keep your kind invitation in mind and will write you again.

W. C. B.

Naval matters interested my father more than military, and I find him writing from Naushon, on August 31, to his friend Mr. George Ashburner, who had left Calcutta and settled in England: —

"I feel as if I had been very negligent in not before thanking you for your most thorough and useful data about iron plates, which will be of great help to the department when they come to decide upon how to build. Red tape, I fear, is not confined to the Crimea! And where there are real difficulties about the iron plates, and lots of plain work to be done in other directions, the plans mature slowly!"

He then goes on to describe two iron ships still on the stocks which could be got at cost by the government, and to ask his correspondent to "get at the views of some experienced man" as to the efficiency of a plan which he had conceived for plating, and making turrets on these; and ends a long letter with, "We are gradually recovering our self-respect, and shall get some good out of much evil," referring to the stampede at Bull Run.

During the summer and autumn of 1861, prior to the seizure of Mason and Slidell, a number of letters passed between my father and his old correspondent, Nassau Senior. I give some of these as showing very forcibly the different points of view of Americans and English on the same subject.

NASSAU W. SENIOR TO J. M. FORBES.

CHÂTEAU DE TOCQUEVILLE, August 20, 1861.

MY DEAR MR. FORBES, — I write from a place in which your name is often mentioned, and always with great gratitude. Madame de Tocqueville, after an illness of thirteen or fourteen years, is better than I

have seen her since 1848. The first use that she
has made of returning strength has been to unite a
little party of her old friends, — the Beaumonts,
Ampère, and ourselves, — and we are passing charming mornings in walking and driving, and evenings
in talking and hearing Ampère read Molière, —
which is better than most acting.

I find the general opinion in France and in England as to your affairs identical.

It is a general conviction that the secession is one
of the wildest and wickedest acts that has ever been
committed; that you will beat the seceders, but that
you will not so far conquer them as to make them
your subjects, or even portions of your federation;
that having humiliated and punished them you will
dictate your own terms on which you will allow
them to go; that those terms will probably be that
you will keep New Orleans and Western Virginia;
that you will deprive them of any right to territories, and probably prohibit their having a slave
trade. As you are fond of tariffs and have not yet
found out that they do more harm to the nation
that makes them than to the nation against which
they are directed, we suppose that you will enact
against them a hostile tariff.

We all bitterly deplore the defeat at Bull's Run,
believing that it will prolong the war.

We also think that our conduct to you has been
perfectly right, and that your complaints of it are
the childish folly of a democracy which has never
met with a check before, and like other spoilt chil-

dren beats the chair over which it has fallen. You will not agree with me, I know, for even your good sense has not saved you altogether from participating in the unreasonableness of those about you.

The state of this country is painful. France is a witch, who has sold herself to the devil, on the condition that he shall give power to hurt others. L. N.'s offer to her was made to our Saviour, when Satan, having shown him all the kingdoms of the world and the glory thereof, said, "All this will I give thee if thou wilt worship me."

The indignation, shame, and depression of the higher and educated classes is indescribable.

We intend to wander over the east and south of France, and return to England in the beginning of October. Kindest regards.

Ever yours,   N. W. SENIOR.

J. M. FORBES TO NASSAU W. SENIOR.

NAUSHON ISLAND, *September* 30, 1861.

DEAR MR. SENIOR, — Your note from the Château de Tocqueville reached me a few days since. It must have been a most agreeable reunion there.

We here feel more and more each day the miracle of M. de Tocqueville's prophetic vision of our history. It seems almost like clairvoyance! Our Channing's *prévoyance* of the results of our Texas land thefts is almost as strange. Such men of genius may well be called seers.

I am sorry that you still class me with the crowd who always seek to forget their own sins in abusing their neighbors. The fact is, all my prepossessions were in favor of England, and I had watched with the greatest satisfaction the subsidence of the old animosities, growing out of the two wars, and the growth of that good feeling which ought to animate the two nations who are, or might be, the bulwark of free institutions against the despotisms of the Old World.

When we cast off the nightmare despotism, which had so long ruled us, the slave oligarchy, which sympathized with Russia because of serfdom, and dismissed your minister to show their homage to the Czar, and which refused you a limited right of search, because it favored the slave trade; in fine, when at last we placed ourselves right on the question of slavery, which has always been a reproach from you to us, I thought the *entente cordiale* was complete. I did not look for material aid nor want it, but only such forbearance of countenance towards our " Sepoys " as would help to discourage them, and would bring our two nations still more into harmony.

Perhaps I feel the disappointment more bitterly than the mob does, because my hope and prejudices were strongly for a warm English alliance — now, I fear, deferred another twenty years. Your " Times " I expected nothing better from than we have had in its cold sneers at the breaking of our bubble of democracy, but from your ministry I did look for something better than a proclamation of strict neutrality, putting us upon precisely the same footing with our "Sepoys," forbidding either party to bring prizes into your ports, prohibiting your subjects aiding either; and this, too, issued just as our new minister was arriving, thus giving him no opportunity to confer upon mutual interests; for I contend that it is our mutual interests that have been endangered, not ours alone.

I beg your Sepoys' pardon for naming them with ours. They at least had foreign conquerors, and a hated religion to conspire against, and yet we watched your Indian battles with a brother's eye, and canonized your Havelocks, Hodsons, and other martyrs, as if they had been our own. Even our press, loose as it is, uttered no sound of exultation at what seemed at one time to be the downfall of your Indian empire.

Had your Sepoys brought a prize into our California ports, we should have known only the British owner, and restored her. Once more I beg your Sepoys' pardon. They were not guilty of the deep crime against their nationality and the principles of government which marks our more barbarous rebels!

One word about the Morrill tariff. It is a labored, clumsy production, and it will fall by its own weight. Some of its blunders have been partially corrected; but you mistake the intention of those who passed it, or at least of the majority of them.

Its aim was to substitute the steadiness of specific duties for the vibrating, cheating system of *ad valorem*. Certain high duties were doubtless smuggled in under guise of specifics, and the extreme difficulty of so framing our specific duties that our poorer classes shall not pay the same duties, per yard or per pound, on their cheap cloth or tea, will probably cause a repeal of the tariff. Yet I think British experience and opinion favor the principle of specific rather than *ad valorem* duties. One tends to cheat the people who buy the poorest qualities, the other tends to enormous frauds against government and profits by false swearing, and encourages the use of poor, showy goods, as against the more substantial ones which come in under specifics.

You are a little more encouraging as to results than you were, but I still think you do not properly appreciate the fact that we are not fighting to subjugate the South, but to put down a small class who have conspired against the people, and who are a thousand times worse enemies of the mass of the people at the South than the North.

The only pinch is our finances. Cannot you help us upon the text of the cutting within, if you find that sound? Our moneyed men continue to take their tone very much from England, and confident views of financial success coming from your side have great weight. . . .

Very truly yours, J. M. FORBES.

NASSAU W. SENIOR TO J. M. FORBES.

13 HYDE PARK GATE, KENSINGTON,
November 20, 1861.

MY DEAR MR. FORBES, — I am going to republish my articles in Reviews; they will form about four volumes. Among them is one, called " European and American State Confederacies," in which I consider whether the American Union be a national union, or a confederation, whether allegiance be due to the State, or to the Union, and I decide that it is a national union, and consequently that secession is rebellion and treason. Pray look at the article : you will find it in the number for January, 1846. But I admit that the question is one of difficulty, and that there are great authorities on each side. If my opinion on this legal question be wrong, if the Union be a mere treaty like the German Bund, every American owes allegiance to his own State, and if that State secede, he would be guilty of rebellion and treason if he did not secede too. Now Lord Russell did not feel competent to decide this difficult legal question — and I think that he could not decide it. Yet it is for not deciding it at once, and declaring the seceders rebels, that you have been abusing him and us for three months. I think that on consideration you will feel that the most certain means of destroying our sympathy with the North, and turning it towards the South, were your threats that as soon as you had settled the affair with the South you would turn on us and punish us, by war, for our want of sympathy.

One thing has tended much to embitter us, your different treatment of France and of us. The conduct of the two governments has been identical, but you have been as civil to France as you have been rude to us. Now I happen to know that the French feeling is with the South. They say that the New Orleans people are their brethren. They are all friends of slavery, and I have peculiar reasons for believing that Louis Napoleon proposed to our government to join him in breaking the blockade. You know that I have access to accurate sources of intelligence, and you may believe this. My only wish, from the time that the enormous armies and the military success of the South showed (at least it so seemed to me) that you might beat, but could not conquer her, has been for the termination of the contest, and as I think that loans to either party would tend to prolong it, I own that I hope that none will be made.

We hear little from the South, but the little which we do hear leads us to think that you are mistaken in believing that there is a strong Union party there. They seem to be as determined as you are.

Can you tell me anything of our Sault Ste. Marie prospects? I suppose that the war adjourns all sales.

Ever yours,　　N. W. SENIOR.

BOSTON, *December* 10, 1861.

MY DEAR MR. SENIOR, — I have yours of the 20th ulto.

I shall read with much interest your article upon the nature of our government, and am glad you came to the same conclusion which everybody here long since arrived at except Calhoun and his gang of conspirators.

I don't blame Lord Russell for being puzzled at any question which *you* say has two sides to it; but I do blame him for jumping at his conclusions in such hot haste that he could not await the arrival of our new minister, whose explanation might have given him some light.

You don't blame the doctor (Medico) when, called to a serious case, he happens to take the dark view of it, and sentences the patient to " dissolution;" but you do think him a blunderer if he hastens to tell the victim that he has only to make his arrangements for his funeral!

Louis Napoleon, by quietly holding back his opinions and then uttering them covered up with sugared words, puts himself, with the masses of our people, where England was a few months since, our natural ally! Of course it is an enormous humbug, and thinking men are not gulled by it, but none the less [the situation] operates to inflame the old animosities that had grown out of two wars and that had been just forgotten.

Another thing must not be forgotten. The

French press has not the chance, even when it has
the will, to do the mischief that yours and ours
has. We hardly read anything from the French
papers; they still less read American papers, and
this makes the grand difference between our situation as relating to the two countries.

You read our New York " Herald " edited by a
renegade Scotchman . . . and you take it for the
representative of American journalism! The " Herald " is really the organ of the seceders, it was so
openly until after Sumter surrendered; and only
came over nominally to the Northern side under the
terrors of mob law. It has since served its masters still better by sowing the seeds of dissension
between us and England.

We, with perhaps equal blindness, permit the
" Times " and half a dozen other papers to stand for
" England." I look for a grand paper duello upon
the Trent question, and shall be relieved if it goes
no further. Should the questions assume a warlike
aspect, we shall only be driven the sooner to our last
desperate resort, emancipation. We are now only
divided into two parties at the North, viz.: those
who would use the negro when we can see no other
way of conquering; and secondly, those who would
use the negro at once, wherever he can be used to
strengthen us or weaken the enemy! The logic of
events has been from day to day settling this question, and if our talking men in Congress can only
be patient or self-denying in the outpouring of patriotic words, we shall go on fast enough. . . .

You cannot believe we shall subjugate ten millions of people. Nor I; but classify these ten millions and all is changed. At least two are avowed loyalists in the border States; four more are blacks ready to help us when we will let them; three more are poor whites whose interests are clearly with us and against their would-be masters. How long will it be before the avowals of their masters, aided by the suffering of the war, will open their eyes?

This leaves one million, of all ages and sexes, who, through owning slaves and connection with slaveholders, may think they have a class interest in the success of the rebellion. This class we can crush out — or what will be left of them after the war debt of the rebels reaches its proper value — whenever we can divide the four million of poor whites, by an operation upon their *eyes!*

But if I underrate the difficulty, the necessity for doing it now is all the greater! If hard now, how much harder will it be after we shall have, as you desire, permitted them to separate. Now they have no manufactures, no foreign alliances, no warlike stores except what they stole from us, and these rapidly diminishing. They have missed their first spring in which lies the strength of a conspiracy; while our cold Anglo-Saxon blood is just getting roused from the lethargy of a long peace and of overmuch prosperity. We are just ready to begin to fight. We all feel that what is now a war between the people and a small class would, after a separation, become a war of sections. As for peace, nobody believes it possible; a truce we might have, to give them time to gather breath! It is only a question between war to the end now and a chronic state of war with two standing armies, two navies, two corps of diplomatists seeking alliances in every court in Europe, to end in another death struggle. There is no peace for us, unless we either conquer the arrogant slave-owner classes who have so long ruled us and bullied you, or permit them by a compromise to continue and extend their combination with our baser class and to drag us into a grand slave empire which shall absorb the West Indies and Mexico and Central America.

A bold stand at the polls by the North in 1850 would have given us the victory peacefully; now we must fight for it, or yield to the basest faction that ever ruled a country. Better a ten years' war than this; but it will not be a long war.

The conspirators counted upon an early success in arms and a division of the North. Foiled in this, their only hope is in foreign intervention. I have no doubt what you tell me is true of Louis Napoleon, still less that he secretly gave the rebels hopes of aid, nor that they have construed your course to favor them. Had you squarely taken the same ground that we did towards your Canadian rebels, this hope would have been extinguished; and now, if you want cotton, if you want trade, if you want to pave the way to a real alliance with the only free nation besides yourselves on the globe, you ought to help us in all legitimate ways.   You should encourage our loan, you should sharpen your police to detect the outfit of hostile vessels, you should hold the Nashville strictly accountable for her acts of pillage and destruction, giving her the experience of a long trial in your courts, if only to discourage other pirates from being their own judges of what property they may appropriate.

Do this and the war will be short.   Four months ago an offer from you to do what we should have readily done when your Indian empire was threatened, had it seemed necessary or proper, would have ended the war before this, — namely, to throw open to us for purchase your armories and your ironclad shipyards.   We might not have accepted the offer, but it would have destroyed the rebels' last hope. I don't complain of your not doing it, but simply indicate what for the sake of both countries I wish might have been your policy!

As for the Sault Ste. Marie, the pine lands must wait for the prairie farmers to build again; but the developments in our mineral lands are said to be magnificent, and to promise results next summer.

Very truly yours,   J. M. FORBES.

CHAPTER X

THE SANITARY COMMISSION

In November, 1861, my brother applied for a commission in the First Massachusetts Cavalry, and my father felt justified in supporting his application by the following letter to the governor : —

J. M. FORBES TO GOVERNOR JOHN A. ANDREW.

BOSTON, *November* 4, 1861.

MY DEAR SIR, — I beg leave to second my son's application for a commission in the First Cavalry Regiment, and to say that nothing would induce me to seek so perilous an honor for him but a conviction that he is morally and physically well adapted to do good service to the good cause. Moreover, I know that he is actuated by the highest motives in seeking service: such motives as alone can reconcile parents to offering their sons!

I do not seek for him any specified position, but only ask that he should have a chance, before he is fixed in the lowest grade, to show whether he is fit for anything higher; in short, that he shall be judged by what he can do, rather than by his age, which is only just past twenty-one.

Very truly yours,   JOHN M. FORBES.

In due course my brother received his commission as lieutenant, and soon afterwards joined his regiment at Readville.

News came, in the fall of 1861, of the great hardships of our men in the Southern prisons, and especially at Richmond, where Colonel W. Raymond Lee, Paul Revere, and C. L. Peirson were confined. Governor Andrew had no appropriation available; and the legislature was not in session; but my father offered to send to Richmond whatever sum the governor thought best; and accordingly sent, through some of his semi-loyal Baltimore friends, a draft for $1000, to be paid there to Colonel W. Raymond Lee, or Adjutant C. L. Peirson, of the Twentieth Massachusetts. This promptly reached its destination, and was of great use in mitigating the situation of many of our officers and men who were in want of blankets and other necessaries. In due time an act of the legislature was passed at the governor's suggestion, reimbursing this outlay.

The seizure of Slidell and Mason came on the 8th of November, 1861. This event and all that followed are matter of history. On what thin ice the two countries had come is manifest by the following extract from one of Mr. Ashburner's letters to my father : —

"I feel in the deepest anxiety regarding this unfortunate affair of the St. Jacinto. I cannot believe that anything so horrible as war with the United States will result from so inadequate a cause, yet

the whole country rings with it; and as the feeling
of irritation on your side seems to be equally great,
I fear that every possible advantage will be taken of
the passions of two great nations to bring them into
collision, in spite of their interests, which are so
deeply involved in the maintenance of peace. That
the danger is looked upon as most imminent you
may judge by the course of the government with
regard to the exportation of saltpetre. The Du-
ponts, of Delaware, came over here last week and
cleared the market of that article. They bought
up the whole stock, some 3000 tons, and were about
to ship it when the affair of the Trent transpired.
Within twenty-four hours government laid an em-
bargo upon it, — a very extraordinary and extreme
measure here, where the utmost freedom in trade
is now the established rule for the country, even
in war."

How the Trent affair as a whole appeared to my
father, after the first excitement of it all had passed,
will be seen from the following letter : —

J. M. FORBES TO NASSAU W. SENIOR.

BOSTON, 20 *December*, 1861.

Nothing from you lately. You will be glad to
hear that our people here are within the control
of the government in regard to the difficulty with
England, and unless the demands are made in such
a spirit and manner as to make it seem that war is
intended sooner or later, we can tide over the present trouble. If our government or people are made

to feel that the Trent affair is merely a pretext, and that after making disagreeable concessions there, we shall only be called upon the sooner to " eat dirt " in some other case, we shall of course fight at first, *coûte qu'il coûte.*

This I do not anticipate, but I hope you statesmen will look ahead beyond the immediate horizon and try to treat this case so that it shall not further embitter the feelings of the two nations, and thus lay the foundations of a future war, whether of tariffs or cannon!

It will be unfortunate, for instance, if you make stringent demands for reparation of a wrong which to our common people, and to the common sense of the world, will in so large a matter between nations look like a technical or legal quibble.

You cannot convince our people that you are justified in humiliating us in this our extremity upon the ground that our frigate exercised an admitted right in a wrong manner, the wrong growing out of a generous motive toward your ship or your nation.

I know it is an important principle that no naval officer should take the office of a judge, and I shall be glad to see our officers and yours put upon their responsibility to conform, in manner and in substance both, to the Law of Nations, — but you ought not to push the legal advantage, if you have one, too far, where the substantial equity will seem to be with us! If you do, it will be considered like striking us while we are down, and will be remembered and resented long after this generation has passed away.

One cannot yet fairly judge how far our government and people may be pushed in the way of concession. If we do give way much beyond what seems to us fair, you may put it down to our inveterate earnestness to whip our domestic enemy.

I hope and believe we shall get over this near danger of collision with you, but I want to see the future guarded too.

If, for instance, you propose to leave the whole question to arbitration of parties as nearly disinterested as the case admits of, I think it will be received as an earnest of a better state of feeling. The king of Italy and the Czar, though opposed to republican institutions, would, I think, be accepted as fair referees, of course after proper argument being heard from your jurists and ours.

On the other hand, to insist upon your own interpretation of the international law, or upon referring it solely to Louis Napoleon, will, even if we concede it, leave a sting that will rankle for half a century! It will confirm all our worst fears that your rulers are ready to catch at any pretext, and risk any amount of suffering to your own people if they can only thus make sure of the failure of republican institutions. The prevailing opinion is that such is the disposition of your government, and I daily hear men of property and of general worldly prudence advocate the necessity of absolute resistance to any demand for concession. They reason that it would break down the spirit of our people and create internal divisions to a degree that is worse than foreign war! Their policy would be to let the foreign demands intensify our efforts against the rebels, and the moment it is ascertained that actual war will result, let loose the blacks, cut the dikes which confine the Mississippi, and deluge New Orleans and the whole of the flat country on its banks; an easy task!

A spark may thus ignite all the elements of war, while public opinion is so nearly balanced that it is only to-day that one can speak for! To-day peace is probable — to-morrow it may be impossible.

Happily the balance turned in favor of peace. I find my father's recollections next referring to a movement, by that time well under way, in which he took a great interest: —

" The National Sanitary Commission was one of the wonders of the war. Its idea may have been suggested in New York State, but it dragged along a good while there without coming to anything, and they sent to Boston for help. A very few men met, either at the city hall council chamber or at the green room of the state house, I forget which; there were not over a half a dozen, and it was a question what to do. But time pressed, and some one suggested that it was still a meeting and could appoint a committee. So, without giving particulars, we prepared a circular stating the object of the meeting and our appointment of a very large committee (picked out of the whole Massachusetts public), with J. Huntington Wolcott[1] as president, to carry into effect a resolution (also prepared by us) for raising and spending money in concert with the New Yorkers. Mr. Wolcott was then a man of business, but was not present, and I doubt whether to this day he has ever known or dreamed of the smallness of the constituency which appointed him and his very respectable associates. However this may be, they took hold with a will, did their work just as well as if a full meeting at Faneuil Hall had called them into being, and laid the foundation for the great success of the Sanitary Commission, which was extended all over the loyal States, with W. G. Eliot at St. Louis commanding its Western wing. They raised several millions of dollars, spent the money judiciously, and not only by active operations, but by the stimulus given to the slower but much more extensive work of the Surgeons' and Commissary departments had great effect in meeting the emergencies of the field. Its very irregularity gave the Commission speed, and it often got ahead of the efficient army arrangements, hampered as they were by red tape and system. To hear the praises of its advocates, one would think that the chief supplies to the wounded through the war came from the Volunteer Sanitary. This is simply absurd, but we can hardly overrate the real good which the Commission did in the field, nor its reflex influence in keeping patriotic men and women busy all over the country doing

---

[1] Father of the present governor of Massachusetts.

their part of the great work. I remember Charles
H. Dalton and Miss Abby May and Miss I. Gray
working zealously in this direction. Dr. Henry W.
Bellows was the nominal head of the Commission,
and did much. The practical work was in the
hands of F. L. Olmsted, the landscape gardener,
and of his deputy, the Rev. Mr. Knapp, of Plymouth."

Some of the questions which had to be dealt
with by the Sanitary Commission, and its influence
on legislation, will be gathered from the following
letters which I find among my father's papers : —

FREDERICK LAW OLMSTED TO J. M. FORBES.

U. S. SANITARY COMMISSION,
WASHINGTON, D. C., *December* 15, 1861.

MY DEAR SIR, — I have just received your favor
of the 12th, and am exceedingly glad there is so
good a prospect of financial aid to the commission from Massachusetts. Your contributions of
goods have astonished me and overrun all my calcu-
lations. You have done in a month nearly four
times as much as the New York association — of
which we had been quite proud — in six months!
If the present rate of supply continues, I shall soon
be in concern to know where to put it.

I shall refer that portion of your letter which
relates to the surgeon-general to Dr. Bellows. The
simplest statement of the case would be perhaps
that with an army of 600,000 fresh men, with im-
promptu officers, it is criminal weakness to intrust

such important responsibilities as those resting on the surgeon-general to a self-satisfied, supercilious, bigoted blockhead, merely because he is the oldest of the old mess-room doctors of the old frontier-guard of the country. He knows nothing and does nothing, and is capable of knowing nothing and doing nothing but quibble about matters of form and precedent, and sign his name to papers which require that ceremony to be performed before they can be admitted to eternal rest in the pigeonholes of the bureau. I write this personally rather than as the secretary, and from general report rather than personal knowledge, but if it were not true is it not certain that as secretary of the Sanitary Commission, after six months' dealings with these poor, green volunteer sawbones, I should have seen some evidence of life in and from their chief?

You may contradict the report to which you refer, that the contributions made to the Sanitary Commission for the benefit of the soldiers' sick have been diverted to the aid of the exiles of the rebellion. To this date no funds of the commission have been disbursed in St. Louis. Probably the local commission there has done something which has given rise to the report.

I have directed Dr. Ware, in visiting Fort Monroe, to ascertain the condition of the refugees there, and report, but to give them no aid except under advice or in an emergency.

Very respectfully yours,
FRED. LAW OLMSTED.

DR. H. W. BELLOWS, INCLOSING THE ABOVE, TO J. M. FORBES.

NEW YORK, *December* 19, 1861.

MY DEAR MR. FORBES, — Mr. Olmsted sends on his letter for approval, and it finds me flat on my back, which accounts for this delay. Since Dr. Van Buren sent on the memorial for signatures, things have taken on a much more active state of quarrel between the Sanitary Commission and the Medical Bureau. General McClellan sent for me and asked me to draw a bill for the reorganization of the Medical Bureau, which I did. He carefully considered and wholly approved the bill, and personally went with me to the President to ask his support; to the Secretary of War (not at home), to the Assistant Secretary of War (much the wiser man), who heartily approved. By their advice, the bill was brought forward in the Senate by Senator Wilson a week ago. Several of the leading senators warmly approve it. The bill strikes at all the senility and incompetency in the bureau and would put about eight first-class men, selected by the President out of the whole Medical Staff, into the control and management of affairs. It would lay on the shelf, on full pay, all the venerable do-nothings and senile obstructives that now vex the health and embarass the safety of our troops. . . . The Medical Staff (that is, all but the Medical Bureau and the twenty men in right line of succession) must feel the bill to be a great boon to them, as it opens eight prizes for merit and competency, in their stupid seniority system, where folly at seventy was put in absolute control of no-matter-what-amount-of skill, knowledge, reputation, and fitness at forty! I told the President, who enjoys a joke, that the bureau system at Washington, in which one venerable noncompos succeeded another through successive ages, reminded me of the man who, on receiving a barrel of apples, eat every day only those on the point of spoiling, and so at the end of his experiment found that he had devoured a whole barrel of rotten apples. If there were any radical difficulties about obtaining signatures to our letter, they will all disappear when our report to the Secretary of War comes out, which will be in your hands in about a week.

We are very much delighted with your financial *report*, which will be *louder* still when we feel the silver bullets or golden balls pouring into our nearly exhausted exchequer.

Commend me to our active and disinterested friends, Mr. Ward, Mr. Norton, and the all-alive gentlemen of your monetary circle.

Yours gratefully and truly,

HENRY W. BELLOWS.

I give extracts from my father's reply to Mr. Olmsted, but the whole of his letter to Dr. Bellows, as the latter shows his characteristic way of raising funds for the Sanitary Commission: —

J. M. FORBES TO FREDERICK LAW OLMSTED.

BOSTON, *December* 21, 1861.

I only received yours of the 13th yesterday, but to make up for the delay, it came indorsed by the Dr. with good news of your medical bill, and with a good story. I gave parts of it to our committee to-day, much to their edification, and it will help me in getting the right names to a petition which I have drawn up to Congress, and of which I will send you a copy on Monday. My idea is to attack, from this distance, the system of seniority rather than to make personal attacks upon individuals, and in this way we can get all the good names in Massachusetts. The real trouble is that so many of the bureaux of the government have degenerated into mere receptacles for files of red tape, that the moment you attack one, it becomes personal to all fossildom, and arrays it against changes.

Can I write personally to anybody to help the bill? I know of course our Massachusetts delegation, and can if necessary make some influence with Vermont, Maine, Michigan, Illinois, Iowa, possibly Missouri; but I don't want to waste my powder by stirring a hair beyond what is necessary, having my hands overfull. . . .

All our women are eager; it is only organization and direction that is wanted; and this is one of the best offices of the Sanitary Commission. . . .

J. M. FORBES TO THE REV. DR. HENRY W. BELLOWS.

BOSTON, December 22, 1861.

I read your message about funds and some other
parts of your letter to our committee, and we voted
to send on $10,000 at once. Hope to have some
more, but it would help us if you would stir up
New York a little more, and have a movement
going on there at the same time. We have in
hand, or promised, $2000 more, especially given to
your Ladies' Society. For the two we are good for
$15,000 in all probability, and Roxbury $1500
more for their Ladies' Society. A strong effort
might, if essential at this time, bring still more, and
we are going on with our systematized levy. Possibly something of our system might help you in
New York. We got a committee of about twenty
business men, lawyers, ministers, and doctors, having as great a variety as possible, and with power
to add to their number. I then had a list made of
all who could afford to pay $25 and upwards (from
tax-book) adding to it out-of-town names of known
wealth; then called a meeting of committee, read
off the list (alphabetically arranged), asking each
member to accept promptly the duty of calling upon
such persons as he is willing to — also assigning to
absent members a fair proportion. We then fixed
upon $200 as the maximum to be asked for, and
the first week called upon all who were likely
to give $200 and $100, not refusing $50 when
offered. We had an address, of which I give you
a copy, and provided members with slips printed

from the newspapers to hand to our friends, and save talking. The large givers exhausted, we came down to $25, not refusing $10. Now we send a *pleasant* collector known to ball and theatre goers, to pick up smaller sums. Those who have refused the large sums may give $10 to the collector. I had doubts about asking more than $100 of any one, but it has worked well enough. It has been considerable work, and I sometimes feel as if the money could have been earned almost as easily as begged. Our committee have worked with great spirit, and now we look for the application of our earnings. I hope, whatever you do with other money and things, that you will be rigid as iron in applying ours strictly to the comfort of *our soldiers, sick and well*. No matter how strong appeals may be made for other good objects. *One instance* of deviation will check the enthusiasm of hundreds. People feel as if there was some hope of making an impression on the extra needs of the army through your organization, but if you are tempted to try to do anything for other good objects, it will seem like risking a certain good for a doubtful success. The loyal refugees, for instance, do or may form such an enormous object of charity, that if we mean to help them at all it must be done by a separate and very large organization.

Your prospect of success with the medical reform is most cheering; if you can effect it, that one act will be worth all the rest of your results.

I speak without any knowledge of persons, but

it is clear that it would be the most wonderful chance ever heard of, if the oldest army doctors proved up to the mark! We are preparing an address to Congress which I think all who are asked will sign, simply because it attacks the *system* of seniority, and protests against its application to our 650,000 men. I will try to inclose a copy of it. A suitable medical board ought to be second in importance only to the commanding generals. One is great to destroy, the other ought to have power to save. The operations of the generals, so far as life is concerned, cover only one quarter or one fifth of the numbers which the medical board with sufficient powers ought to have an influence over. The generals cause the death of, say one quarter, but even upon this quarter killed and wounded, the skill of the surgeons must have a marked influence. When you add to this the power of preventing or palliating the diseases which carry off the other three quarters, you make a sum which ought to dwindle down to the faintest line any claims of any persons, even for meritorious services to be rewarded! How much smaller the claims of those who ask high places as a reward for longevity, and for keeping their precious bodies out of harm's way so long! The case needs only to be stated, to be decided in your favor; if you will only keep personal quarrels out of it.

N. B. — Of course, you have figured out the importance of the allotment system?[1] 500,000 men

---

[1] The allusion is to a plan for securing from the volunteers "allot-

get per month $6,600,000 wages, of which one half, $3,300,000, is a large allowance for necessary expenses of men well clothed, and fed, and doctored by government? Whether the other half shall go to frolicking or be used to prevent pauperism of the soldiers' families, is a great question! If you have any spare time, I hope you will give some help to the perfecting and passing of the bill for securing the payment of the allotments at the expense and risk of the United States.

All hands, sanitary inspectors, chaplains, surgeons, and all decent army officers, should use their influence with the men to further the allotment.

The following letter to Mr. Olmsted refers to army sanitary reform : —

J. M. FORBES TO FREDERICK LAW OLMSTED.

BOSTON, *December* 23, 1861.

MY DEAR SIR, — I have not seen your bill. Would not this be a good time to provide in it for a statistical report upon the sanitary condition of the army — frequent enough to be of use for this war, as well as for future times? With a proper system, and one or two clerks at headquarters, the reports of sanitary measures of prevention, of medical and surgical cases, of deaths, etc., might be tabulated on a certain day in each month, and while laying the foundation for future statistics, would be

ments" of their pay for the benefit of their families. A law providing for this was enacted on December 24, 1861. — ED.

a great check upon the regimental surgeons, and help reform many immediate abuses. It would also give the surgeons a chance to make suggestions, independently of their colonels. For instance, I hear of a surgeon saying, " I wanted the colonel to order so and so done as necessary or valuable for health," but the colonel does not think it "worth while to harass the men," etc. A well-organized medical board ought to have influence enough to procure general orders for any measures of clear sanitary reform, if they only have the disposition, and can insist upon certain detailed reports for each regiment at fixed times.　　Truly yours,

J. M. FORBES.

CHAPTER XI

ANOTHER call for exertion and for frequent journeys to Washington now came, owing to the extremely crude ideas of finance that existed among the legislators there. My father writes in his notes : —

"During the summer of 1861, an extra session of Congress had been sitting, and measures of the utmost consequence were discussed and passed, including financial ones. . . . Our Secretary of the Treasury, S. P. Chase, was a good lawyer, full of patriotism and brains, but with no practice as a financier, and it took all the influence we could bring to bear from New York and the other business centres to hold him back in the use of paper money, which was his easiest but most dangerous resource. We fought hardest on his first plan of issuing fifty millions of greenbacks, which were made 'legal tenders,' unnecessarily as we thought at the time, and as I think now. Our idea was that paper money should be held as a last resort, and then should be issued as treasury notes and offered as a temporary payment to our creditors who chose to take them, instead of which Mr. Chase forced their circulation by making them a legal tender for all debts.[1]

"Mr. William Gray[2] was the boldest and best coadjutor I found in this contest. The first issue was only fifty millions, but when I had fought it at Washington to the bitter end, and it passed into law, I could only express myself by a telegram, saying, 'We are beaten, and the best speculation now would be to buy a paper-mill, which must now take the functions of a gold mine.'

"Issue after issue followed, and the best we could do was, when the bond question came up, to get provision made in the bill for paying interest in gold, which alone saved our finances. As it was, paper ran down from bad to worse, so that at one time the gold dollar was worth $2.80 in paper, and three years treasury notes were sold bearing $7.30 interest per annum, it being fixed at this rate for the convenience of computing at exactly two cents per day for the three hundred and sixty-five days of the

[1] Compare Mr. Chase's changed views, when in the case of Hepburn *v.* Griswold, 8 Wallace's U. S. Reports, p. 603, in 1870, as chief justice of the United States, he declared all the legal tender legislation not only unconstitutional, but also economically and practically a mistake. — ED.

[2] Mr. Gray's daughter writes of one of these trips to Washington : "Those days, with all the pressing questions about the financial policy of the government, are as clear and vivid in my mind to-day as they were then, and I always associate your father and mine in the remembrance. I went with them both to Washington once, in the time before sleeping-cars were invented, and I remember how they talked all night and I listened, sitting up in a common car all the way. It took us twenty-four hours to get to Washington then, I believe."

year, which was a certain help towards making it a popular loan, as the $7.30 formed a very simple savings bank for any body who could save up a hundred dollars."

Mr. Fessenden was then chairman of the Ways and Means Committee of the Senate, and to him my father wrote in a tone which shows his extreme uneasiness at the turn affairs were taking : —

J. M. FORBES TO WILLIAM P. FESSENDEN.

New York, January 13, 1862.

My dear Sir, — I see that the financial question is pressing, and before I turn my face eastward I cannot help repeating some of the suggestions which I have already made, the soundness of which is chiefly the discussion here, where so many are opposed to them.

1st. Taxation for interest and current ordinary expenses; on this all agree now, but many will oppose if you once get into the "irredeemable gulf."

2d. Your main reliance for carrying on the government must be upon selling your long bonds at the best prices they will bring after a fixed policy has been announced, and of course using proper judgment as to the time and manner of bringing them forward.

3d. Avail of short loans, exchequer bills, or emission of small notes for currency, under the advice of experts in whichever manner or form promises to give greatest relief temporarily; but it will be a fatal error to rely upon it as your chief dependence. It is limited in amount and liable to great mischief the moment it is pushed beyond a certain and very moderate amount.

4th. Make this currency, or short paper, or demand paper, in whatever shape you put it, as good as possible by providing for its being received by government for all dues, by fixing a mode of its redemption, and by making it fundable at a good rate of interest. Raise it all you can, so as to make it good, and cause it to be received by all classes voluntarily in payment of debts already existing, but avoid making it a legal tender unless you want to see it depreciate. To make it a legal tender will be to give notice to capitalists to get their capital out of the country as fast as possible, and to foreign capitalists to keep from sending money here, and to sacrifice what available stocks they have, government included, as early as possible before the depreciation has got very bad.

5th. Finally, avoid pledging anything but the faith of the government for your debt.

It will be urged to pledge your revenues, or certain specified parts of them. If this pledge covers all your issues, past, present, and future, it amounts to nothing. If confined to the present debt and to certain specified loans it will be urged upon you by those who hold the present loan and wish it secured, and who wish to see the war ended, even at the cost of disunion or submission, whenever the loan now authorized is expended.

If our policy is to be war until we succeed, whether it cost us five hundred millions or five thousand millions (about England's debt), let us have no pledge of our revenue. Even if the loan was sure to be limited, it would be unworthy the dignity of government to pawn our revenue for it, like a Mexican or South American state, and would defeat its object if that object really was to raise the public credit.

We are rich and strong, and it only requires strong action and wise measures of finance at this crisis to carry us through.

Most respectfully and truly yours,

J. M. FORBES.

I fear the interest of the banks in keeping up for a little while the price of the long bonds (1881) may influence them to other and temporary expedients. If you follow their advice you will soon see them slipping out of their long bonds at the best prices they can get.

If one doubted about the true policy, the opposition to it of the "Herald," the organ of the seceders, should turn the scales. It goes for irredeemable currency and for short expedients. It wants to see the war short — and disgraceful! J. M. F.

J. M. FORBES TO WILLIAM P. FESSENDEN.

WILLARD'S HOTEL, WASHINGTON,
February 13, 1862.

Mr. Gray has gone home not very well and rather discouraged. I gave him your message. . . .

Suppose the stain of bad faith hurts the eight hundred and fifty millions of bonds five per cent. by discrediting it at home, and keeping out of our reach the great reservoirs of European capital (which in my opinion is a very small estimate of the pecuniary damage), the nation loses by the operation five per cent. on eight hundred and fifty millions, say $42,500,000.

But this low and mean view of the case only discloses a small part of its mischief. We shall have the stain and irritation of repudiation of the many millions due to foreigners which we promised in specie and are to pay in paper, and if we are not successful during the few weeks for which time we purchase ease by this expedient, we may in consequence of it find such obstacles to our next financial move (beyond the one hundred and fifty millions) that the legal tender clause may terminate the war, a consummation which some of the bankers and others advocating it will not weep for!

I must say I shall consider it our financial Bull Run.

With our strong constitution we may get over this astounding quackery, but it is a trial I hope we may be spared.

On the other hand with Napoleon holding back from interference, with England reacting in our favor, with the navy pushing the war into the interior, and with Stanton waking up the army, and putting out a declaration of Independence of the Satanic Press, it only needs good Anglo-Saxon pluck in this the very pinch of the game of finance, to put us on firm ground.

The Senate bill, with the legal tender struck out, and with a good tax bill, will do this as surely as there is a sun in heaven.

I hope to get off this afternoon, having done my best against the monsters.

I have given almost at full length my father's financial arguments, addressed to Mr. Fessenden, against "paper money;" and so I confine the following extracts from letters to the editor of the New York "Evening Post," to an argument in favor of adhering to a sound currency, not urged in his letters to the chairman of the Finance Committee in the Senate. Of Senator Fessenden in this capacity, Mr. Sumner said that he was, in the region of finance, what our best generals were in the field.

J. M. FORBES TO WILLIAM CULLEN BRYANT.

BOSTON, *January* 22, 1862.

. . . I have not seen set forth so distinctly as it deserves the point that while speculators, and gamblers, and indeed shrewd men in active business can take care of themselves, no matter how vicious the currency tinkering may be, it is the women and minors, the helpless and the poor generally, upon whom a vicious currency and its consequences are sure to fall hardest. The savings banks represent the accumulations of the poor, and the effect on them ought to be strongly painted;

but in point of fact the savings in the hands of the people are larger than those in the banks, and these belong to a still poorer class, who do not accumulate enough to make deposits, or who have not the habits of thrift of the savings bank depositors. Upon this poorer class the loss is going to be still sharper. . . .

THE SAME TO THE SAME.

BOSTON, *January* 27, 1862.

I have your note. I knew you always as the champion of sound finance. Your article sets forth the effect on the poor; others have been solely looking to its injury to the rich. . . . In great haste, yours truly.

I find my father, during this winter of 1861–62, with more irons in the fire than one would have thought it possible for any one man to keep there; again stirring up his friend Mr. Sedgwick (who was now on a naval investigation committee of Congress) to check the corruption and abuses of the navy yards; applauding Stanton for his Declaration of Independence of the Satanic Press; and still urging the throwing out of the Legal Tender bill. But as to this it is clear he begins to see that the inflationists are getting their own way, for he says in a letter to Mr. Bryant : —

" I am glad to see the bill still hangs, but suppose it will go. The interest in coin, and above all the removal of the restriction as to selling bonds at par, will, if insisted on, do much to modify it, but, after all, it will be like a merchant suspending payment in a panic, and behaving decently thereafter. His assets will be depreciated, and his credit suffer, but after a while he may by prudence recover position."

There is also a letter from him to Mr. Fessenden, discussing different ways of raising revenue, of which I quote a part : —

" There seems much force in the suggestion made in a communication to the ' Evening Post ' of January 21, that an income tax, being a 'direct tax,' can, under the Constitution, only be levied upon the citizens of each State in proportion to the basis of representation, and consequently will amount to very little. Indeed, if this legal objection be sound, the tax becomes impracticable.[1]

" But we must reach the rich, and especially that large class who hoard more of their income than they spend, for they do not pay anything near their share of indirect taxes upon importations or excise. We cannot reach them through their tobacco or whiskey or wines, or broadcloth or silks. A stamp tax is one obvious mode of reaching them. Every receipt they give for their semi-annual interest, or for the principal when paid them, may thus be taxed. Every fire or marine policy ; every rent bill they render or

---

[1] An income tax law was passed, however, at this time and in 1864 ; and its constitutionality was upheld in the case of Springer v. U. S., 102 U. S. Rep. 586, in 1880. But afterwards, in 1895, the Supreme Court of the United States reversed its former decisions, and laid down the doctrine which is here referred to by Mr. Forbes. — ED.

lease they grant, or contract for sale or lease of property; every settlement in probate; every investment they have in railways or canals may be thus taxed through the sources of income.

"Even if there were no doubt as to the income tax being a direct tax, and thus objectionable, the arguments would be very strong for tapping the sources of income rather than the income itself. For there are a thousand ways in which income, once in the hands of individuals, will evade taxation. We must therefore seize it in the hands of corporations if possible, before it reaches the individual."

Another to the same correspondent opposes vehemently the agitation which had sprung up under the irritation caused by the Mason and Slidell incident, for prohibiting the export of specie, a proposal which he characterizes as "suicidal and barbarous," and "worthy of the political economy of old Spain or her colonies."

These and many other letters of great interest in their day I have been prevented from giving at length for lack of space, or have omitted altogether, and I only give the following, to the New York "Evening Post," because it is so short, and shows so clearly the deadly earnestness with which my father was helping to fight what he now felt to be a life or death battle for the Union: —

WHAT HAS BECOME OF THE CONVICTED SLAVE CAPTAIN ? [1]

Is he, like the rattlesnake in camp, and the crowd of detected spies in Washington, to have the oath put to him, and to be released ? [2] or to be sentenced to imprisonment till sympathizing political friends ask his pardon ? The great want of the hour is to see one spy — the higher his social position the better — hanged, and thus begin to protect the lives of our soldiers from these secret enemies. But if this wish of the nation must not be gratified, can not we at least hang one of the pirates who have sacrificed such hecatombs of Africans ? and thus hint to the civilized world that there has been a change of administration since slavers were protected, England bullied, and Cuba plotted against in the interest of slaveholders !

The English government may continue to ignore

[1] Captain N. P. Gordon, of the slaver Erie. He was afterwards executed at New York, in February, 1862. (4 *Reb. Record*, Diary, 37.) Knowing the President's tenderness of heart, and believing it very important to make an example of this criminal, my father visited Washington with Henry Ward Beecher and Dr. Bellows, to urge upon Mr. Lincoln the course which was finally taken. — ED.

[2] The reference is to a story of the period which has recently been given in the newspapers in the following form : —

"There had been a good deal of bushwhacking along the Virginia border, and it was thought that some of this was done by men who professed to be loyal. The Union troops naturally felt rather sore about it. On one occasion a private soldier called out : 'Sergeant, I have caught a copperhead, a real snake this time ; what shall I do with him ?' 'Oh,' said the sergeant, 'd—n it, I suppose the only thing you can do is to swear him and let him go.'"

this change, and to visit upon us the sins of our Southern rulers, as they have heretofore done; but we might as well begin to enlighten their people, if in earnest. JUSTICE.

The next five letters speak for themselves, and with sufficient vigor, on the topics of the hour: —

J. M. FORBES TO W. H. ASPINWALL.

BOSTON, *January* 21, 1862.

MY DEAR MR. ASPINWALL, — Some of our infernally weak-backed bank men as soon as they had got back here went to overturning all the work they had done (under Gray's inspiration) in Washington, telegraphing in favor of the hundred millions legal tender. Many of the House committee were in favor of it before, Chase only half fixed in its favor, the horde of contractors, speculators, and debtors, headed by your Satanic "Herald," pressed for it. It is my conviction that the Senate committee is the chief safeguard against its being passed, and they cannot stand alone. You must back them up by private letters and public opinion! Here our bankers are troubled by the demand notes, and, not content with having them made practically good by their restriction, want them made a legal tender under the delusion that this will make them better! Once abandon the sound principle, and the pressure will soon sink the restriction.

Cannot you rally the "Evening Post" and some other sound papers and get them to stand by their guns? I still wish you and Mr. Minturn and Green felt like going to Washington. It looks as if all our labor is likely to be thrown away unless some more is put in.

Truly yours in haste, J. M. FORBES.

BOSTON, *January* 24, 1862.

. . . Barren proclamations to those beyond our reach will just now hurt Kentucky and the Northern harmony more than it will help the cause; treating slaves well that we do reach is the best preparation, and best proclamation to others. I saw in New York one of the blacks (yellow), [who was] carried off and sold from the Star of the West when captured. He said the slaves knew in the most distant plantations how we used those who came to us, and that much stress was laid upon the return by our soldiers of a few fugitives! He says intelligence runs fast through the plantations, and he thinks a proclamation of freedom, following up well-attested good faith to those who had come in, would have great effect. In the same "Post" you will find an editorial upon the sinews of war: containing much good financial doctrine.

We were just going over the dam into an irredeemable currency about a week ago, when a few of us made a rally for the doctrines of that editorial! and we saved it for the time, brought Chase over half way, where he would by the logic of events have been soon forced to come all right, but the horde of debtors, and gamblers, and fools, with the " Herald " at their head, are at it again, and the result is still doubtful. With such leaders, what but a sturdy Anglo-Saxon people, or a miracle-dealing God, can save us from destruction! If we survive the military and diplomatic and financial blunders, it will be because we are the strongest people and have the strongest government on the face of the earth!

I was in New York last week seeing Will off to the war, — to Beaufort with his regiment, the First Massachusetts Cavalry; a hard trial for his mother — but we must do our share, and if he goes to the Spirit Land, we may not be long behind. . . .

J. M. FORBES TO JOHN H. CLIFFORD.[1]

NEW YORK CARS, January 27, 1862.

MY DEAR CLIFFORD, — I am going on to Washington by " telegraph," and may stay a few days. You once gave me a line to Secretary Stanton, but I could not find him, after several calls, he being in court. I wish you would give me such a letter to him as will convince him that I do not come on to steal anything from Uncle Sam. In fact my object is quite the reverse — viz. : to help fight the " legal tender " mongrel, a cross between a folly and a fraud! I may also want to talk coast defense with him.

I have a line to him from the governor, but I also want one from you, to let him know I am no self-seeker, nor office-seeker, nor politician!

____

[1] Formerly governor of Massachusetts, and a leading member of the bar in that State. — ED.

Thanks to your suggestions, I gave the joint Committee on Federal Relations a good screed of doctrine, and now hope they will act promptly.

Very truly yours, J. M. FORBES.

J. M. FORBES TO GEORGE RIPLEY, OF THE NEW YORK TRIBUNE.

BOSTON, *February* 17, 1862.

MY DEAR SIR, — I address you not for publication, but in the hope of influencing the " Tribune " for the good which I know you and it aim at.

I regret your continued onslaughts upon Gideon Welles. If they succeed, you will be sure to have some wretched political hunker in his place, and to drive out Fox, the best executive secretary of the navy we ever had; better where he is than if head secretary, with politics too to manage!

As to the M. matter I can speak from knowledge and experience. I was employed in Boston, as he was in New York, minus the commissions. I corresponded and conferred with him; I know the difficulties he had to encounter, by experience. I say, after full reflection, that his work was, without being perfect, the best done of any that the government have yet done, always excepting Stanton's slaying of the Satanic! As compared with buying through a naval officer, I have no sort of question that M. saved five or ten times his commission. There is no sort of question, either, that the commission was too high, and that Gideon blundered! and that M. deserves some scorching for not disgorging the surplus or the whole ; but still, as a whole, the thing which might have been better done was well done : to blame it too severely is a premium upon routine.

Had Welles spent twenty-five per cent., or about a million, more, through the regular channels, he would have been all right. Take care, or you will drive him out on this issue, and have harpies and do-nothings in the place of an honest old man and of efficient Fox.

Fox was too good for the old navy, and was successfully transferred to the head of a large manufacturing company. He projected the reinforcement of Sumter when it could have been done, in the winter, undertook it when desperate, in April, and thus precipitated the glorious rising. He put younger men at the head of our expeditions, which have saved the country, and will save it if salvation be possible. He has the old-fogyism of the navy to fight, and yet has done much where *more* remains to do. Let him not have to fight the fire in the rear, of the head of the liberal party, the " Tribune."

Pray note : I don't say M.'s work was perfect, nor he blameless of greed, but that you may lead to a worse evil by pushing Welles further !

Truly yours,   J. M. Forbes.

I pray you not to embalm my name in print.

BOSTON, *February* 27, 1862.

MY DEAR SIR, — I think you are wrong in opposing the new order of Stanton as to telegrams. I have had much experience with the telegraph as a business engine, and I know what it must be in war. The weakest and most discouraging point in our war management up to this time has been the looseness with which the telegraph has been left open : and Stanton's move to control it seems to me one of the best things he has done. I only hope he will have a sharp censor or superintendent, and do the thing thoroughly. I urged this measure very strongly in the spring, and was disgusted at the apathy of the higher powers. For with Baltimore and Washington and the public offices ever full of traitors, the free use of the telegraph seemed to me to put Washington in the power of the enemy.

The telegraph is a mighty *engine of war*, and, if used up to its capacity, is enough to turn the scale.

Upon our single track railroads we find that the erection of a telegraph is worth to us more than a double track would be without the wires. It increases the availability of our engines, cars, and men enormously, besides the value for safety. I mention this as an illustration of what good it may do to the army if put under sharp systematic management; and beyond all, how dangerous, if the enemy are permitted to share its use and our secrets!

Very truly yours, J. M. FORBES.

CHAPTER XII

WORK and anxiety had to be lived through by
all good citizens during that winter (1861–62)
while the gigantic machine, which afterwards was
surely and steadily to grind up the "peculiar institution," and prepare the way for what became
really, and not only nominally, the United States,
was still in course of making and getting into gear.
None could have worked harder or been more anxious than the subject of this memoir. The navy
continued to ask his help; and how much was asked
of him, and left to his judgment, may be seen from
such a letter as the following:—

GIDEON WELLES TO J. M. FORBES.

NAVY DEPARTMENT, 20 *January,* 1862.

SIR,—It is understood that one of the iron boats
built to run to New Orleans is ready for sea at Boston. You are requested and authorized to charter
this vessel on the most favorable terms, for three
months or more, to go in pursuit of the pirate
Sumter. Before closing the arrangement, however,
telegraph the department the price of charter.

The government will furnish a lieutenant commanding and three acting masters, guns and ammunition, — all else to be provided by the owners. You can authorize such preparations to the vessel as are necessary without sending her to the navy yard.

You may suggest to the department a proper person for the command and three others for acting masters. The commander can probably obtain a good crew from volunteers. Let the owners take all but the war risks, and have a favorable proviso to enable government to take the vessel at any time.

Answer by telegraph.

When will the other boat be ready?

I am, respectfully, your obedient servant,

GIDEON WELLES.

A succession of such calls could not fail to tell: my father was now nearly fifty, and it is not to be wondered at that his chronic enemy, which would have killed a weaker man before he arrived at middle age, should have taken advantage of its opportunity. Accordingly I find him writing in his notes: "As the winter dragged on I was attacked by a bad cough, and ordered to go South for a milder climate." By this time my brother was with his regiment, the First Massachusetts Cavalry, stationed at Beaufort, South Carolina, which had been occupied by Federal troops since the Hilton Head forts, commanding the mouth of its river, had yielded to the guns of the fleet. The relations between

father and son were peculiarly intimate, each heartily
enjoying the other's society; "as glad to meet
as if they were lovers," one who knew them well
has said. To Beaufort, therefore, the father now
went, in search of the prescribed " milder climate,"
making the voyage on the paddle-wheel transport
Atlantic, then commanded by his friend, Captain
Eldridge. The letter which follows was addressed
to his wife : —

STEAMER ATLANTIC, 4th March, 1862.

There is nothing like beginning a journal early,
so I take it up where Alice will have left me, on my
way to the ship. Cousin Sim[1] would n't hear of my
plan of ordering a carriage for me and my baggage,
but would have a wagon for the trunks, and drive
me down. So I dispatched all my things, bag included, to wait for me at the Atlantic, and followed
soon after. Arrived there, all was bustle and confusion, but our wagon was missing ! — gone probably
to some other Atlantic at some other Canal Street,
existing in the driver's fertile brain! Mr. Cary, and
William, and Sim, and little Johnny, and William
Russell all started in different directions, while I kept
guard in the drizzling northeaster for the wagon.
Baggage and miscellaneous heaps of things gradually disappeared into the maw of the monster ship,
whose wheels were turning and churning up the
water as if impatient for a start. Frantic women,
unprotected females, appealed to the captain and to
Mr. E. L. Pierce to let them go and teach young

---

[1] His cousin, Paul Sieman Forbes, of New York.

nigs ; others in despair about their traps, some tear-
ful at parting, the collector busy as a bee swearing
in the passengers. Finally he bundled up his papers, the wharf was emptied, and the ship full. The
captain mounted the paddle-box, and still my precious trunks came not. I determined to leave them
and trust to the captain and Mr. Heard for clothes,
— yet lingered on the ladder to the last. Imagine
my " phelinks " at the idea of not having even a
tooth-brush! and at the vision of what Mary's cake
would be when turned out of my trunk a fortnight
hence ! At last back came Mr. Cary with the wag-
oner in his clutches, who protested that he brought
all and that it had gone on board, deep, alas, into
that bottomless pit of a baggage hole, now full to
the top. Thankful even for this forlorn hope, I
bade our friends good-by, and took refuge in the
cabin, where Mr. Heard's things were snugly stored
in our little state-room ! I leave you to think of
the anathemas uttered against cousin Sim, against
the whole race of wagoners, and above all against
my own feeble-minded self for trusting any of them!

Once fairly started I seized the head porter and
insisted on having my trunks, if the whole had to be
turned out of their stowage ; then by going down
myself I luckily managed to get my *sea* things, and
so that adventure ended in comedy !

Our passengers consist chiefly of the " villain-
tropic " society, as dear little Sarah's friend, the
housekeeper in Miss Edgeworth's " False Keys,"
would call it ; bearded and mustached and odd-

looking men, with odder-looking women. . . . You
would have doubted whether it was the adjourn-
ment of a John Brown meeting or the fag end of
a broken-down phalanstery! Among others Mr.
Mack (Stillman's father-in-law, who says he knew
and liked William H.), Ned Hooper and young
Phillips of Will's class, and Fred Eustis and son;
an officer stationed at Beaufort, Captain Eliot, son
of the oculist, introduced to me by or through the
Shaws, Tim Walker's sister, whom I have not yet
seen; William Bacon and young Brooks, a scattering naval officer or two, and the usual *quantum
suff.* of nondescripts and nonentities, valued doubtless by somebody, but offering no salient points to
fix the eye.

We made a grand show at dinner, — a terrible
waste of good things for most of them, and then
plunged into the fog and drizzle of a dirty northeaster, which doubtless visited you in snow, and
gave you some twinges at having let me go! Tea
and cards in the evening. Mr. Heard seasick, and
only a few of us haunting the long dining-room.
A fair night's sleep, variegated with sore throat
and some coughing, and then a bright morning
with a westerly gale blowing. Passengers very
scattering. We had an alarm of a countess, but
neither captain nor purser know of her, so it is
doubtless a mistake, unless, like a wolf in sheep's
clothing she had smuggled herself into Mr. Pierce's
troop of fifty! I should not forget to tell you
of Whist, who was consigned to a porter, nor of

Billy,[1] the occupant of a box such as you saw horses hoisted in. As he was much exposed to wind I luckily found an old sail belonging to the little boat Mr. Cary sent on board for me, and went and got one end of his box tented in. The top was already covered, so he seemed pretty well provided for, although the blanket Luther got for him looked mighty thin and cottony!

This morning after breakfast I was forward by the pilot-house, watching the old ship pitch into the sea and the gulls following, and the bright sky and blue and white waves, when an unlucky billow took us at the wrong time, like a boxer hitting his adversary when down, and instantly the whole deck below, nine feet down, was full of water; and even where I stood it came ankle deep, and even found its way, a *little* of it, down my back as I clutched at a rope and turned to avoid it! The next moment I looked down upon poor Billy. His box had been lifted bodily, turned around, and the iron anchor stock driven through it! Billy had plunged forward and got his fore feet outside, and was struggling violently among the flukes of the anchor to keep his footing, and then, with the intelligence of a pony, tried to get back into his box from the slippery deck, — his box, now shared with the anchor stock and generally knocked into a cocked hat! They got him out with whole legs, and he is now standing, or trying to stand, on the deck, while the

---

[1] A little Naushon island horse, taken down as a charger for Lieutenant W. H. F. Whist was a setter. — ED.

carpenter is mending his box. It was for a time a bad sight, and, the water being still surging about below, I could not without thorough ducking help him, except by advice and consolation offered through the singing of the gale !

So I have brought you up to the present time. Alice can well finish the picture, if she remembers our old seat near the captain's end of the table, where I am sitting, with my feet on the warm steam pipe under the table and my outer man guarded by a coat stolen from Mr. Heard to replace my wet one, — the spray still dashing against the saloon square windows, but the sea going down ; and now we are sure of good weather for the rest of our trip.

Four P. M. Thursday, March 6, 1862. I left you day before yesterday, well posted up to that time. We had just begun to feel comfortable when another gale sprang up, worse than the first and right ahead, — lasting all day yesterday and up to this morning, when it was again smooth and sunny ; but we had lost our chance of reaching Port Royal in time for high tide on the bar. At noon we passed Fort Sumter and Charleston spires in the distance, and were boarded by one of the blockaders for news. It is now blowing half a gale again, and we have got to lie off the bar all night, and until noon to-morrow, making a four days' passage. Yesterday I had nothing to tell except of headache, etc., which made me too miserable to read or write. To-day I am about well again, under the more genial air, though still coughing.

We expect to be boarded in about an hour by the pilot-boat, which will take the mail ashore, and I make up my package for the chance of its finding a vessel ready there to go homeward. I should go ashore myself, but that I should there be all adrift, and might be exposed to catching cold; so with my usual prudence I hold on. . . .

To-morrow night I hope to see Will; and now with lots of love to the children and to all who love me, I am as ever,

Yours,   J. M. F.

P. S. — Tell Mack, Billy looks all right after his adventures, though rather sleepy! Whist, too, is bright. Mr. Heard, as I see more of him, seems very feeble. I hope the yacht will get down, so that I may make him comfortable. This rough weather looks rather formidable for her, but she may hit upon a smooth time.

On arriving off Hilton Head my father took to a river steamer, and, on her grounding on an oyster bank, to the little sailboat brought with him, and after some small adventures arrived at Beaufort at midnight, " in the sharp stage of an attack of bronchitis, not improved by the Southern night air of the swampy river, and barking like a very hoarse dog." But he adds, " We got passed through the lines, and knocked up Lieutenant W. H. F. out of his sound warm nap, and soon were rejoicing in a cup of hot coffee; and before long I was resting my weary bones on his bed. He had no more idea of seeing me when my voice awoke him than of meeting the angel Gabriel."

My father enjoyed his first reveillé and all the camp experience which followed. Beaufort was on high ground overlooking the river. Before the war it had been the Newport of South Carolina, and when the Hilton Head forts were threatened by the Federal fleet its inhabitants had gone down the river in boats to see it pounded and driven off; and when, instead of this, the Union flag had promptly gone up on the fort, they had lost no time in getting off from Beaufort, leaving their houses just as they stood, a great convenience for the incoming tenants. These tenants in the first instance were the soldiers, and through the military commandant my father at once found a house which quite answered his purpose. But military rule was now to be qualified by that of the commissioners who had come down on the Atlantic, authorized to claim all abandoned property on government account; and these, consequently, became in the eyes of the army and their hangers-on " the most unpopular set of Christians ever seen." They were nicknamed " Gideonites " by the military.

Apropos of this feeling, my father, in the interest of fair play, had to write in the following month to Mr. Sumner in Washington : —

" The undercurrent against the commission here is very strong, even among those who ought to know better. First, the cotton agents think their interests, and their personal use of negroes, horses, and houses, hurt thereby; then the sutlers, and finally the military, are all prejudiced, especially the subordinates; the lower you go the worse the feeling, the generals and those high up doing, I believe, all they can, and showing, so far as I can judge, a good spirit. . . .

" I don't believe in having two sets of treasury agents here with equal and sometimes conflicting powers, but suppose this has been made so apparent that Mr. Chase must have stopped it ere this, and put Mr. Pierce distinctly above the cotton agents. . . . He is here with enemies all around, and in his own association weak brothers and sisters, — his only friend being the general commanding; and if you hear criticisms you must, and of course would, always make allowances.

" I think, so far as I can judge, the experiment must be practically a success; not equal to the expectations of sanguine friends, but making a good beginning, giving most valuable data for other quarters and doing great positive good to the blacks here, and to the confidence of good men in our power to make the blacks useful."

As a matter of fact, the commission did turn out a practical success and a "positive good to the blacks;" as any one can learn who will pay a visit to their descendants on the Sea Islands at the present day. In the same letter to Mr. Sumner, my father returns to the negro question as it then stood, and adds : —

" There is one thing that I would especially urge

upon you and your (our) more extreme Republicans: while struggling for the whole, why neglect to secure half a loaf when you can get it?

"In the present stage of the negro question, you cannot for months to come get the emancipation of all rebel slaves. . . . Meantime, cannot you get an almost unanimous recognition by Congress of the principle that any slave once employed to work for the government (by spade, or hoe, or mattock, no matter which) shall from that moment be free, with his family, — providing compensation for loyal masters?

"If you can do this, clinch it by a registration of slaves called into the government service, which shall hereafter constitute their free papers. Then let all those Sea Islanders now working under government orders be so registered.

"If you get general emancipation, this will be unnecessary; but if, under either success or disaster, some wretched compromise is made, you may hereafter, without it, have a hard struggle to prevent these freemen here being given back to their rebel masters, with thousands of others who have dug our trenches, or otherwise struck a blow for the Union!

"Do not despise the small things within reach while aiming at the large ones you may miss."

Meanwhile my father and his guests, Messrs. Heard, Bacon, and Brooks, had been enjoying themselves much in the company of his son William and his fellow officers. At first they had to draw supplies through the sutlers, but a few days later my father was wakened early in the morning by his "plucky and trusty Captain Smith," who had brought the little Azalea down from Naushon, with a crew of three, in five days; after which there was plenty in the land, and there were yachting excursions to Hilton Head and rides along the sands there on the chargers of his friend, Major Henry Higginson, who was quartered there. The mails, too, always one of his first considerations, could now be brought up the river promptly, and altogether the Azalea was a great comfort. During one of his trips to Hilton Head, he made the acquaintance of the mulatto, Robert Smalls, on board the little Planter, which he had run out of Charleston under the guns of Fort Sumter, and was now apparently running on his own account. At that time he was slight and wide-awake, — afterwards to become, in carpet-bag times, a very different personage.

Early in April came the time when his friends, Messrs. Heard and Bacon, had to turn their faces homeward. What was done then by a man still "coughing like a dog barking" my father confesses without contrition in his notes : —

"I took them over to Hilton Head to embark, and a fit of homesickness coming over me I just stepped on board the Atlantic, with my hand bag and coat, and ran back home, leaving the Azalea to do transport service for General Hunter, and a line to W. H. F. to give notice of my intentions. We reached home in very cold weather, and the doctor at once pronounced me insane to come North, and ordered me back by the return trip of the Atlantic; and my wife, in spite of her seasickness and the cares of the family, determined to go with me. Luckily we had a very smooth passage down, and she really suffered less than I have seen her do in going from New Bedford to Naushon against a southwest breeze. We stopped in at Fortress Monroe to get some ordnance stores. Our visit there was at the great crisis when McClellan's army was collecting for its movement on Richmond, and already 100,000 soldiers were around Fortress Monroe. It was a gay spectacle. Just before this, the great sea-fight between the Merrimac and the Monitor had occurred, and the little Monitor lay there with steam up, expecting hourly to see the great Merrimac come out from Norfolk (fifteen miles distant) to renew the attack on our fleet. Our friend, Admiral Goldsborough, was then in command of the fleet, and the ships which had suffered (without being sunk) in the late battle had not yet repaired damages. I was too ill to go about, but Goldsborough came to see me, and my wife visited some of the vessels. After a few very exciting hours at Fortress Monroe, we put out to sea and reached Hilton Head and Beaufort without adventure. I had given up my house on leaving, so when we reached Beaufort, Dr. De Wolf, the assistant surgeon of the First Cavalry, took us into his hospital, giving us his room for a night; and the next day, armed with an order from General Stevens, I managed to get on horseback, and with Will's servant went in search of other quarters. After examining all the most prominent vacant houses within the lines, we pitched upon a very nice one outside the camp, at the extreme point where the river branches, or two rivers meet. This, though now dismantled, had the advantage of a veranda, garden, and, best of all, a water tank, shaded by some fine live oaks; and was only inhabited by some of the "Gideonites," who promised at once to make way for us. A messenger was sent out for some negro woman to sweep and scrub the floors, and my shawl, laid over a board for a sofa, made me a temporary bed; for the short ride had exhausted my strength. After the work had gone on some time I received a very unexpected visit from the captain of a revenue cutter, who came in with a companion, and told me he was sorry I had taken so much trouble about cleaning up the house, as he had "just determined to take it for his own use." He had an air of authority, a good many brass buttons, some gilt braid, and seemed to think he had settled the whole matter; he kindly promised to pay for the work done, and even criticised the brick andirons, which he told his friends would be replaced by some better brass ones. I was rather angry and very tired, and listened till my patience gave out, when I told him that he must leave the room, as I was not well; and when he brought me an order from General Stevens countermanding the one I had, he should have the house, and not till

then.   Our friend, Tom Motley,[1] had come in while
the fine gentleman was making his remarks, and I
just asked him to take my horse, which stood saddled
in the yard, and go to headquarters. My naval
friend had hardly gone, when Tom returned with a
message from General Stevens to the effect that the
house was mine, and that if anybody interfered with
me he would send a corporal's guard to protect me;
and here ended this little skirmish.

"By dinner-time my wife came round, and with
a trunk for a table we made our first meal and got
to housekeeping; some of the officers sent us pieces
of furniture which they had "borrowed" from
former owners, and we were soon reasonably comfortable."

With the little Azalea close by, they felt quite at
home, and, with the exception of one scare of a
raid, spent a quiet and happy time watching the
negroes, young and old, busy over their spelling-
books, "getting education;" making excursions in
a rickety wagon, one day picnicking with their son
while he was on picket duty, and another listening
to the twenty-miles-off bombardment of Fort Pulaski,
and finally, just before leaving for home on the 14th
of May, enjoying the delicious blackberries which
the colored folk had begun to bring in heaping
baskets on their heads. Looking back upon this
time in 1886, my father writes: —

"My two visits to Beaufort seem like a dream
with only a few distinct points; the yellow jasmine,

---

[1] Brother of John Lothrop Motley. — ED.

and the other flowers of the woods and gardens, being the most pleasant. Among the comic incidents my exhibition of the Spencer rifle may be worth telling. I had brought with me in the Azalea one of the first specimens of the Spencer six-shooter; had tried it at Naushon, and was confident it would turn out the great success which it afterward proved. Telling Admiral Dupont about it on his ship (perhaps the frigate Wabash) at Hilton Head, he asked me to show it and sent a boat to the Azalea for me. It was about noon, when the 500 men of the ship were being mustered on deck, and all eyes were upon me as I snapped the gun, aiming through an open port. It was the first time the gun had ever missed, but either my nervousness or the devil intervened and it stuck fast; I could not get it off and had to drop it in disgust.

"As a whole our recollections of this trip are very pleasant; we found the climate delightful most of the spring; my cough gradually yielded, and about the middle of May we again embarked on the Atlantic and made our way home."

But before leaving, my father had become quite intimate with General Hunter, who commanded at Hilton Head. He had found him on his first trip "a wonderful specimen of an enlightened army officer who had been converted by secession into an abolitionist." They had long and confidential talks together, and he appears to have sympathized with the general's enlisting colored soldiers "long before Governor Andrew was allowed to do so in Massa-

chusetts," and with his issue of a proclamation of
freedom, in May, 1862, which, however, brought
down on him a rebuke from the President. He was
evidently privy to the following pungent answer of
General Hunter to inquiries made by Secretary
Stanton, in consequence of resolutions introduced
into the House of Representatives hostile to the
emancipation or enlistment of the slaves : —

"Question 1st. Whether I had organized or was
organizing a regiment of 'fugitive slaves' in this
department?

"To the first question I reply, that no regiment
of 'fugitive slaves' has been, or is being, organized
in this department. There is, however, a fine regiment of persons whose late masters are 'fugitive
rebels,' men who everywhere fly before the appearance of the national flag, leaving their servants
behind them to shift as best they can for themselves. So far indeed are the loyal persons composing this regiment from seeking to avoid the presence
of their late owners, that they are now one and all
working with remarkable industry to place themselves in a position to go in full and effective pursuit of their fugacious and traitorous proprietors."

On his return to Boston came a letter from Mr.
Sedgwick : —

C. B. SEDGWICK TO J. M. FORBES.

WASHINGTON, 18 May, 1862.

. . . I hope God will give his servant Abraham
the grace to stand by his general and not let the

border state men sacrifice him. I cannot say, however, that I have the highest degree of faith in a president who thinks it necessary to salvation to allow the enforcement of the Fugitive Slave Law in this District at this time. . . .

My father had been much exercised during both trips to Beaufort by the prejudice against the Educational Commission, and the unfair treatment of them; and immediately on his return home he wrote the following letter to the treasurer of the commission : —

J. M. FORBES TO EDWARD ATKINSON.

BOSTON, *May* 23, 1862.

MY DEAR SIR, — . . . I would gladly do anything, except come before the public, to help your good work. You may use my testimony in any other way than over my signature, and the indorsements of the " Daily "[1] and other journals would seem to answer all purposes. I have watched the Educational Commission from its very inception with the greatest interest, and, while in *Secessia*, had every opportunity to gauge it, not only by the criticisms of its many enemies, and by the statements of its friends, but by personal observation. It was started very late, and when only the most prompt and even hasty measures gave it a chance of success. These measures were taken chiefly at Boston, with that efficiency which marks our good city and State. A large number of

---

[1] The *Boston Daily Advertiser.*

volunteers were hurried from various pursuits, down into South Carolina, where, in about ten days after the enterprise was first thought of, they found themselves landed, with bare floors to sleep upon, soldier's rations to eat, and the obloquy and ridicule of all around them for " sauce piquante."

Under all their inexperience, and all these disadvantages, they have worked their way quietly on, and up to the time when I left, May 14th, when the new rule of military governor was about beginning, they had accomplished the following results.

First and foremost. They had inspired confidence in the blacks by their kindness, and especially by their bringing the first boon which these forlorn creatures had received from us, namely, an opportunity for education. In all else the negroes have been materially worse off than under their old masters, — with only their scanty ration of Indian corn, no shoes, blankets, clothing, molasses, or other necessaries, and no luxuries given them, of which they formerly had a moderate allowance. Against all this they had had only the doubtful advantage of idleness or precarious employment, and the promises of the cotton agents. It was a great point to put over them intelligent and Christian teachers, and this they have fully appreciated.

Second. The material benefits which have resulted, namely: beginning very late, the forces of the plantation have been organized to reasonably steady labor; a full crop of food has been planted in common, besides many much larger private, or, as these are called, " Negro Grounds," planted than ever before. I saw repeatedly whole gangs who had finished their plantation work by ten A. M., and had all the rest of the day for their own patches, some of which are four or five times as large as usual.

Third. In addition to the food crop, enough cotton land has been planted to give the negroes, if they are allowed to take care of the crop and enjoy its fruits, more of the necessaries and indeed comforts of life than they have ever had before.

To sum up, we have then for some of the results,

The confidence of the blacks;

The education, so far as it goes;

The encouragement of industry; and

The material advantage of food and cotton crops;

instead of leaving the negroes alone to run into vice and pauperism, or turning them over to the tender mercies of hard speculators.

Of course, the agents of the commission have made mistakes in some cases, and some of them have been ill chosen, and have helped the enemies of the enterprise to bring it into local discredit; but generally the whole has been a most successful undertaking, and most of those sent from this quarter have, by their patience, faithfulness, and disinterested zeal, been a credit to Massachusetts. They, as a whole, form a noble band of men and women. They have had everything to contend with, especially the opposition of many with whose

interests they interfered, and of others whose prejudices they offended. Their predécessors on the
plantations, the cotton agents and military, had
begun to look upon themselves as the successors to
the planters, entitled to the use of all that was left,
houses, horses, negroes, crops.

When the agents of the commission came down
to take charge of the plantations, they were looked
upon as interlopers, and in most cases every obstacle,
short of absolute disobedience to the orders of the
commanding general, was thrown in their way. All
the little mistakes of the new-comers were magnified;
all the good they did ignored, and a local public
opinion thus created against them, which many of
our own soldiers, who ought to have known better,
gave in to. "What a ridiculous thing for these
philanthropists to come down and teach the stupid
negroes, and occupy the plantations, and use the
secesh ponies which had been so convenient for our
pickets !"

Such was the natural feeling of the unthinking,
and of some who ought to have reflected. This false
opinion was largely availed of by the " Herald "
and other kindred papers, to create prejudice at the
North against an enterprise aiming to improve the
condition of the blacks. How much more satisfactory to this class would it have been to have had the
negroes left to their own devices, and then given all
the enemies of improvement a chance to say, " We
told you so ! The negroes are worse off than before, — idle, vicious, paupers. The sooner you reduce

them to slavery again, and the more firmly you bind the rest of their race to eternal slavery, the better!"

It would take too long to go into the question of what is to be done hereafter; but there was an emergency three months ago which has, in my opinion, been successfully met; and among other results I believe you will have the testimony of all who have been engaged in the experiment, that it has distinctly proved that the negro has the same selfish element in him which induces other men to labor. Give him only a fair prospect of benefit from his labor, and he will work like other human beings. Doubtless hereafter this selfish element must be appealed to more than it could be by the agents of the commission. There must be less working in common, and more done for the especial benefit of each laborer. It is much to establish the fact that this element of industry exists.

In conclusion, I consider the Educational Commission up to this time a decided success. I congratulate you and your associates upon having added another to the good deeds of Massachusetts, not by any means forgetting the share which New York has had in the good work; and I sincerely hope that General Saxton, coöperating with you, may in a manner worthy of his high reputation complete what has been so well begun.

Very truly yours, J. M. FORBES.

CHAPTER XIII

THE PROSECUTION OF THE WAR

DURING my father's stay at Beaufort, S. C., he had been impressed with the inadequacy of the Union forces stationed on the Sea Islands for any forward movement; and so, soon after his return home, I find him (with the view of averting if possible the consequent trouble) trying to stir up the press on the subject. The following letters show with what eagerness he was using every means of influence within his power, in this and other matters of public welfare : —

TO PARKE GODWIN, EDITOR OF THE NEW YORK "EVENING POST."

BOSTON, June 23, 1862.

MY DEAR SIR, — . . . The " New Bedford Mercury," under its new management, is getting to be quite a live paper. I wish as much could be said for our administration, which seems to be carrying a millstone about its neck in its dread of the border States and of " Hunkerism " generally. I believe to-day that the old Union Democrats, and even the true men of the border States, are ahead of Lincoln upon this question of hitting the rebels hard — with the negro or any other club. It is strange when a rattlesnake is attacking us that we should be so delicate about the stick we hit him with!

I look with much anxiety to our operations in South Carolina. Beauregard's army, on its way from Corinth, passes directly by Charleston. Our force is ridiculously small for attack, the Key West troops included — if they can get there. Our negro brigade amounts to nothing until trained. We need prompt reinforcement there, or we shall have another blow half struck, or possibly a recoil there.

TO CHARLES B. SEDGWICK, WASHINGTON.

June 2, 1862.

MY DEAR MR. SEDGWICK, — I see I forgot the 21stly, as the old parsons used to say, of my sermon; my amen to your emancipation speech.

If you have such a devilish poor set in Congress that they are afraid to pass your bill, for freeing such slaves as come to our aid, you had better give up trying for any emancipation bill until Parson Brownlow, General Rodgers, and other pro-slavery border state men have cultivated the manliness of Congress up to the Tennessee standard! Why, I hear that the border state Unionists everywhere are in advance of Congress, and go for strangling the rebellion through its vitals, not pinching the ends of its toes! Rather than take anything worse than your bill, I would trust to old Abe's being pushed up to the use of the military powers of emancipation. What infernal nonsense is your present law, making freedom the reward of those who serve the enemy, while their masters only promise them hanging and burning if they serve us.

You carry on the war in such a manner that either slaves or other loyal men in the border and rebel States have one plain road to safety open ; namely, to help the rebels.   You reward the slaves with freedom for such help : you offer them no reward, except the chance of being shot by us and hanged by their masters, if they come into our lines ! . . .

Your lame confiscation bill will be no terror to the rebels, but rather an indication of the mildness with which you will treat them hereafter, and the many exceptions you will make if you pass any confiscation acts.

I only wonder with such a policy that any Union men show their heads !   All your efforts seem to be to make rebellion cheap and easy, and loyalty hard and dangerous.

In great haste, I bide yours,

J. M. FORBES.

TO THE SAME.

BOSTON, June 7, 1862.

MY DEAR MR. SEDGWICK, — Cannot you get some ingenuous Hunker . . . to offer a little simple amendment to the emancipation bill that shall provide for the freedom of any slave (and his family) who may serve the United States, a certificate from the military officer cognizant of such service to be his warrant for free papers from any court of record, etc., etc., loyal masters to be compensated — rascals not? Such an amendment, coming from a radical, disorganizing red Republican like C. B. S. of Syracuse, would be of course summarily put down; there must always be a ferocious cat, or royal Bengal tiger rather, under *his* meal! but such an innocent and proper provision would be, I suppose, unanimously adopted if offered by some moderate Republican. Our good friend Horton now would carry it *nem. con.*, unless you radicals, from the mere force of habit, oppose him. . . .

General Hunter hit the nail on the head when he said to me, " I want to find out whether we, as well as the rebels, are fighting chiefly for the preservation of slavery!"

Trebly conservative as I am, I sometimes get so disgusted with the timidity and folly of our moderate Republicans that I should go in and join the Abolitionists if these last were not so arbitrary and illiberal that no man of independence can live in the house with them. Yours,

J. M. F.

TO CHARLES SUMNER, WASHINGTON.

BOSTON, *June* 21, 1862.

MY DEAR MR. SUMNER, — The inclosed is from a Russian who was once, I believe, in the Czar's service. Thinking it possible that you might have a chance to show it to the President, I have had a fair copy made of the substance of it, and inclosed. Please return me the original. I used to think emancipation only another name for murder, fire, and rape, but mature reflection and considerable personal observation have since convinced me that emancipation may, at any time, be declared without disorder; and especially now when we have two white armies in the field to prevent mischief. The Russian, you see, is of this opinion from his experience. We now have, too, for the first and perhaps only time, the power to emancipate, under the emergency of war, without infringing upon the Constitution.

The only question, then, is as to the necessity. Of course we are not to wait until the last deadly necessity comes. We have spent millions upon millions of money and thousands of lives. Shall we wait until the deadly fevers of the South have stript off more thousands, and until our credit begins to totter under the load? I am no philanthropist, but I do want to see the promptest and hardest blows struck. I only ask that the weakest point of the enemy shall be assailed before throwing away more valuable lives.

TO THE SAME.

BOSTON, June 27, 1862.

MY DEAR MR. SUMNER, — The inclosed[1] will explain itself. If you don't object, you may think it worth sending to the "Evening Post," with our

---

[1] A squib in the form of a supposed letter from a business firm to Senator Sumner, referring to the acknowledged acceptance of a bribe by a United States senator, and frankly proposing to bribe Mr. Sumner into obtaining government contracts for them. — ED.

names struck out! I do not see how the Senate can sit with a member who acknowledges such operations, unless a majority of the senators are rotten. Even then I should think the honest ones could stuff it down their throats. If you don't do something, the public verdict will be that you dare not denounce what has been a senatorial custom. . . . Whoever it hits, Republican, Hunker, or pro-slavery Democrat, the knife ought to be applied, and all the sooner because the immediate sinner is a *soi-disant* Republican.

TO C. B. SEDGWICK, WASHINGTON.

BOSTON, *June* 27, 1862.

MY DEAR MR. SEDGWICK, — I have not heard a word from you since I wrote you an abusive letter because you did not go far enough in your bill. I will take it all back if you are offended, and make the most abject apologies! What is the present market price of a senator? S. was rather dear at fifty, but I suppose he was rather high up on the committee!

When are you coming this way, and when will you and Mrs. Sedgwick give us a visit at Naushon? We shall go there some time next month.

I was sorry, but not surprised, to see that we had had a rebuff at Charleston.[1] When I returned from Port Royal, I wrote to Senator Wilson urging reinforcements and predicting disaster if we went

---

[1] Probably referring to a skirmish at Secessionville, S. C., in which the Union forces were defeated.

without them. I don't think now our forces are safe on the Sea Islands, outside the guns of the navy, without reinforcements.

> Very truly yours,   J. M. FORBES.

How beautifully easy you legislators have made money! How valuable your restriction to one hundred millions!

C. B. SEDGWICK TO J. M. FORBES.

WASHINGTON, 29th June, 1862.

MY DEAR MR. FORBES, — Well, by Jove, if this is n't the luckiest escape I ever had! I have been swearing at myself the last fortnight for abusing you like a pickpocket, taking no notice of your friendly letters which by way of penance I have kept on my table where I should see them on coming in or going out, on lying down and rising up, expecting every day to hear that you had denied on 'Change having ever seen me, and now comes your letter offering an apology. Good! make it! it shall be accepted, although your last letter was abusive. The truth is I vowed never to write you until I had settled for you the inclosed account,[1] which you sent me just twenty-seven days ago. They tried to send it back, but I said no, I wanted it paid, and I have only just got it, although it appears to have been made out several days. Please sign it in all the places where you see room for your name and return it to me, and I will hand over the money to the Sanitary, if you still remain charitably inclined.

. . . I showed H. your letter about generals

---

[1] Of expenses incurred on the Ship Commission.

giving certificates to loyal blacks who had served the government, which would serve as manumission deeds to them and their families. It seemed to go through his feathers as a good practical idea, and he has taken the letter home to Ohio to consider of it and sit on it !

I have yet some hopes ; I think the tone of Congress is improving, but very slowly. If Mallory don't succeed in hanging me, as he proposes, I may bring them up to something practical yet.

Grimes is crowding the principle of your suggestion in the Senate and says he shall pass it. There is a scriptural objection, however, to success; it is written that " you may bray an ass in a mortar, she will not be wise." How would firing them out of Porter's mortar answer? After we have been whipped a few times, as we were on James Island, I think our ideas on the subject of natural allies will be improved. Do you see that your friend Fremont has been kicking out of the traces again? I fear J. has been putting him up to this folly. You will have to give him up as one of the impracticables, and go in for some more steady and less mercurial general.

About Naushon ; I should like to swing a hammock under a beech in the forests there about 15th August and sleep for two weeks. I am tired out ; we have pretty much reorganized the whole Navy Department. I have worked hard upon it and am fatigued. After making it all over new, would it not be well enough to give it a new head ? . . .

After being home three or four weeks I want to come down to your kingdom by the sea to rest. I will bring my wife down to talk. Please let me know what time in the last half of August it will be convenient for you to see us.

I am very sorry for that reverse in Charleston. I shall try and make a row about it, but I suppose it will do no good until Richmond is taken. If you find money hard to be got let us know and we will get out another batch of greenbacks. The next bill will make provision for a large government paper-mill, and so we will save all the profits. With kind regards to Mrs. F. and the children.

The following letter to my mother from the doctor of my brother's regiment may serve to indicate how she seconded the efforts of my father, and to show that part of their time at Beaufort must have been spent in finding out the needs of the hospital there. Later on in the war, the Armory Square Hospital in Washington, three wards of which were presided over by our friends Miss Emma Ware, Miss Lowell, and Miss Stone, could have given a similar account of care and thought.

DR. DE WOLF TO MRS. J. M. FORBES.

HILTON HEAD, SOUTH CAROLINA,
July 9, 1862.

MY DEAR MRS. FORBES, — Your box reached us safely this morning. A steamer leaves for New York in two hours, and I make haste to tell you how much I wish that every regiment in the service had a Mrs. Forbes to look after its hospital department.

When the doctors began to look around after the engagement at James Island, they found themselves destitute of a great many things they needed to make their wounded comfortable. The cavalry regiment had more material suited to the occasion than any other five regiments in the expedition. Our chests and boxes were opened wide, and our reputation as always looking out for No. 1 was never less selfishly exhibited. The credit does not belong to us, but more than to any one else, to you. I have written Lieutenant Forbes to-day telling him of the boxes we have received, and begging him to thank you for us. Without seeing it personally one cannot imagine how much the want of such material embarrasses an army on the march or the field. At best, men must suffer a great deal; but without constant attention to the clothing, bedding, and dressing of the sick and wounded, their condition is terrible. At present we have need of nothing. The fifty sheets you have sent us have made our measure full; those we wanted; the rest will be packed away against our time of need. . . .

Of the summer of 1862 my father writes in his notes as follows: —

"In that summer I had the satisfaction of getting up the Committee of a Hundred for promoting the use of the blacks as soldiers, and acted as chairman

of it.   We raised, I think, about $100,000 by sub-
scription among the most conservative Republicans.
The first two Massachusetts regiments of colored
troops were in course of formation (54th and 55th),
in which I was able to do something towards the
choice of the right officers, as well as in raising the
men, Colonel Shaw having the 54th and N. P. Hallowell the 55th."

The actual appeal for funds for raising the colored regiments was not made till February, 1863.

Another enterprise in which he took a great interest is disclosed in the following letters to a prominent lawyer in New York : —

TO WM. CURTIS NOYES, NEW YORK.

Boston, July 28, 1862.

My dear Sir, — Hardly a day passes that I do
not see some article which ought to be republished
in each of the loyal States : Evarts's letter, your
New York resolutions, one day, something from the
" Evening Post " or " Tribune," another, something
better from the rebels, proclaiming themselves " aris-
tocrats and masters bound to rule us."

It seems to me that we need a publishing committee with headquarters in New York, and a
member at each principal point.   When anything
good comes out, it can always be copied without
cost, and a quantity of slips struck off at insignifi-
cant expense.   These should be sent with the indorsement of a member of the committee to each
important newspaper.   The chief cost would be in

postage, and this might fairly be obviated to a large extent by calling upon members of Congress for franks for an object of such public interest. If you approve of the idea, perhaps you will talk with Mr. Bryant and other leading men, *and act*. I shall be away all summer, but I suggest for Boston James B. Thayer, a lawyer, brother of W. S. Thayer, formerly connected with the "Evening Post," now consul-general to Egypt. Party and personal interests ought to be carefully kept out of it, and the vigorous prosecution of the war made its chief object. Such an article as I inclose would just now be of great value in raising recruits, and opening the eyes of the people to the real nature of the contest, aristocracy *vs*. popular government, and slave labor *vs*. free labor. It is pretty clear that your leaders are "marching on" in New York, and it is now mainly important to enlighten the working classes.

If they could see where the real support of the war lies, it is my belief that they would force the administration and the generals to fire into the enemy's powder magazine, and then we should soon come down to Mr. Seward's sixty days' duration of the war! Please return me the inclosed cutting, which I mean to make worth several recruits, and oblige,

Yours truly,   J. M. FORBES.

TO THE SAME.

NAUSHON ISLAND, *August* 12, 1862.

MY DEAR SIR, — Your favor of the 7th has been sent me here, where I am established for a month or two, with a chance to visit Boston only occasionally. I am very glad that my plan strikes you favorably. Governor Andrew made me a flying visit yesterday, and seems to like the idea much; he had already made use of the slips I sent him of the " aristocracy *vs.* popular government " by sending them to the recruiting stations.

I sincerely hope a thorough system may be inaugurated under your personal oversight in such a manner as will shut off any attempt to use it either for personal ambition (*i. e.* for lauding political or military aspirants), or even for pushing the views of our most extreme Republicans. To do its best work, it needs to be broader than any one set of men, even the best, belonging to our wing of the Republican party. In other words, its aim should not be anti-slavery, except incidentally, but should be " the vigorous prosecution of the war." How would it do to style it " the committee of correspondence upon the vigorous prosecution of the war " ?

Mr. George W. Curtis, who is here, and has considerable experience with the press, thinks there is some danger of jealousy from the press at the appearance of dictation there would be in my original plan of sending with each article a circular from the committee, suggesting its republication. If this be so, perhaps the best mode would be to have our organization complete, but informal ; that is to say, not appearing before the public as a committee. The articles we wish to have republished would, in most cases, if well selected, be adopted in each State, either at the individual suggestion of our committeeman for that point, or they might be sent anonymously with a printed or written line, saying, for instance, that a " fellow-countryman calls your attention to the inclosed important article as valuable for circulation."

One of the most important ends that could be gained by a judicious organization would be to sink and obliterate the old party names and prejudices, especially those connected with the name of democrat.

You and I have fought under the Whig banner ; one of our strongest allies is Mr. Bryant, the leader of the only really Democratic party which ever existed. Yet we constantly find our best Republican journals even now fighting " Democracy." It seems to me of vast importance to sink these old distinctions, and to put before the voting and fighting masses, in the strongest light, the real issue — of the war-Democratic or Republican [government], (whichever we may call the government of the people) *vs.* Aristocratic government ; in other words, the people *vs.* a class. . . .

I give you a rough sketch of an organization, and am very truly yours,

J. M. FORBES.

The idea thus expressed took form in a small organization called "The New England Loyal Publication Society." Before the society was formed, my father was working out the plan in his own office, using his clerk for the business of sending out hundreds of printed slips all over the country, and through Governor Andrew to the army. By degrees, however, the work became too much for a man as busy as he was at this time, and, as I have said, the society was formed. Supported by him, and other patriotic men,[1] it developed by degrees into an organized and efficient agency for the distribution of sound doctrine on finance and politics. The editor collected the best articles and speeches that met his eyes, and these were printed on a broadside, and sent to nine hundred different newspapers all over the country. Many local editors were glad to find part of their work ready to their hands, and availed themselves eagerly of these sheets. After careful inquiry, the society felt assured that their publications reached something like one million readers.

The whole thing gradually grew into a regular publication, issued once a week, keeping as its name the title of the society; it was under the charge of Mr. C. E. Norton, now Professor Norton of Harvard University. The yearly cost of the whole came to

---

[1] The executive committee was as follows: J. M. Forbes, President; Wm. Endicott, Jr., Treasurer; J. B. Thayer, Secretary; C. E. Norton, Edward Atkinson, Martin Brimmer, Rev. E. E. Hale, Henry B. Rogers, Professor W. B. Rogers, S. G. Ward.

something under $4000. My father used to say
that he accomplished more in this way than in any
other during the war, — a statement which indi-
cates, at any rate, his interest in the work and his
confidence as to its success. The practical management of the work was in the hands of Mr. Norton
and the secretary, Mr. J. B. Thayer, now Professor
Thayer of the Harvard Law School.

In the fall of 1862 the following memorandum
was sent to Governor Andrew. It was " probably
used," says my father, " with members of Congress,
and not sent to the War Department : " —

" Minor Reforms Needed. September, 1862.

" 1st. Drunken officers. The public, rightly or
wrongly, attribute part of the mischief at Bull Run
to one, Colonel M., commanding the reserve. . . . .
If there be no time for courts-martial, why not
quietly shelve every drunkard ?

" 2d. Skulkers. The President found at Harrison's Bar half his army unaccounted for. The
papers tell of crowds of stragglers helping to make
panics in each battle. The enemy shoot their
stragglers. We might at least drop, if not from a
tree by a rope, at least from the army list, every
skulking officer. . . . . The inclosed cutting gives a
hint of where the record can be found (the Mar-
shall House and City Hotel, Alexandria) of the
doings of 135 officers on Sunday, August 31, when
our army was in its greatest peril. Why not call
on each to account satisfactorily for his being there

on that day?   In short, **why** not have an efficient police system to correct this crying evil?

"**3d.**   Spies.   **The spies have thus** far slain more than any other **arm of the enemy.**   **We** hear of one, **a famous** guerilla, being condemned **to** die in Missouri; **but it looks** like a mere excuse **for** punishing other crimes.   Several have been imprisoned, **some** compelled to take the oath!! **but not one choked to** death, — they probably being practised in swallowing hard oaths!   We see accounts from **Nor**folk of three rebel mail carriers caught passing our lines 'with private letters only, nothing of public interest,' and these will **doubtless** be leniently dealt **with!**   **Who can say what dangerous cipher** those private letters **carried? or whether the real object of** their **mission — a short military dispatch — was not** swallowed or destroyed? . . . **Shall we encourage** spies and informers by continued leniency **toward** mail carriers from our lines to the enemy's?   **Wash**ington thought **it** necessary to hang the noble André.   **Can it be doubted** that the **enemy** destroy **without any compunction any of our spies or** 'mail **carriers'?**   **We hang a man for** the doubtful military crime of hauling **down a** flag, **and we let pass free, or punish** lightly, **men who, by all military usages, and** by **the** dictates of **common sense, de**serve the heaviest punishment.   **Half a dozen spies** hanged **would have saved as many thousand** lives, and have **given** confidence **to our own** people and **soldiers in the earnestness of** their leaders, civil and **military.**   It is **not too late to** begin.

"4th. Robbers, in the shape of contractors, and of army officers receiving commissions [on purchases or sales for the government]; in short, the army worms of our military wheat. Of course, eternal vigilance is the only remedy for this disease. How would it do, as a sort of scarecrow at least, to insert a clause in each contract, that the contractor becomes by signing it subject to martial law, both as to his person and property? Without legislation it would not be binding, but many, nay, most of the new contracts will run beyond the meeting of the next Congress, when we may have a law for it, and by signing such a contract, agreeing to be amenable, the party could not complain that the law was *ex post facto*.

"We who are paying taxes feel that the army contractors and the commission-receiving officers are eating us up. The soldier feels it in his bare feet and back, and sometimes in his empty stomach, and a hint from the Department would surely give us such a law during the first week of the session. The enemy does not tolerate drunken generals, stragglers, spies, or thieving contractors. Let us remember the old proverb, '*Fas est et ab hoste doceri.*'"

GOVERNOR ANDREW TO J. M. FORBES.

BOSTON, September 13, 1862.

MY DEAR SIR, — I like your suggestions very much, but I venture to suggest: 1st, that having perused the report of the testimony . . . printed

. . . by order of the **Senate, I** do not think **any** part of the disaster of **Bull Run was** due to Colonel M., and I think **that on the weight of** the evidence he was sick, **but not intoxicated.** . . .

2d, as to contractors. I think **the** department can do nothing in the direction you propose; Congress might. And I think General Meigs might properly be appealed to for an opinion. Stanton can know but little about the matter directly. And I think a part of the rage against him is due to the contractors who like a long war and were angry that Stanton tried to shorten it.

3d, as to skulkers and spies. Unless the General-in-Chief is in earnest, these reforms are impossible. The department may fulminate regulations, but in vain, as long as imbecility, disobedience, evasion of duty, neglect of duty, coldness towards the cause itself, distinguish the General-in-Chief.

The department is powerless for reform while the army is led as it now is led and has been led hitherto. It can only give rules and orders, but it remains for the officers in command to enforce them. The President persists in retaining those who will not do what you and I think zeal and faithful service demand. The reform is only possible by a new commander in the field. Thus believing, I have not the heart to write of these details to the Secretary.

I am ever faithfully and most respectfully yours,

JOHN A. ANDREW.

One of the great difficulties in the war is dealt with in the following passage from my father's notes, in regard to his work in recruiting : —

"After the first enthusiasm of the war had died out, it became much more difficult to get new recruits, and drafts were resorted to; which induced various towns called upon to resort to large bounties. This money element naturally drew out the worst men from the cities; many of the rough customers enlisting with the intention of deserting and getting new bounties. At one time when recruiting for the Second Cavalry, we had in a single day a squad of about a dozen recruits brought in from New York by the Fall River steamer, who appeared at our recruiting office and seemed about to sign, when a whistle from their leader took them all off and we saw no more of them. This experience was more or less repeated as long as the war lasted. . . .

"During this period Mr. Amos A. Lawrence and I were acting together, and I persuaded him to join me in what proved to be a very successful experiment. The large bounties brought into the field a great number of middle-men, whose business was to collect recruits, and who often took the largest part of the bounties themselves. Mr. Lawrence and I, with the governor's assent, decided to become our own brokers, and got an order that any engagement of ours should be accepted by the draft officers as equivalent to men. We then engaged with the large towns, agreeing to furnish them with men at the best prices they were willing to pay; so enabling them to settle their share of the draft without supplying **any more men.** When we had **got** a considerable fund, we engaged **the** men directly ourselves, **or through our** enlisting officers, among whom **George Quincy was** prominent, paying them a smaller **price than we** received **from** the towns, but giving it them direct; and **thus they got a great deal** more benefit out of it than **when** they **treated** with **the** brokers. In this way we **filled up** our regiments and had a fund, which was used to continue recruiting, for the regimental band, **and for various** other useful purposes, until the end **of the war. My** impression is that **we** enlisted in this **way over two thousand men, and had a fund of seven or eight thousand dollars left."**

I find from my father's files of letters of this time that he **must have done a very inordinate** amount of writing in regard to the recruiting of troops. Some of his correspondents got at **logger-heads** with **one** another, insisting on laying complaints of each other before him, **as to** trespassing on the other's district. **This was one** of many tedious and petty **vexations that troubled him** in the midst of his intense **work.**

His notes continue : —

"Antietam, with its drawn game claimed **as a** victory, came September **the** 19th, 1862, **and, after** that, a period of reorganization in regard **to our** army which **only** some historian can record. At this time the public, through **the press** and in many other ways, took a hand in the game, and had great influence on the action not only of Congress, but still more upon that of the administration of President Lincoln, who was always disposed to follow public opinion rather than to be a bold leader in the strife.

" After trying Burnside, who failed at Fredericksburg signally, and Hooker, who while a brave and energetic corps commander lost his head completely at Chancellorsville, chaos followed till Grant was put at the head of our whole army, — notwithstanding some faults which alarmed us at the time when he was thus selected ; but he had the strength to overcome them, and by his genius, his firmness, and above all his magnanimity towards other officers around him, he fully justified Lincoln in his selection, and left a record which will place him among the great men of the world."

The letters that follow indicate the anxieties, the plans, and the efforts to shape the course of events in the great drama that was going on, of my father and of some of his correspondents who were among the most influential men of the time. A great step had been taken in September, when the President issued his preliminary proclamation as to emancipation.

W. C. BRYANT TO J. M. FORBES.

OFFICE OF THE EVENING POST,
NEW YORK, October 16, 1862.

MY DEAR SIR, — What your friend says of Grant may be the truth, so far as he is acquainted with his history. But I have friends who profess to be acquainted with him, and who declare that he is now a temperate man, and that it is a cruel wrong to speak of him as otherwise. I have in my drawer a batch of written testimonials to that effect. He reformed when he got or was put out of the army, and went into it again with a solemn promise of abstinence. One of my acquaintances has made it his special business to inquire concerning his habits, of the officers who have recently served with him or under him. None of them have seen him drunk, or seen him drink. Their general testimony is that he is a man remarkably insensible to danger, active, and adventurous.

Whether he drinks or not, he is certainly a fighting general, and a successful fighter, which is a great thing in these days.

W. P. FESSENDEN TO J. M. FORBES.

PORTLAND, *November* 13, 1862.

MY DEAR SIR, — I have received your letter, and also the newspaper puff, for which I am probably indebted to you. McClellan's removal is a great step, but it should have been taken a year ago. There was no excuse for giving him the command of the army after his Yorktown campaign, and the President cannot defend himself for so doing. He knew his unfitness and admitted it. If it had not been proved before, the failure to win Antietam (for he did not win it), and to attack Lee on the day following, demonstrated either his incapacity or his treachery. Fear of offending the Democracy has been at the bottom of all our disasters. I am not clear that the result of the elections is not fortunate for the country, for it has taught the President that he has nothing to look for in that quarter, a fact which any sensible man might have seen. The only way to get the support of the Democracy is to show that you don't fear them. It is a mistake to suppose that you will gain anything of such people by conciliation, or by admitting them to your councils.

As to the cabinet, I have no belief that there will be any change. Seward will never yield his place willingly, and the President never will ask him to do so. But, whatever may happen, no man could be of much use in a cabinet office, for no man could carry out his own views. You cannot change the President's character or conduct, unfortunately; he remained long enough at Springfield, surrounded by toadies and office-seekers, to persuade himself that he was specially chosen by the Almighty for this great crisis, and well chosen. This conceit has never yet been beaten out of him, and until it is, no human wisdom can be of much avail. I see nothing for it but to let the ship of state drift along, hoping that the current of public opinion may bring it safely into port. For myself, I can only say that there is no political calamity I should look upon with so much dread as the being asked to share the responsibility of guiding it. I have neither the strength nor the wisdom requisite, and if I had, it would be useless. No, my friend, I can, perhaps,

render my country some service where I am. In the
cabinet I could no nothing, and no friend of mine
should ever wish to see me there.

TO W. P. FESSENDEN.

BOSTON, *November* 15, 1862.

MY DEAR SIR, — Your note received. I must
differ from you about the President. He has been
in the hands of a vacillating, undecided man like
Seward!

With your decided opinions, if you were once in
the cabinet, he and all the political aspirants there
would form into line and march to your music.
Even Chase would be glad to see some one else put
at the head to take the responsibility. His opinions
are firm enough, but he lacks your uncompromising
directness of will. The only possible doubt is your
health, and you may as well die at the head of the
nation a few months hence, after saving it, as at
the head of the Senate a few years hence, fighting
the compromisers and rebels combined.

A prominent New York man ascribes, in a private
letter, the late failure there[1] to Seward and his
friends, and says the President ought to know and
act upon it. He adds, "The accession of Mr. W. P. F.
would delight me." He [my correspondent] is a man
who, perhaps, next to you, ought to be there himself,
though known at the bar rather than in public life.

---

[1] Referring to the defeat of the Republican party in New York,
and the election of Seymour, the Democratic candidate for governor.
— ED.

TO JOSHUA BATES, OF BARING BROS. & CO., LONDON.

Boston, *November* 11, 1862.

MY DEAR MR. BATES, — Nothing from you lately; and I suppose even your steady nerves and heart are shaken by our long supineness. We have awaked at last, and if we had only a William Pitt to put over our cabinet, we should be all right.

Mr. Chase, I hear, shows some signs of returning sanity by inquiring (outside of the clique who had his ear) as to his future course. Our friend Hooper has a good deal to answer for in leading him into the legal tender labyrinth; it will take wiser heads to guide him out. We are not quite lost yet, and if the report due next month shows that he has sounded the depths of the currency issue as a resource, and is coming back to sound principles of finance, we may, with large revenues from our tax bill (reported to be very large), and with some military vigor, still save ourselves from utter ruin, — financially, I mean.

Somehow or other, in spite of weak-kneed friends and open traitors at home, and a sharp enemy outside, we can and will keep the old ship together.

To fail now is to establish the most dangerous military government for our neighbors that the world ever saw. Five or six millions of whites despising labor, and having a black slave race to work for them, while they fight! If we disarm, with such a neighbor unconquered, and our so-called democracy ready to ally itself with them, we may as well give up our government at once and return to feudalism.

I hope you will give me the benefit of a hint now and then from your deep stores of financial experience, and am, with best regards to Mrs. Bates,

  Yours, very truly,   J. M. FORBES.

My father's notes of this period go on to say : —

"Besides the military situation during 1862, came the alarm in regard to the extension of the system of outfitting cruisers against us in European ports, — which had got to sea and were driving our ships out of the carrying trade ; and especially the building of two powerful ironclad warships by Laird, at Liverpool, which not only threatened our cities and ports on the coast, but seemed to render foreign intervention probable. My relations with the Navy Department and with Mr. Fox, the assistant secretary, who carried on the executive work there, were very close, and led to a good deal of consultation by letter and otherwise ; which communications were kept very carefully to ourselves."

I give here three of these communications, showing how alive to the danger the Navy Department had become, and how unprepared the northern seaports were to withstand any attack from ironclads :

G. V. FOX TO J. M. FORBES.

NAVY DEPARTMENT, *November* 22, 1862.

DEAR SIR, — . . . As to our defenses, I believe this is about the truth. The Alabama can be kept out by our present forts. She is doing a better business, with less risk, than attacking Boston. No forts can keep out ironclads. We must have obstructions easily raised. There are no big guns to spare. Parties cannot make guns who are not experienced. We have started half a dozen new foundries in New England the last year, and got only one good gun. Any man for a year past, and now, who wishes a contract for big guns can have it. No one has ever been refused. As to ironclads it is the same. Every one is invited and has been, and no one capable of doing the work has been refused. So with marine engines. We will build a vessel for every party who will take an engine. Washington is reported to have said, "In peace, prepare for war." We didn't, and here we are. It is of no use to sacrifice anybody; we are caught uprepared, and must pay for it. . . . We are building some wooden-bottom turret ships in the navy yards to carry four 15-inch guns. We fired the 15-inch gun at nine inches of iron. It did not penetrate, but it shook the whole affair nearly to pieces. We are in the hands of the contractors, who are doing all they can, but it is far short of public expectation. In the mean time, if harbor obstructions are not provided, our cities are not safe against ironclads.

THE SAME TO THE SAME.

NAVY DEPARTMENT, *December* 9, 1862.

MY DEAR SIR, — I have your letter of the 3d inst. The matter of purchase of vessels fitting out in England has frequently been under discussion, and, as a matter of precaution, is expensive, as it would involve us in unlimited purchases without entirely curing the evil, since every steamer could not be obtained. There are but very few of the English steamers that escape our cruisers. I think it safe to say that not one in twenty has landed a cargo and returned safely to England.

The Kate, an iron steamer, has been the most successful, and she could not cross the ocean. She has just been lost at Wilmington by running into the obstructions at New Inlet. With regard to two ironclads (one at Glasgow and one at Liverpool), I think it very important to purchase them if they can be obtained for money. Mr. Welles favors the idea, and Mr. Seward simply urges it. If Mr. Upton could do this, I think it would be well to send him out. If you will talk the matter over with him, and it seems feasible, Mr. Upton had better come on. No one but Mr. Seward, Mr. Welles, and ourselves need know it. Their vessels fitting to run the blockade can be disposed of, but the ironclads (if rumors in regard to them be true) are a more serious matter, deserving of instant action at any price, since we have not a port North that can resist an ironclad of very moderate power.

THE SAME TO THE SAME.

NAVY DEPARTMENT, December 19, 1862.

DEAR SIR, — I have yours of 17th inst. I fancy there can be no ironclads for the rebels put into the water before May. But they require strict watching and ample measures to guard against their coming over here. Mr. Seward is of the opinion that the English government are very anxious for us to come into their market for the purchase of vessels, that we may be put upon an equal footing with the South. The reclamations in the matter of the Alabama have disturbed them very much. With this view of the matter, Mr. Welles rather inclines to some doubt about making any purchases. I think you and Mr. Upton better come on after the holidays; it would be good to discuss that and other matters.

When a superintending Providence deprives us of all means of recruiting our armies, I believe we will call upon those who, at least, will, by their desertion, paralyze the rebels. The President remarked to me the other night that he was very anxious to have us take Sumter, and that he would man it with negroes. When the Nahant leaves, we shall have the number of ironclads fixed upon as the least number to go into Charleston. That vessel will not probably leave before the first of January.

There is a good deal of depression felt at the repulse at Fredericksburg, and the President is exceedingly disturbed; but it seems to me that, looking over the whole ground, the movements contemplated West, and the probability of getting possession of the remaining ports South, we should hardly deserve success if we allowed our faith to waver now. It is a matter of regret, however, that the whole military force of the country is not used to expel the enemy from Virginia.

Of this period my father says in his notes : —

"It was the darkest time of the war, though its grand turning point (outside of what the army and navy could do) was approaching in the Proclamation of Emancipation," — the final proclamation promised in the preliminary one of September, 1862.

The following letter from Mr. Sedgwick gives a lively account of the state of feeling in Washington at the time of writing. It led to my father's drawing up an address to the President from the presidential electors of 1860, and forwarding it to Mr. Sedgwick, who obtained the required signatures, and then sent it on to Mr. Lincoln. It is inserted in its place below.

WASHINGTON, 22d December, 1862.

MY DEAR MR. FORBES, — I have shown your letter (copy) to Mr. Fessenden to several conservative gentlemen of my acquaintance. They all agree in saying that it would be well to send on a strong delegation of clergy and laity to urge on the President. Some doubt his intention to issue the proclamation of 1st January; I do not. Many assert, more fear, that it will be essentially modified from what is promised. I do not fear this; but what I do fear is, that he will stop with the proclamation and take no active and vigorous measures to insure its efficacy. I say he will issue it, because it is his own offspring, which Seward tried hard to strangle at its birth, and failed to do it. If the President don't tell you all about it some time, I will, as I heard the story from the chief himself. Judge Kelly told me this evening he had just come from Stanton, who told him that the President and Burnside had been there but a little while before, and this subject coming up, the President said " that he could not stop the Proclamation if he would, and he would not if he could; that just as soon as the first of January dawned it would be issued."   So I cannot doubt that it will be issued.   There are other facts within my knowledge which convince me that it will certainly go forth.   Every conceivable influence has been brought to bear upon him to induce him to withhold or modify, — threats, entreaties, all sorts of humbugs, but he is firm as a mule.

Now if Banks can start from Mobile or New Orleans with a sufficient army, or send Butler, which will be equally well, perhaps, armed with this proclamation, and enlist every able-bodied, willing, loyal negro, as he progresses into the country, until he has 100,000 of them under arms, the great work will be accomplished.   If Banks was sent South for some such purpose, the expedition is a sensible one; if not, it is pure strategy, and not worth, in the aggregate, so much as one of the rotten ships in which it was embarked.   I say by all means come on and be here in force the last of this month.   Be ready to shout Hallelujah on the morning of 1st January, and let the President know that he is to have sympathy and support.   By all means, put him up to practical measures to make it successful.   Tell him the world will pardon his crimes, and his stories even, if he only makes the proclamation a success, and that if he fails he will be gibbeted in history as a great, long-legged, awkward, country pettifogger, without brains or backbone.

We have had a nice row in the cabinet. The Senate had a secret caucus and resolved to get rid of the President's evil genius, Seward. Preston King, fearing Seward, loose, would endanger his prospects for senator, slipped out and told Seward all about it. Seward tendered his resignation Wednesday evening. By Thursday morning his friends began to pour in, to threaten the President if he accepted it. The world in general only found it out on Friday. Chase, like a good boy, on Saturday went out to bring little wandering Willie back. The telegraph is forbidden to carry the startling news to the country, except, now, to my Lord Thurlow [1] and some others; and on Monday all goes " merry as a marriage bell " again. So the Senate is snubbed, Seward is more powerful than ever, Chase's radical friends are disgusted that he has been used to save Seward from his folly, and the great chasm into which the administration was to fall is bridged. Vive la Humbug !

The electors' letter above referred to was as follows : —

[1] Thurlow Weed, editor of the *Albany Journal*, Mr. Seward's right-hand man. — ED.

December 24, 1862.

To ABRAHAM LINCOLN, President of the United
States, Washington : —

Sir, — The undersigned, as electors, performed
two years ago the pleasant duty of certifying to
your appointment to the chief magistracy of this
country, by the choice of the people.

Believing that the approaching new year brings
with it a crisis in the life of our nation, they beg
leave to congratulate you upon your having begun
the greatest act in American history, the emancipation of 3,000,000 of blacks and of 5,000,000 of
whites from the power of an aristocratic class.

It is admitted upon all sides that the transfer of
three millions of slaves from the productive force
of the rebels to our scale in the balance would instantly end the rebellion ; it follows that each slave
so transferred will proportionately contribute to that
end.

It is only a question of time when emancipation
must take place, and it is believed that no time
can ever occur so safe from unnecessary violence as
when the slaves have the strength of the Union to
rally behind, and when a large army of rebels can
and ought to be thus withdrawn from opposing the
laws, to the more fitting work of keeping order
around their own homes.

For these and other reasons the undersigned believe that emancipation is the weapon which, effi-
ciently used, can not only strike at the heart of the
Rebellion, but lay the foundation for a true and
permanent republic ; a consummation even more

beneficent to the moral and material interests of the
people of the South than to those of the Northern
people.

They therefore earnestly pray you to complete
now your great work by taking every possible measure to carry into practical effect the promise of your
Proclamation of 22d September, and especially by
demanding imperatively of every person in the military, naval, and civil service of your government to
obey strictly the regulations by which you will enforce your new settled policy.

They believe that by so doing you will place yourself among the great benefactors of your country
and of the human race, and that you will live in
future ages by the side of the Father of his Country
— George Washington.

Respectfully submitted,   [ELECTORS.]

With the view of placing the Proclamation of
Emancipation in the hands of the negroes themselves, my father had 1,000,000 copies printed on
small slips, one and a half inches square, put into
packages of fifty each, and distributed among the
Northern soldiers at the front, who scattered them
about among the blacks, while on the march. Sumner approved the idea, as will be seen by the following letter : —

WASHINGTON, *Xmas Day*, 1862.

MY DEAR FORBES, — Your letter of 23d was on
my table when I returned from an interview with
the President, where much had been said about the
Proclamation. He is now considering how to pro-

claim on 1st January. It will be done. He says of himself that he is hard to be moved from any position which he has taken. He let me know last evening of his plan to employ African troops to hold the Mississippi River, and also other posts in the warm climates, so that our white soldiers may be employed elsewhere. He seemed much in earnest.

I did not write at once on the receipt of your letter of 18th December, because it found me excessively occupied, and because I had been already assured by the President with regard to the Proclamation. I see no objection to printing the extract from Stephens [1] on the sheet with the Proclamation; and I like much the idea of distributing the Proclamation through the army. I have exhorted the President to put into the next Proclamation some sentiment of justice and humanity. He promised at once to consider it.

Why not send to all the hospitals, camps, posts? The more the better.

Ever yours,   CHARLES SUMNER.

It would seem that this letter must have crossed that from my father, which follows: —

TO THE HON. CHARLES SUMNER.

BOSTON, *December* 27, 1862.

MY DEAR MR. SUMNER, — I had hoped to have sent you to-day communications to the President

---

[1] "This stone (slavery), which was rejected by the first builders, is become the chief stone of the corner in our new edifice." (Speech of Alex. H. Stephens, Vice-President of the Confederate States, delivered March 31, 1861.)

from the rest of our electors (except Mr. Morey, absent in Europe) all indorsing the Proclamation and begging for its enforcement; but the electors are so widely separated, from Nantucket to the Connecticut, that concert of action is difficult. Whittier will probably write a letter instead of signing with us.

May I ask of you the favor to present the letters already sent you, carefully including Judge Chapman's cordial assent.

I sincerely hope that you and others will have sufficient influence with the President to insure his giving us on 1st January such a Proclamation as will only need the "General Orders" of his subordinates to carry into effect not only emancipation but all the fruits thereof, in the perfect right to use the negro in every respect as a man, and consequently as a soldier, sailor, or laborer, wherever he can most effectually strike a blow against the enemy.

It seems to me very important that the ground of "military necessity" should be even more squarely taken than it was on 22d September. Many of our strongest Republicans, some even of our Lincoln electors, have constitutional scruples in regard to emancipation upon any other ground, and with them must be joined a large class of Democrats, and self-styled "Conservatives," whose support is highly desirable, and ought to be secured where it can be done without any sacrifice of principle.

I know that you and many others would like to have it done upon higher ground, but the main thing is to have it done strongly, and to have it

so backed up by public opinion that it will strike
the telling blow, at the rebellion and at slavery
together, which we so much need.

I buy and eat my bread made from the flour
raised by the hard-working farmer; it is certainly
satisfactory that in so doing I am helping the
farmer clothe his children, but my motive is self-
preservation, not philanthropy or justice. Let the
President free the slaves upon the same principle,
and so state it that the masses of our people can
easily understand it.

He will thus remove constitutional scruples from
some, and will draw to himself the support of a very
large class who do not want to expend their brothers
and sons and money for the benefit of the negro,
but who will be very glad to see Northern life and
treasure saved by any practical measure, even if it
does incidentally an act of justice and benevolence.

Now I would not by any means disclaim the
higher motives, but where so much prejudice exists,
I would eat my bread to sustain my life; I would
take the one short, sure method of preserving the
national life, — and say little about any other motive. . . .

Forgive me for writing so much, and for asking
you to try to urge my poor ideas upon the President,
but I feel strongly that we all need encouragement
and hope; and a good strong Proclamation full of
vigor, of freedom, and of *democracy,* would almost
compensate us for the dreadful repulse of Fredericksburg.   Truly yours,   J. M. FORBES.

Mr. Sumner writes the next day : —

WASHINGTON, 28th December, 1862.

MY DEAR FORBES, — Last evening I handed to the President a memorial from clergymen, calling on him to stand by his Proclamation, reading it to him aloud.

I then handed him your slip *Audax*, which he commenced reading.

Then a slip from a Boston paper, advertising a musical celebration in honor of the Proclamation, 1st January, with all the names, yours among the rest.

Then the unsigned address[1] from the electors, which he proceeded to read aloud.

I then read to him Mr. Chapman's letter, which I enforced by saying that he was now a very able judge of our Supreme Court,[2] once a Hunker, and not much of my way of thinking in times past.

I then proceeded to dwell on the importance and grandeur of the act, and how impatient we all are that it should be done in the way to enlist the most sympathy and to stifle opposition. On his account I urged that it should be a military decree, counter-signed by the Secretary of War, and that it should have something in it showing that though an act of military necessity and just self-defense, it was also an act of justice and humanity, which must have the blessings of a benevolent God.

---

[1] This was an address slightly different in form from that sent through Mr. Sedgwick. — ED.

[2] Afterwards the chief justice. — ED.

The President says that he could not stop the Proclamation if he would, and he would not if he could.   Burnside was present at this remark.

I find Stanton unusually sanguine and confident. He says that he shall have 200,000 negroes under arms before June, holding the Mississippi River and garrisoning the ports, so that our white soldiers can go elsewhere.   The President accepts this idea.

Let the music sound, and the day be celebrated.

www.ingramcontent.com/pod-product-compliance
Lightning Source LLC
Chambersburg PA
CBHW051216120726
47905CB00004B/1148